TOWARD THE MIDNIGHT SUN

ALSO BY EOIN DEMPSEY

Finding Rebecca

The Bogside Boys

White Rose, Black Forest

TOWARD THE MIDNIGHT SUN

A NOVEL

EOIN DEMPSEY

LAKE UNION
PUBLISHING

This is a work of fiction. Names, characters, organizations, places, events, and incidents are either products of the author's imagination or are used fictitiously.

Published by Lake Union Publishing, Seattle

www.apub.com

ISBN-13: 9781542008426
ISBN-10: 1542008425

Cover design by Faceout Studio, Derek Thornton

Printed in the United States of America

This book is for my son Sam.

Arctic Ocean
Bering Sea
Alaska
Yukon R.
US
CANADA
Dawson City
Anchorage
Northwest Territories
Yukon
Gulf of Alaska
Chilkoot Pass
CANADIAN ROUTE
Skagway
RICH MAN'S ROUTE
POOR MAN'S ROUTE
Coast Mountains
British Columbia
Alberta
Pacific Ocean
Edmonton
Vancouver
CANADA
US
Seattle
Washington
N
0
250
500 mi
0
250
500 km

Chapter 1

Seattle, August 20, 1897

The dreamers gathered. The throngs of idiotic unprepared, fueled by hope, driven by the despair of low wages and bread lines, by the newspapers' talk of recession, by the future that had been promised to them, and by the gold. All talk was of the gold, or "the color," as those who boasted of having more experience had taken to calling it. It was suddenly everywhere. It gleamed in the storefronts of Seattle and in the haversacks of smiling prospectors stepping off the gangway into a life they had only hoped for but never believed they'd possess. It had overtaken all else in the minds of the men and women gathered here. There was nothing else now. It was their hope. It was the light at the end of the dark tunnel their lives had become. They had forsaken everything for its promise.

Everyone was here—doctors and lawyers, bakers and students, servants and masters, musicians and whores. None was immune to the lure of the color. Its universal promise had brought them all here on a fool's errand to a land they'd never heard of or certainly never thought to mention just weeks before—the Klondike, just far enough away to elicit a palpable mysticism and just close enough to make that dream a possibility. They had gathered here.

Anna's eyes swept through the crowd that had assembled to send off the steamer. Perhaps it might have been better not to look, but she couldn't resist. Hundreds of pairs of eyes peered back at her. Mustached men, their hats casting the shadow of the afternoon sun on their faces, sang songs of the Klondike and of the bounty that awaited those fortunate enough to make the journey up to collect it. A few feet along the railing, a young man stated that he was looking forward to returning as a millionaire. His conviction was real. All on the steamer felt it.

The smell of hay filled Anna's nostrils, and below her feet, the horses thrashed in their thrown-together enclosures like fish in a net. Her eyes remained trained on the baying crowd below. The faces of her family tore at her heart, and tears welled in her eyes. Their time as her chaperones was over. They had been compensated for the expense of their journey with her as they passed her off. Her mother was stoic, her eyes unmoving, but even from her lofted position, Anna could see the sadness there. She had her arms around Anna's sisters, one on each side. Each girl had her head bowed, and as they brought their faces up, Anna could make out the streams of tears shining on her sisters' cheeks. She raised a hand, but her gesture was not returned. She saw her mother draw her sister Mary into her bosom. Her other sister Henrietta continued peering up at the ship. Anna called down, but her voice drowned in the cacophony of cheers. It seemed there was no room for mourning in the revelry.

The cheers came to a crescendo as the ship broke free of its mooring, and the good ship *Mercury*, newly fitted out for the most profitable journey in its long tenure on the ocean, set out for the hitherto unknown. The faces on the dock faded, and she lost sight of her mother and sisters. The noise of the crowd reverberated, tracking across the white peaks of surf the steamer left in her wake. Some of the crowd on board moved to the stern of the ship for one final farewell to their old life. Most did not. Most looked out toward the clear blue of the horizon as if the goldfields would appear at any moment.

Anna was still crying, wondering if anyone noticed. Her chaperones, Bryce and Stevens, perhaps the only two men on board who had any idea what lay ahead of the stampeders, were sitting on a bale of hay a few feet away playing cards. Bryce threw a glance up at her before raising a flask of whiskey to his unwashed mouth. She wondered if she need tell them that she wanted to take a walk around the ship but recognized they didn't care what she did. She pushed her way through the crowd. Some of the people on board were dressed for the goldfields already in their brand-new iron-toed boots and plaid flannel shirts as yet unsullied by the sucking mud of the Klondike. Others seemed dressed for a pleasant summer jaunt, in moccasins and corduroys.

She pushed through the crowd, standing elbow to elbow. Bales of hay strewn against the railings became armchairs, and eager stampeders sat down to discuss the ease with which riches would be theirs. It seemed that the ticket on the steamer was the real prize—for the gold in the Klondike had only to be scooped up upon arrival. She had heard that her place on board this bucket of rust could have been sold ten times over. The bales of hay, the piled-up sacks of food and supplies, and the plethora of people made it difficult to move across the deck. She tried not to think about what a violent storm might do to the ship and to instead draw on the energy the crowd was emitting. This wasn't the life she wanted, but it was her life now, and she was determined to make the best of it.

Her life was dedicated to her family. She thought back to the night her father had broken the news to her and the letter from a place she'd never heard of before. The thought that she was doing this for her family would be reward enough. Her father was reluctant to agree. The conversation he'd had with her came back now. She'd never quite seen him like that before—all his strength drained. He'd floated the possibility of her traveling to the Klondike and marrying this man she'd never met as a choice, but it was no choice at all.

He'd called it a "bride price"—an ancient tradition that would be the saving of their family. His idiotic gambling on the stock market had ruined them, and the medicines that Mabel needed daily for her illness were expensive. His business was foundering like a raft adrift in the storm of the recession, and this was her family's last chance. She was their last chance. Her knuckles were white on the railing. He had sacrificed her future. She would do this for her mother and sisters, and, of course, Mabel. This wasn't for him. She had made her father swear he wouldn't lose the money he received for her. She would do this, but not if it was going to be in vain.

Perhaps she could find happiness thousands of miles from anything and anyone she'd ever known with a man she'd met so long ago. It was impossible to form a clear picture of what he looked like. He existed in her mind as an essence, constructed from a memory she'd long since deemed unnecessary to bear. How could she have known that the man she'd met so briefly as a ten-year-old child would be the man she'd marry? He'd seemed so inconsequential then. To everyone. Even just two years ago, he'd been nothing, but that was the power of the color. Now he was the King of the Klondike, and she was to be his queen.

The smell of smoke wafted past her. Music and laughter lilted through the air. The ocean below was a benign bluish brown and seemed to stretch out forever. Within minutes, the city of Seattle had disappeared, and the loneliness inside her expanded until she almost felt it was choking her. She had the thought to return to Bryce and Stevens, the gruff prospectors her future husband had paid to escort her the rest of the way to her new home in the Klondike. She caught a glimpse of them through the crowd as they sat in silence, playing cards and gulping from their flasks. She scanned the multitude below. There were few other women. Those who were there linked arms with their stampeder husbands, listening in to the conversation. No children were on board, but she'd heard of entire families purchasing tickets to travel together.

Few people seemed to know much about the conditions that awaited them once they arrived in the Klondike. The little she'd heard had been from Bryce and Stevens, but they were men of few words, many of them unintelligible. All they'd imparted was that life was hard there, but she would be comfortable. Unlike most, they would be sailing all the way to Dawson, the town that was to be her new home. Most couldn't afford the fare for the so-called "rich man's route," but money was no object for her future husband. Not when it came to travel expenses or the matter of purchasing a wife.

She wiped the tears from her face, making her way over to the railing. The passage of time seemed to stutter. She was staring down at the boat's wake, the curvature of the white water thrown up by the rudders as it faded back into nothing. They had all been together on the pond just a few days before, rowing the old boat their father had bought them when he'd been able to spend precious money on such things. Mabel wasn't well enough to go out on the water, or so Mother had said, and so they'd taken turns sitting with her watching the others in the boat. Lost in this memory, Anna startled when she heard a voice beside her.

"Quite the menagerie on board, isn't it?"

She looked up at a young man in his late twenties, perhaps five years older than she. His well-trimmed brown beard almost covered a scar on the side of his face, and his gray-blue eyes were reddened, with black rims underneath. It had been years since she'd spoken with someone as handsome as he was. The opportunity had rarely presented itself. None of the suitors her parents had considered looked like this man.

"I've never seen the likes of it before," the man said.

He stood beside her at the railing for a few seconds before he spoke again.

"That man over there," he said, pointing to a stout man with a gray beard standing in a group behind them, "was the chief of police in Seattle two days ago. He resigned his role when he got a ticket for this steamer."

She allowed herself a furtive glance at the man beside her again. He was staring out at the Puget Sound, which would lead them to the ocean. She was formulating an answer when he spoke again.

"I still remember the first time I saw the ocean," he said. "I'd never felt quite so small in all my life. It seemed so limitless, so unknowable. That was the Atlantic Ocean, of course."

"You sailed across the Atlantic?"

"Yes, from Ireland, back in '76."

"Alone?"

"No. My parents were with me."

The sound of a dog barking caused both to turn. A German shepherd surged toward them, but neither cringed. The owner yanked the leash around its neck, explaining that she only wanted to play. The man reached down to pet her before Anna did the same. The dog's owner pulled her away, and they turned back to the railings.

"You were saying, sir?"

"Yes, my journey to the United States—that was a different atmosphere, as far as I remember anyway. I was only just turned six."

"How was it different?"

"The air of desperation, I suppose. My parents tried to shield me from it, but I could see it. People died on that ship. Their bodies were blessed and tossed over the side. It's not the type of thing one forgets easily."

"That's horrible."

"I'm sorry, ma'am. I don't mean to speak so gloomily. I don't mean to sound pitiful."

"Oh, no. I can't imagine how hard that must have been."

"This is different. This is a ship of hope. These people around us aren't leaving home forever, never to see loved ones again."

"I wouldn't assume anyone else's intentions."

"Perhaps I shouldn't either." The man reached into his pocket for a packet of cigarettes, placed one in his mouth. Then he placed it back into the pack and his pocket without lighting it. "I can say for certain that journey was different from this. There was no one singing at the dock when we left."

A fiddler sitting on a bale of hay began to play "The Yellow Rose of Texas."

"Do you know this song?" he said.

"Of course." She smiled despite herself. Bryce and Stevens were still playing cards and drinking. Somehow, she suspected they wouldn't be doing much else for the next ten days of the voyage. "So you were born in Ireland?"

"Yes, I was."

"Where did you grow up?"

"I'd love to say somewhere more original, but we settled in Boston."

"You didn't get too far, then."

"My parents got jobs in the city."

"Are they still there?"

"No. Where are you from?"

"I'm from just outside Chicago."

"I've never been. Will you miss it?"

"I will. I'll miss the colors of the fall and the warm summer rain. I don't expect we'll see much like that where we're going."

The people leaning against the railing beside him were speaking French. He gestured to them. "You see—everybody's here. From all four corners of the earth."

"What brings you here, Mr. . . ."

"I'm William Leary," he said.

"Anna Denton. Pleasure to make your acquaintance, Mr. Leary."

"And yours, Miss Denton. In answer to your question, I'm here because my brother asked me to come with him. I'm his grubstake."

"Please excuse my lack of understanding of mining terminology."

"He's backing me financially, funding my trip in return for a share of any resulting profits we make together once I've paid off the cost of my passage."

"Do you have any experience prospecting for gold?"

"Miss Denton, I'm sure you could count the combined hours of mining experience of almost everyone on board on one hand."

"And what about you?"

"You could count mine on no hands." She laughed, and he continued. "What about you? Will you be staking your own claim, or are you traveling with others?"

"I'm traveling with those two bastions of culture over there," she said, pointing at her two escorts. As if on cue, Stevens reached down to scratch himself. Anna felt safer with this man who she'd only just met than with her two so-called minders. It was ironic; her father had spent years trying to protect her from the likes of them. Until the price was right, and then he'd handed her right over.

"Now I can say I'm truly confused."

"I'm not going to prospect. I'm going to get married. My betrothed awaits me in Dawson."

"I do apologize. I hope you don't feel I was acting improperly by approaching you."

"Not one bit. It's a pleasure to have some stimulating conversation for a change. God knows I won't be extracting much from those two over the coming ten days of our voyage."

"Will you be disembarking with us at Skagway? The thriving center of the sunny northwest?"

"We will be, albeit briefly. We'll be taking the next steamer to St. Michael and then up the river to Dawson."

"That's not for us. We're for the way known as the Chilkoot. I believe it's a few days across the mountains, and then we take a boat downriver from there."

"Do you know the way?"

"We'll follow the crowd."

"So you've no experience as a prospector and little idea of what lays ahead of you. What chance of success in the north, then, Mr. Leary?"

"Ask my brother, Miss Denton. This was his idea. I'm merely along for the ride."

A taller man with a full beard walked over. He was bigger than Mr. Leary, well over six feet, with powerful shoulders bulging from beneath his checked shirt. Mr. Leary nodded to him as he approached.

"This is where you've been," the man said.

"Not too many places to hide on this ship," he answered. "Silas, I'd like you to meet someone. This is Miss Anna Denton."

"Silas Oliver. A pleasure to meet you, Miss Denton. I hope Will hasn't been boring you too much."

"Quite the contrary. You must be the brother he mentioned," Anna said, wondering why they didn't share a last name but thinking better of pressing the issue.

"So you're referring to me as your brother again now. I'm glad to hear that."

"Miss Denton is going to Dawson via St. Michael to get married."

"Many congratulations."

Reacting to people's congratulations was something that Anna had come to terms with. Best to answer with a simple "thank you."

"Your fiancé is in Dawson? Have you been?"

"No. I haven't."

Anna felt awkward. This was so new that she'd not had time to prepare answers to questions as to her motivations for going to Dawson. It was embarrassing, but she wouldn't lie about it. Her mother had assured her that lying would be the worst way to approach any conversations of the agreement that had brought her here.

"Is he a new arrival? How long has he been there himself?"

"He's been there quite a while. He was one of the first to stake a claim on the gold up there. He's gathered quite an amount, by all accounts. His name is Henry Bradwell."

"You've heard of him?" Will asked Silas.

Silas nodded. "The newspaper article I read about him called him the 'King of the Klondike.'"

"I have heard him referred to using that moniker. I don't expect a royal wedding, however. If you do have questions about Dawson or the way ahead, I will direct you toward my colleagues over on the other side of the deck. Mr. Bryce and Mr. Stevens came down from Dawson to escort me back. They've been up there for a year or more."

"An introduction would be graciously appreciated," Silas said.

"Of course."

Anna pushed off the railing, passing several older men with gray mustaches who looked more fit for the smoking lounge in a gentleman's club than a steamer bound for the goldfields. Bryce threw an indifferent glance at her as she arrived beside them. Stevens didn't look up from the cards in front of his face. The pot between them ran into the hundreds.

"Excuse my interruption, gentlemen, but I'd like to introduce my new friends, William Leary and Silas Oliver. They're on the way to Dawson to make their fortunes."

"As opposed to everyone else on this tub?" Bryce said. His colleague sneered his approval.

"The young lady informed us that you've been in the Klondike for a while. Can you tell us about it?" Silas asked.

"It's cold as a witch's tit, and when it's not snowing, it's raining."

"Mind your language, sir," Will said.

"It's fine," Anna said.

Coarse language was one of the many hardships she would have to bear, and if that were the worst, it would be an easy time indeed.

"Is there gold?" Silas said.

"Oh, there's gold all right. More's the pity that it's all claimed already, though." Bryce threw down his cards.

"What exactly do you mean?"

"You understand the notion of a legal claim, don't you, son?" This man was perhaps five years older than Silas, although his pitted complexion suggested a man much older.

"Of course."

"Well, let's just say that all these people are in for quite the shock once they get over the Chilkoot and all the way downriver. If any of these fools make it that far." He threw a callous hand toward the crowd around him. "All the claims are long since taken. The gold is gone. All they're going to be doing is working for the likes of her future husband, just like us."

"Ridiculous stories," Silas said, "to frighten women and deter honest men from staking their own claims, I'm sure."

Bryce grinned. "You ever prospected before? No? I didn't think so. Firemen, teachers, store clerks, politicians, and office workers. Suddenly, these people, who have never labored a hard day's work, think they can do what we've been trying to our whole lives? They can strike it rich? Because of a story they read in the newspaper as they sat in their front parlor?"

"I think you underestimate the will of these people and the determination and ingenuity of the American worker."

"Perhaps I do, but not the cruelty of the Klondike herself. Look around you, my friend. Many of these joyous people—those smiling and counting their fortunes already—are going to die there. They'd do well to turn around and come back once we reach Skagway, and so would you."

Chapter 2

Stories circulated the ship as the days wore on. There was little else to do but talk. Stories of the great riches that awaited them and of people who had gone ahead and struck it rich were standard fare. The stories were always hearsay. No one could name a friend or relative who was now a millionaire, but all seemed to know of people who knew these lucky souls. Their stories became legend in the confines of the ship.

Bryce and Stevens stayed quiet. Anna kept her distance from them, preferring to share her company with her books or some of the more enlightened passengers. The two men she had made the acquaintance of on the first day were never far away and tipped their hats with polite smiles as they passed her on deck. Although she and Will hadn't shared more than a few sentences since that first day, she had sat in on a couple of the card games that seemed to build around him whenever he sat down. She returned his smiles and bade him luck every time he asked for it, which was almost every hand he played. His brother seemed more intent on planning for the trip and was often seen talking with other prospectors about plans upon their arrival.

She had gone down belowdecks to see the horses, but the smell and squalid conditions kept her from spending more than a few minutes with the bony animals, driven half-mad by the cramped confines of a ship never designed to transport them. Most had bite marks on their necks and shoulders from the next unfortunate beast tethered inches away. It was hard to see them being in any fit state to haul the mountains of supplies that littered the ship upon their arrival in Skagway. The smell of manure permeated the ship. Some took to shoveling it overboard, but it did little good. The pungent odor clung to everything, making the already unappetizing food served in the crowded mess hall almost unbearable. She ate beside other ladies on board at mealtimes, some of whom complained so much as to have her wishing for solitude and the refuge of her books as soon as they sat down.

Retreating to her bunk offered little comfort. The newly installed beds were lumpy and hard, and she found that being belowdecks during the day did little to allay the seasickness that threatened her. Many succumbed to it. Most were not used to ocean travel, and the sound of vomiting over the side was as common as the sight of men as they relieved their bladders into the ocean below at the bow. The bathrooms could not facilitate the 150 passengers on board or even half that number. An unwritten agreement was put in place that the bow of the boat was for men while the bathrooms were to be for the ladies—unless other types of relief were needed. The stern of the boat was for card games, daily exercise, boxing matches, and sing-alongs.

The pain of leaving her family was with Anna in everything she did. The dawn of each new day brought the memory of her mother and sisters crying on the dock in Seattle and the pain that provoked in her. She knew that what she was doing was for the greater good and that she was the savior of her father's business and family fortune. That was some comfort, but no more than a cup of water on a raging fire. The thought of their imminent arrival still filled her with dread. This man, Henry Bradwell, at fifty-two, was thirty years her senior. She tried to comfort herself with the thought that children could bring fulfillment—that some happiness could spring from there—but that dream dwindled to nothing as quickly as the water in the wake of the steamer.

She was alone on the seventh day when Will's voice interrupted her gazing at the wonder of the islands and inlets of British Columbia.

"Breathtaking, isn't it?"

"It is that, Mr. Leary. I'd always imagined Ireland would look something similar. Would I be right in that assumption?"

"It's certainly beautiful from what I can remember. It's green also. That's what the relentless rain will do for a place. I suspect it might be the same case here. It lends an undeniable beauty."

"What do you remember about Ireland?"

"Being evicted from our house. I remember that. The landlord put the rent beyond our means and did the same for our neighbors too. The police came in the middle of the day and forced us out at the point of bayonets. I remember my mother clinging to me and my father as they shoved him to the ground."

"I'm so sorry . . ."

"I have good memories also. I remember my grandmother—God rest her soul—as she held me by the fire, the peat burning and the kettle howling. I remember my cousins and my friends. Most of them are still there. But the memories are fading. They come only in flashes now."

She thought to ask more but didn't want to push this man she had only just met.

"Have you thought much of what my personalized goons said to you on the first day we met, about the Klondike and its dangers?"

"I've seen danger before. I had nothing in the States. I've nothing to lose, not even the cost of my fare on this ship. Silas is the one who's spent money, not me."

"They said many on board would die there."

"Silas says they're telling stories to scare the other passengers away. The other people I spoke to on board delivered a swift rebuke to what your friends Mr. Bryce and Mr. Stevens said."

"I don't know. They seemed serious. I asked Bryce about it in private. He said none of the other passengers has a notion of what hardships truly await them."

"Perhaps they don't. Perhaps they've been blinded by the lure of the gold. We will find out soon enough."

"May I ask what your profession was before we came to meet?"

"Jobs have been hard to come by. I was in the army years ago, but I'll not speak of that. I've been working when I could these last few years. I labor. I play cards. Life hasn't been easy since the Panic. I was in San Francisco when Silas found me. He asked me to be his partner and to come along with him to the Klondike, where we would find riches beyond the dreams of Croesus. What about you, Miss Denton?"

"I was trained as a seamstress, taught by my mother at home along with my sisters, but that was merely a sideshow. My fate as the eldest daughter was to be married off early."

"And such has befallen you now? Is that the way you'd have it?"

"My uncle is a lawyer. I saw no reason why I couldn't follow in his footsteps. The bar association did, however. Ladies are meant to drink tea, darn cloth, and bear children, not to discuss matters of the law. Things are beginning to change now, ever so slowly, but my fate is sealed. I'm to be married to the King. I'm to be the queen of a place I never wished to go."

"Should I start calling you 'your majesty'?"

"I certainly think so. I also believe you should arrange a throne of hay at the stern of the ship where I can watch the boxing matches while I lay down decrees."

"That would seem fitting."

"It's the role I was born to play." They paused a few seconds and gazed out at another wooded green island that looked like no human had ever set foot upon it. "I did have another question for you. I do hope you don't find me impertinent, Mr. Leary."

"Quite the opposite."

"You mention Silas as your brother, yet you have different surnames and different accents. May I ask why?"

"We have different names because we have different parents. We have different accents because he's American. His family, the Olivers, has been here for several generations. Mine were new immigrants." A large man in a tweed suit squeezed past them, and Will stopped talking until he was out of earshot. The sky above was concrete gray, the ocean below a mirror of it. The sumptuous green of the island stood out like a jewel.

"My parents died. I was eight at the time. My mother worked for the Olivers, and I was friendly with Silas, who is two years older than me. They took me in when I had nowhere to go. They treated me as their own. Silas and his older brother and sister are the only siblings I've ever known, and his parents were as my own for many years. Although, to my shame, it's been a long time since I've seen them."

"I'm so sorry for the loss of your parents. I can't imagine what it must have been like to bear such grief at an early age."

Every question she asked seemed to drag up two or three more in her mind that she struggled to hold back. It wasn't proper to make such an acquaintance with her wedding in the offing. Or was it? It was hard to know without direction from her mother.

"It was a fire. They were caught in the tenement building we lived in. Entire families perished. I managed to get out the back window, jumping into the arms of a neighbor from County Clare below. With no other relatives in the country, I was taken in by Mr. and Mrs. Oliver. I owe them everything."

"Did you see them before you left?"

"It's been a long time since we spoke in person. Not since I came out west four years ago, just when the Panic hit."

"I can't imagine when I'll see my family again. I feel the lack of them already."

"I'm sorry, Miss Denton."

"No need to apologize. There's nothing to be done about it. It's all down to my father's business troubles. We were in church praying for a solution, and then a few days later, we received the letter from my future husband. It came with the first ship. I hadn't even heard of the gold rush. I hadn't seen the newspapers. My life was about to change completely."

"What does your father do?"

"He runs a toolmaking factory—garden implements and the like. He suffered from the downturn in the economy as much as anyone else. More, even. His business was about to go under before he received the proposal from Mr. Bradwell." She paused a few seconds to clear her throat. She reached into the tiny bag she was carrying for a handkerchief. "He told me the news that night."

"Did he give you a choice?" He seemed to stop himself. "I'm sorry. I shouldn't ask such questions. We don't know one another."

"Sometimes speaking to strangers is best. I appreciate your listening to me, Mr. Leary." She placed the handkerchief back into her bag. "He showed me the letter and expressed that this was the miracle we had been praying for. It was the only way to get Mabel the treatment she needed. My father told me then that he'd remortgaged the house, and he laid out for me how much Mabel's medications cost."

"What is Mabel's sickness?"

"She has cancer in her chest. She and my mother took a trip to Johns Hopkins Hospital in Baltimore earlier this year to try a new therapy called 'radiation.' The doctors want to try it on her, but we didn't have the means—until the letter arrived from Mr. Bradwell."

"Does your family have money for her treatment now?"

"Some. Mr. Bradwell sent some back with my mother and sisters when they met with Bryce and Stevens."

"Is that enough? Will Mabel need the balance of Bradwell's money for her treatments?"

"Much of it, and with the balance, my father will be able to pay off the mortgage he took out on the house and pay off his business debts. Absent this offer from Mr. Bradwell, my father would have lost his business, and we would have lost our home."

"What did your mother say?"

"She told me to do as my heart dictated. She told me not to go unless it was something I was willing to commit to fully. 'Marriage is forever,' she said. 'This decision will live with you every day for the rest of your life.' I had three days to decide. Bryce and Stevens met us in Seattle and took me to catch the steamer."

"I admire your courage and your commitment to your family. Most wouldn't have done what you did. I hope you can find happiness in the Klondike. Maybe once the rush is over in a year or two, you can persuade your husband to move back to Chicago with you and be near your family."

"Maybe, but it's hard to speak for a man I've only ever met once in my life before."

"When did you meet him?"

"He was at our house in Evanston many years ago, for one afternoon. I had to be prodded to remember, but I can just about picture meeting him. I remember meeting a man with a thick mustache, a prospector, who was introduced to me as a distant cousin of my father."

"Why did he choose you? He only met you once, many years ago. I understand there's a dearth of women in the Klondike, but why you?"

"I wish I knew. I know he and my father maintained correspondence over the years—when Mr. Bradwell was able to. I'm told he spent many years in the wilds of the Yukon and Alaska before finally striking it rich in the Klondike."

"Did your father share the contents of the letters Mr. Bradwell sent him?"

"I never saw one of them. I was presented with a choice. There was little time for investigation or contemplation. Part of the deal was that I reach the Klondike before winter set in, so there was no time to waste."

"From what I've heard, we've little time left even now. It's almost September, and we've perhaps a month or two left before the rivers freeze over."

"What do we do if the rivers are frozen when we arrive?"

"No one seems to know the answer to that particular question."

The rays of the setting sun bathed the deck in gold. At the stern, a fiddler began his song. The sound of clomping shoes on deck signified the beginning of the night's dancing. Bottles were uncorked, and songs of the Klondike soon followed. It was a beautiful evening, and the deck would soon be packed with enthusiastic revelers. Neither Anna nor Will moved to join them.

"This is the last night before we dock at Skagway," Will said. "How long will you be there before your ship leaves for St. Michael?"

"A day or two. I'm not entirely sure. I'm very much on a need-to-know basis as far as my travel plans are concerned. Perhaps Bryce and Stevens don't want me to concern myself with details. Maybe they think I'll furrow my brow with worry over them. Asking them questions rarely ends in my gaining any answers. They're masters of saying little."

"Miss Denton, I don't mean to worry you, but I was under the impression that the all-water route to the Klondike went directly from Seattle to St. Michael. I've asked a few people, including some of the crew on board on your behalf, and they weren't aware of any steamers going from Skagway to St. Michael once we arrive."

"Oh. Perhaps Mr. Stevens and Mr. Bryce know something no one else does."

"I'm sure they won't want to let down their employer either way."

"I'm sure. Mr. Bradwell will be eager to receive his package alive and intact. He did pay top dollar for it, after all."

Will looked out as the trees onshore faded from green to black before their eyes.

The evening drew in. Few retired early, since it was the last night on board. The goldfields were within reach. Stories spread of whole creeks paved with gold. It seemed that one would merely have to bend over to pick it up. People spoke of the trouble of hoarding their gold and whether the banks up there were reliable enough to make deposits. The ladies Anna sat with at dinner spoke of starting schools and giving dance lessons in Dawson. Anna hadn't told them her precise circumstances. As far as they knew, she was going up to join her fiancé, who'd made good. They didn't ask any more questions. They looked past her as she spoke. They would soon forget her.

She walked out on deck as the party was in full swing. Music and laughter swelled the cool night air. Several couples danced in the middle of the deck. Three musicians on their way to Dawson had taken to entertaining the crowd in exchange for all the whiskey they could drink. Empty and half-drunk cups littered the deck in front of the band as they played. The few women on board danced with their husbands, while the rest of the passengers talked among themselves about the new partnerships they'd forged on board. Will played cards in the corner with Bryce and Stevens and several other men. Silas sat beside him smoking a cigarette. She walked over. Will greeted her with a smile as Silas stood to offer her his place at the game. She declined with thanks but then realized she had nowhere else to go.

"Come to bring me luck?"

"Has it worked so far?"

"I'd say so. Look who I'm playing against tonight, though."

Bryce looked up from his cards, flicking his head toward her to say hello. It was the friendliest he'd been the entire journey. Stevens offered a mumbled greeting before sipping from his whiskey bottle. He had been drinking most of the day and almost tipped off the bale of hay he was sitting on as the ship lurched. She stayed a few hands, her eyes drifting over to the couples still dancing on deck.

"Why don't you tell your lady here the real plan?" Will said to Bryce. The older man didn't answer, just held a match to his cigarette. "I spoke to the captain. There's no ship going from Skagway to St. Michael. So when are you going to tell her?"

"Tell her what?"

"Yes, tell me what?" Anna said.

"What happened to the tickets that your employer paid for? Did you lose them playing poker in Seattle?"

"Where are the tickets, Mr. Bryce?" Anna pressed. "It will be easy to prove him wrong—that's if you still have them." Her anger masked the discomfort she felt at the discourse unfolding in front of her.

Bryce stared across at Will. "I don't have to prove anything to him."

"What about to me? Can you produce the tickets for my benefit?"

"We'll get you to Dawson."

"Excuse my brother," Silas said. "It's been a long journey, and we're all tired. He means no disrespect."

"I'm not sure I agree with you, sir," Bryce spat through gritted teeth. "I'm failing to see how he doesn't mean to disrespect my partner and me while implying that we gambled away our tickets to Dawson."

"That was the deal, wasn't it, Miss Denton? That your future husband paid for the all-water route—a route more suitable for a lady of your refinements than the trip we're all about to embark on through Skagway. Why have you been so silent about the rigors ahead of all of us, except for a few brief sentences on that first day?"

"What's the point?" Stevens said. "They'll all find out soon enough."

"We'll get the lady to Dawson, just as we were told to," Bryce said. Lamplight shone in his eyes.

"If we're not taking the all-water route, then how exactly are we going to get to Dawson?" Anna said.

"We'll get you there," grumbled Bryce.

"Of course you will," said Will. "I'm sure Miss Denton has the utmost faith in you. You won't mind if we keep an eye out for her along the way? Just to make sure things are moving along as smoothly as Mr. Bradwell might expect?"

"You won't get away with any impropriety, Mr. Bryce, and I can assure you that your employer will be hearing about this," Anna said.

"I said we'll get you there," Bryce repeated. "The all-water route isn't all gravy anyway. Once that river freezes, those rich pricks will be stuck with no chance of making it to Dawson. This is Alaska we're talking about here. We're better off not relying on that," Bryce said to Anna before bringing his eyes back to Will. "And if you want to waste your time looking out for the only men who have any experience of the hell that awaits us all, you go right ahead."

He threw down his cards and stood up, leaving his money in the pot.

Chapter 3

Will found himself drawn to the magnificent scenery around them. The mountains, which seemed to have been following them all the way from Seattle, came to a crescendo as they pulled into the inlet for Skagway. The hulking black peaks, barely visible through the fog over the bay, were peppered with snow, their summits extending into nothing beyond the line of puffy clouds. Above them, the sky was bright white, the clouds not granting any sight of the sun. All were on deck as the steamer slowed to a halt. Anna stood beside Silas, with Will on his other side. No one spoke. There had been scarcely a word said since they'd arrived. Bryce and Stevens stood at the back, smug in their private knowledge of the rigors they'd promised were to come.

Several other steamships puffed into the bay with the *Mercury*. The tiny wharf in Skagway was wholly insufficient to cater to the ships thronging the harbor, so they anchored in the bay. A fleet of lighters—rowboats, Indian canoes, and barges—rushed out to meet the steamers. The town of Skagway was visible as a line of white tents in the distance. The mountains rose all around it, encircling it in a narrow fjord. It seemed as if the newcomers were utterly surrounded.

Within minutes, barges and canoes encircled the ship. The men on the canoes shouted up prices to take the passengers ashore. Members of the crew threw ropes over the side and began to pass down their supplies to be loaded on board. The men on the barges and canoes made sure to remind the passengers embarking that there was no money back and that all goods were loaded at their owners' risk. With this license to be careless in place, the men on the barges threw around the supplies the passengers had so carefully guarded on board the ship. In the distance, dozens of rowboats full of stampeders and their goods made their way to shore, the men jumping out as they reached the beach to haul the packages onto the sand. The horses would have to wait for the opportunity to get closer to land before being unceremoniously dumped overboard to swim the last few feet to shore.

Bryce and Stevens hailed a canoe. They acted as Anna's porters, perhaps mindful that Will was staring at them as they loaded up.

"We'll see you on the shore. I'll find you," Will said to her as Bryce held his arms up for her. He helped her down and into the canoe, and a few seconds later, they were rowing toward the shore. Will and Silas were with a group Silas had agreed to join the night before, and they helped each other with their supplies into a waiting barge. Each paid the requisite fare, and they left the *Mercury* behind. Will looked up and around as they rowed to shore. The sun was breaking through a crack in the clouds, and he took a few seconds to behold the sparkling aquamarine waters and the snowy, glacier-capped mountains lofting above. It was hard to remember being somewhere so beautiful or quite so intense. Boats sliced through the calm waters all around them, each full of stampeders, all intent on one thing. He tried to pick out the canoe that Anna was on as they went, but it was lost among the throng trying to get ashore.

Massive heaps of supplies were piled along the shoreline. The stampeders wandered through the jungle of brassbound trunks, suitcases, shipping boxes, and foodstuffs, looking for their own.

"It seems like we weren't the only ones to have this idea," Will said.

"It's coming into perspective now," said Silas. "How competitive we're going to have to be even if the gold is as plentiful as they say."

"What if it's not? What if Miss Denton's minders were telling us the truth, and all the best claims are already gone?"

"Well, then I suppose we'll have an interesting story to tell upon our return."

"Interesting stories rarely pay debts."

"The debts are mine, little brother. Let me worry about them."

"We can always stay up here among the bears, eating salmon and drinking from mountain streams."

"That doesn't sound so bad. No. We're going to make our fortunes here."

The land was only a hundred feet or so away. He spied Anna wading into the shallows, the bottom of her dress wetted as she strode ashore. Bryce and Stevens were unloading her goods. They seemed to have a lot less baggage than most of the other travelers—certainly less than he and Silas.

Broken boxes littered the beach. Ripped-open sacks of flour spewed white over the sands, bleeding back into the bay. Hats, dresses, and pants lay discarded, and broken mining equipment glittered unused in the sunshine. The sound of dogs barking cut through the chatter of the several hundred people on the beach, and a horse galloped through the mountains of supplies, its owner shouting at it to stop. Beyond the beach, the town began—lines of white tents of every size and kind pockmarking the land and stretching back for several hundred yards. The men outside the tents seemed not to notice the new batches of stampeders stowing their goods on the shore and didn't look up from where they sat outside, cooking bacon over the fire or having a smoke. Several wooden-framed buildings were visible among the tents.

Silas was first over the side and jumped into the cold water up to his waist. He didn't wait for the crew and began to ferry their supplies onto the sand. Will passed the boxes to him and watched as he waded to shore with them in hand. An hour later, their supplies were stowed along with the thousands of other sacks and boxes that had been brought from the steamers that morning. The two men helped their new companions with their supplies. Soon all were unloaded, and the canoe was back out to garner more business from another newly arrived vessel.

He clapped Silas on the shoulder. "Welcome to Alaska."

"Yes, welcome, and let's get out of here before all the best claims are taken."

Otto Lind, one of the others they'd partnered with, stayed to look after the supplies as they took a walk into the town with several others from the steamer. Few people on the steamer had gotten on with the intention of sharing their fortune with anyone else, but as time went on, it had become apparent that each stampeder was going to need all the help he could get, and people banded together.

Will scanned the crowd for Anna as he went but was unable to pick her out of the maelstrom. The mud of the streets stuck to their boots as they went past makeshift buildings and tents set up as general stores. They stopped in one of the few wooden buildings—which happened to be a saloon. The room was about fifty feet long and sixty wide. On the right-hand side, an unvarnished board served as the bar. A staircase at the back of the room led up to a balcony overlooking the bar area. Several exotic-looking ladies stood with their arms over the guardrail, surveying the crowd for customers.

Will ordered two whiskeys and handed one to his brother. They clinked glasses before knocking them back. The whiskey was poor—probably two-thirds water, he guessed. Several men drank draft beer from the tap that protruded from underneath the bar. He wondered if that was any better and held up his hand to gain the bartender's attention once more.

"You need to watch your drinking, Will. I can't carry you all the way to the Klondike."

"We won't have time for drinking. Just let me enjoy this one, if that's possible." He put his hand down, the bartender still occupied at the other end of the bar.

Several other patrons leaned against the bar. The grandfather clock on the back wall struck six.

"You been here long?" Will asked the man beside him. The man's face was lined with dirt, his britches brown with mud.

"I'm just down from the Chilkoot."

"The pass over the mountains?"

"I take it you're new around here?"

"Just off the boat this morning. Can I buy you a drink, sir?"

The man nodded and stood back as Will signaled the bartender to pour him two beers.

"So what are the goldfields like? What's Dawson like?"

"I couldn't tell you about a place I've not been to yet. I'm still trying to get there. I've been here a week—that makes me an old-timer around these parts."

"You said you just came back from the Chilkoot?"

"Yeah, but I ain't been to Dawson. Not yet. I was in the Salmon River rush in Idaho, but I ain't seen anything like this. Ten thousand people went that winter, but it had nothing on this. This country's never seen the like of it before."

Silas placed his glass down on the bar. "How far is it to the gold from here?"

"You want to get there before winter?"

"Of course," Silas replied.

"Leave tomorrow." The man knocked back his beer. Silas motioned to the bartender for another round. "It's August thirtieth. The rivers are going to be frozen in about seven or eight weeks. You've got that long to get to Dawson. Otherwise, you're stuck until the spring thaw."

"When is that?"

"May, I'm told."

The bartender shook his head, walking away with a wry grin on his face.

"How far is it downriver?"

"Best part of six hundred miles, but believe me—that's the easy part. The pass over the mountains is the killer. How many supplies did you bring?"

"About twenty-five hundred pounds, all told."

"About the same as my partner and myself—before he departed back to Seattle, that is." The man took out a cigarette. Will lit it for him. "You're going to have to haul that thirty-three miles over the pass. You're young and fit. You might get that done in six weeks if you pay for help."

"Pay for help?"

"From the local Indians or from stampeders who lost their money in the casinos. I'd give it some serious thought. They'll help you haul your load." The stampeder's whiskey glass showed stains from his muddy fingers. "There's two choices. There's White Pass, which leaves from here in Skagway, but that's longer and more expensive. You have horses?"

"No."

"People with horses, and who don't care about the welfare of those horses, tend to take White Pass. The rest of us take the Chilkoot. You won't be short of company up there." The man took a deep drag on the cigarette. "It's a mean trail."

"What are you doing back here?"

"Came to see off my partner. He couldn't take it—said no gold was worth going through that."

"Where are your supplies?"

"Cached up near the end of the trail. I just have to make it over one more time, and I'm through."

"Why did your partner come back if you were so close to the end?"

"He didn't realize what was waiting for us at the end—that once we got there, we'd have to build our own boat."

"Why'd you come back? Why not go on alone?"

"He paid me. Everything around here costs money, mister."

Will drank back his whiskey without reply. A band in the corner began to strum, and several prostitutes appeared from down the wooden staircase, dressed in flaming-red, green, and orange. The prospectors leaned back against the bar with wide grins as the ladies began to work the crowd.

Anna strode behind her two chaperones. They had tried to take all the baggage on the sleds but hadn't been able to fit everything. Rather than make a needless trip back, she had insisted on helping despite their protestations. She assured them getting her to Dawson in one piece would be enough to please Bradwell sufficiently, particularly considering the issues Bryce had mentioned afflicting the all-water route. That seemed to reassure the men enough to let her carry a small amount of her own luggage herself. They made their way through newly sectioned mud-lined streets. Work was going on all around them, and the sound of nails being hammered and saws being applied to lumber filled the air. She saw a few wooden buildings, most of which seemed to serve as saloons. She wondered about sending a letter home to let her family know she'd arrived safely.

"I'd like to send a letter to my family to inform them of my safe arrival." She waited a few seconds until she was sure no answer was forthcoming. "Is there a way to do that? Could I send a telegram, perhaps?"

"There's no telegraph or even a post office here. There'll be time for that later."

The men seemed rushed, flustered, and worried, but they weren't letting on why. Being led around like a child was beginning to vex her. It was time for some answers.

"Gentlemen, may I inquire as to what our plans are from here? I understand that we're not taking a steamer to St. Michael, but I need to know the contingency."

Bryce stopped to turn to her as Stevens continued toward their unknown destination.

"There could be some trouble with that, Miss Denton. We're on our way to see a man who may be able to help us."

So Mr. Leary was right.

"Don't worry. We'll get you to Dawson, one way or the other."

He turned away and continued walking. Her shoes were soon caked in mud, but she slogged after the two men nonetheless. Gangs of men sat outside tents. She felt their eyes clinging to her like limpets.

"Be careful who you speak to around here," Stevens said. "There are more inexperienced, desperate men here than in any place I've ever been to, and they're all carrying double-action revolvers."

"There's not much here that could pass as law," Bryce added. "You stay close to us and you'll be all right."

They carried on through the mud a few minutes longer. She averted her eyes from every hungry gaze cast upon her. No one was to be trusted here. They shuffled past a game of three-card monte, which erupted into a shouting match. A stampeder drew his gun, accusing the man running the game of cheating. The accused man laughed as the other held the gun in his face. Another man grabbed the accuser from behind, and the gun tumbled into the mud. Stevens took her by the hand, hurrying her on as the scuffle behind them developed into a full-on brawl. She walked beside the two men until they stopped at a newly built saloon with a freshly daubed sign above the door. The men led her inside. The saloon was packed, and at least a dozen heads swiveled around as she walked in. A band was playing in the corner, and revelers stood two deep at the bar. She stepped back as Bryce motioned to the bartender. Stevens led her away, demanding that the prospectors sitting at the table in the corner vacate it for her. They did so with a gracious tip of their hats, and she sat down, her baggage heaped around her. Stevens ordered her to stay put and not to talk to anyone. She'd never felt so alone in her life.

Will turned around to face the room, his back to the bar, when he noticed Bryce and Stevens walking up the stairs with another man. He pointed out the two men to Silas.

"Is Miss Denton here?" Silas asked.

"I don't know yet."

Then he saw her. She was sitting silent and alone in the corner, like glinting gold in the dirt. He made his excuses to Silas and the others, who didn't seem to hear, and made his way over to her, music and smoke swimming through the air around him.

"Miss Denton. Are you alone?"

"I am, and glad to see a friendly face. My companions disappeared upstairs a few minutes ago. They've told me little, but I suspect they're having trouble securing our passage to Dawson. They're not proving to be the most reliable of chaperones."

"Perhaps Mr. Bradwell should have chosen more wisely."

"My thoughts exactly. Won't you join me? I'd certainly appreciate some company while I wait. Heaven only knows how long whatever business they have here will take."

"I'd be delighted," he said, pulling out a chair. "I'm here with Silas and a few other fellows from the boat."

Silas raised a glass to her from across the bar before turning back to talk to the others.

"What are your first impressions of this place?" Will asked.

"I haven't seen much, only the beach and walking here, but it seems ghastly. I saw a man pointing a gun in another's face and a brawl just on the way here."

"I have to agree. This is no place for a lady of your standing. I've seen a few wild towns in my life but nowhere quite like this. I didn't think places like this existed anymore."

Silas ordered another round of drinks for his friends from the steamer. John Harmon shook his head. "I can't do this. I'm fifty-eight years of age. I can't haul almost a ton of pack over a thirty-three-mile trail through a mountain range."

"I should have stayed in the store in Connecticut," Ned Holt said.

"Easy money, they said," Harmon said. "That's why we paid so much for those damn steamer tickets and for the gear and what brought us to this craven hole in the ground masquerading as a town."

The men drank down their whiskeys in resigned silence.

"It's pretty clear what this all is—a classic con. We've all spent our money and been taken in," Holt said.

"I'm sorry for you," Silas said. "But I still intend to get to Dawson and stake my claim." The jagged-edge advice that Bryce had imparted on the steamer reverberated through his mind, but he ignored it. "My brother and I will be able to reach Dawson before winter. I'm confident of that much. Any man who wants to come along with us is welcome." Harmon looked down at the floor. The other four men raised their glasses half-heartedly, but none expressed his desire to travel.

A red-haired prostitute in a bright-green dress slipped through the crowd to where Silas stood against the bar.

"Hello there, sir," she said. "Are you new in town?" She put an arm over Silas's massive shoulders. "Maybe you need an experienced girl to help show you the ropes around here?"

"I'm fresh off the boat. I'm as green as that lovely dress you're just about wearing."

The other men seemed quite amused by the sideshow unfolding in front of them.

"Why don't you come upstairs with me, and I'll show you everything you need to know to get by around these parts?"

He put down his drink.

"Go ahead, Silas," Harmon said. "It could be your last chance for a while if you're to take to the pass tomorrow."

The other men stood back. Ned Holt gestured toward the staircase. "I'll be next."

"Well, if you're an experienced hand—perhaps we should convene awhile," Silas said.

She led him toward the stairs. His new companions seemed to approve. The band of six men he left behind returned to their drinks as he moved up the stairs. Will and Anna were still talking in the corner. Where had Bryce and Stevens disappeared to? Why bring the lady here of all places?

The prostitute led him to a room at the end of the hall and pushed the wooden door open. It was decorated in garish red, the bed unmade and ruffled.

"What's your name?"

She looked surprised by the question. "Cheryl. What's yours?"

"Silas. Shall we settle payment now?"

"Sure, honey, whatever you want," she said, pointing to a list of prices on the wall.

"Let's say thirty minutes."

He threw a few notes down on the dresser and moved back to sit on the bed. Cheryl began to undress.

"No. Don't do that. Please."

She looked at him as if he were speaking another language. "All right, it's your money."

"How about we just sit awhile?"

"I'll just sit over here, then," she said and sat in a wooden chair in the corner. He lay back on the bed, his fingers interlocked behind his head. He stared up at the ceiling, falling into a daydream of home. The voices of three men talking next door jarred him back into the moment. He thought he recognized two of them. The springs on the bed creaked as he stood. Cheryl glanced up from the book she was leafing through.

"What's the matter, darlin'? You changed your mind?"

"No. No need to get up."

He moved to the wooden wall between the two rooms and pressed his ear against it. He could hear Bryce's voice.

"What are you, some kind of pervert?" she asked. He shushed her, but she stood up, undeterred. "You've come to the right place, honey. We cater to all sexual prerogatives here." She moved to where he was standing and lifted a small oval-shaped picture from the wall, placing it on the ground by her feet. "The boss had this put in," she whispered. "For those who like to watch. For a little extra."

He took a couple of coins from his pocket and placed them into her hand. He had to bend down to peer through the tiny hole into the next room. The bed had been pushed into the corner, the woman who worked the room nowhere to be seen. Bryce was sitting at a wooden table. Stevens was beside him with another man sitting opposite. Bryce stubbed out a cigarette before he began talking again.

"So we find ourselves in an awkward position."

"Bradwell is going to kill you when we get to Dawson. If anything happens to Miss Denton on the way up there . . . ," Stevens said.

"Nothing's going to happen."

"On the Chilkoot? Are you insane? A lady like her? She's probably never hiked five miles in her life."

"How much money do you have left?" the other man said. He had a thick black beard and was wearing a hat to match. His dark eyes burned underneath bushy eyebrows. "Take it out. Put it on the table. Let's see." The two men emptied their pockets. Stevens took off his hat and ran fingers around the lining, taking out a roll of bills, which he threw onto the table. The man in the black hat took a few seconds to count it. "You've still got about seven hundred bucks. Not bad. That should almost be enough to get you to Dawson. But the problem is your lack of supplies. What are you going to live on? You don't have enough food, and this isn't going to be enough."

"What's your bright idea, Bryce?" Stevens said. "You were the one who gambled away our tickets on our first night in Seattle. What are we going to do now?" He gestured toward the man across the table. "You tell me Denny is an old friend of yours from the Colorado rush, but what's the plan, gentlemen? Mr. Bradwell's not going to be one little bit happy when we arrive back with his bride-to-be haggard and worn after a journey through a frozen hell. And when he finds out what you did with the tickets he bought . . . You're going to have to work hard to worm your way out of this, Bryce."

"Not if no one tells him."

Denny stood up from the table. Stevens didn't seem to notice.

"What are you talking about?" Stevens said. "He dispatched us to do a job, and I intend to finish it."

"What he doesn't know won't hurt him." Denny grabbed Stevens's arms. Bryce pulled a knife from his coat and plunged it into the center of Stevens's chest. Stevens's eyes bulged in disbelief as he brought his fingers to the handle in a vain attempt to pull it out. Crimson blood began dripping down his dirty shirt. "No hard feelings, but I'm taking the money myself. I figured I'd join up with Denny here. We're going to rule Skagway, for a while at least. I couldn't have you telling Bradwell, could I?"

Silas drew his head back, his eyeballs burning. Cheryl was sitting by the dresser filing her nails. She looked up at the clock on the wall and then at her fingers splayed out in front of her. Silas leaned in to watch again.

Stevens emitted a few horrific gargles and went still, the knife jutting out of his chest. Denny gathered the money on the table.

"All right, five hundred for me, two hundred for you. Don't you worry, old buddy. This place is awash with cash just dying to be liberated from the pockets of the idiots who brought it here. We'll be rich soon enough. What are you going to do about the girl?"

"Maybe she could get a job here?" Bryce said. "She'd be about the best-looking hooker I've ever seen. She'd make a fortune."

"So we're doing her a favor?"

"I like that perspective. Maybe I could sell her off to the saloon myself and make a few bucks? You want her?"

"I'd take her on. She's not yours to sell, but if she were desperate, I'd surely do her the favor of offering her a job. Problem would be that Bradwell would send someone after you when he finds out that you've forced his future wife into prostitution."

"Let him. By the time he figures that out, it'll be spring. That gives me nine months. He'll have to send someone down here to look for me, but I'll be gone along with the fortune I'm going to make here over the winter. I'm looking forward to fleecing these fools clambering off the boats every day as green as the dollars bulging out of their pockets. Forget the girl. She can make her own way to Dawson, or home, or wherever."

Bryce moved around the table and put his arms under Stevens's armpits. Denny took his legs, and they laid him out on the floor.

Silas felt the blood drain from his face. He turned to Cheryl. "Did you hear that?"

"What?"

"You didn't hear that?"

"I only hear what I'm supposed to hear, mister. Your time's nearly up."

He went back to the bed and picked up his hat. "If anybody asks . . ."

"I know—you gave me the time of my life."

"And you didn't hear anything from next door?"

"Mister, I do not know what you are talking about. What's going on in there?"

"Nothing. Something weird to me but maybe not to you."

"I doubt it. I've seen—and heard—it all."

He closed the door behind him and made for the stairs. His face felt numb. He tried to calm himself as he descended the stairs back into the saloon. A raven-haired prostitute was nuzzling up to his new companions, going from man to man. Even Harmon was smiling. Silas held up a hand to them as he pushed past. He made straight for Will and Anna, still sitting in the corner.

"Is everything all right, Silas?"

"No. I can't say that it is. I need to speak to you both immediately. Outside."

"You need to speak to me?" she said, but he was already making toward the door. Several clean-suited prospectors pushed past them as they left. He had paced fifty yards down the road before he turned to them.

"I was upstairs. I saw something I shouldn't have."

"I'm sure you did," Will said. "You were upstairs with a lady? You?"

"That's not important. I heard Bryce and Stevens, your traveling companions, in the next room. They were with another man I'd never seen before. Bryce gambled away your tickets for the all-water route to St. Michael. That's why you're here in Skagway. You shouldn't be here at all. This isn't what Mr. Bradwell paid for." He paused for a few seconds, but this wasn't the time for considering her feelings. "They gathered together the money they had left, and Stevens began to berate Bryce for gambling their tickets away. Then Bryce murdered him with the aid of the other man."

"What? How?" Anna said. "Oh my God. The poor man."

"Stabbed in the chest."

"He's dead?" Will asked.

"As Julius Caesar. They were just about to dispose of the body when I left. I came straight to you. This happened not more than five minutes ago."

"Did he mention me? What plans did he have for me?"

"You need to come with us, Miss Denton. You can stay with us tonight."

"What about my passage to Dawson?"

"We don't have time to discuss details. Let's get your luggage and make sure you're safe before we leave." There were no streetlights. The glow from inside the saloons was the only light to see. "Will, get Miss Denton's luggage and drag it back to our cache on the beach. We'll deal with it when we have a moment to think. I'll let the others know we're leaving."

"What are we going to do about the murder you witnessed? To whom do we report it?" Anna asked.

Two men were ambling by. Both had worn complexions and old, torn clothing, stained from use. Will raised a hand to gain their attention. "Excuse me, gentlemen, could I trouble you with a question? Where would one report a crime in town? The lady has had her handbag stolen."

Both men laughed in perfect time, as if they had it rehearsed. "Best thing'd be to get on a ship back to Seattle and report it there."

"There ain't no law in this town. The closest American cops are down in Seattle. I'm sorry for your troubles, ma'am, but this is no place for a lady. You'll find things are different in Canada, but there's no system in place here. It's just a bunch of con men and thieves trying to get rich off all the people passing through."

The men walked on.

Chapter 4

Anna kept her eyes to the floor as they walked back to the beach in silence, never straying more than a foot or two from her protectors. Every shadow she saw seemed to carry an implicit threat. The relentless pounding of her heart continued.

Silas paid for a plot to pitch their tent on. All the ground in Skagway was already staked. Nothing came for free here. They even found someone willing to sell Anna a tent of her own, allaying her fears of having to share with her new chaperones. They found a spot at the edge of town. It was almost nine o'clock, and the daylight had faded to a gritty gray. They set up her tent first, with their own beside it. She had barely said a word since they'd left the saloon. They hadn't time to talk or plan, just to gather their supplies from the beach and drag them up on the sleds they'd brought. It had taken them an hour. It was less than five hundred yards. They would have to drag those same supplies thirty-three miles over the mountains that loomed black all around them. Harmon and the other men Silas had partnered with on the boat were still in the saloon. They didn't need to know what he'd seen, and it seemed doubtful that they were going to attempt the trails through the mountains in the timely manner they would need to. Perhaps their dreams of getting to the goldfields were over already. Many of the men cooking dinner and smoking outside their tents were heading home, not onward. Some had been here weeks, some just days. Some had suffered defeat at the frigid hands of the Chilkoot Trail or had been swindled out of their money by Skagway thieves.

Anna closed the flap on her tent, bringing her knees up to her chest. Her hands were visibly shaking, and she felt a great weight on her chest. Almost all her money was gone. Bryce had taken it from her at the start of the journey for safekeeping. She berated herself for trusting him, for having no way of getting home and no way of getting to Dawson. She laid her head between her knees and fought back the urge to cry. What good would that do? She had to get out of this situation herself.

There was one chance. Will and Silas were decent men. She could sense it. And surely they'd want to make a deal with the richest man in the Klondike? She crawled out of the tent. The two men were sitting, staring into the encroaching darkness, finishing off the dregs of the meal they'd made. She hadn't been able to eat.

"What are you going to do?" Will said. "We need to discuss that. I won't leave here until I know you're safe."

"I appreciate your concern, Mr. Leary. You've been so kind."

"The obvious thing to do is to go back to Seattle," Silas said. "We'll try and get you out of here tomorrow. You can send a telegram upon your arrival, and your family can come for you."

Her heart lifted at the thought of returning home, but she knew she couldn't do so in failure. She was here for a purpose.

"I can't go home. My family is relying on me. Mabel needs that money."

"What are you talking about?" Silas asked. He threw down his plate and pulled up a stool for her to sit down.

"If I go home now, I go back a failure. My family won't receive the balance of monies they were promised upon my marriage, my father's business will fail, and my young sister won't get the medicine she needs."

"You can't stay here," Silas said.

"I don't intend to. Not one more minute than I have to. I feel sullied just by being here."

"So what are you going to do?" Silas asked.

"You could come with us—" Will said.

"Now listen," Silas interrupted. "This journey is going to be difficult enough for us. Look at all these men around us who've given up, defeated. Have you any experience of this kind of physical activity?"

"Don't underestimate a woman's fortitude, Mr. Oliver," Anna said.

"What if we get stuck up there and winter comes? What then?"

"Then I will wait out the winter—just as you will—and make my way to Dawson with you when the time comes. My motivations for reaching the goldfields are different from yours, gentlemen, but I'm just as determined as you to get there. I have too many people depending on me to turn tail and head back."

Will drank from the coffee cup in his hand. "She can make it. If we help her along, she can make it."

"I believe in you. I've not met many in my life with your determination, but the fact remains that you're not prepared to make the journey with us. Have you suitable clothes to travel in?"

"Can't such clothes be bought?"

"Of course, but with what money? You told us yourself that you've none."

"I need your help, gentlemen. I'll set this out as a business proposition. I don't know my future husband. I know him only from what my father told me of their correspondence and by his reputation. I know he is a wealthy man. I will have him pay you five thousand dollars each upon my safe arrival in Dawson."

"Five thousand?" Silas said. "Are you sure you can guarantee us that much of someone else's money—someone who has no idea we're even having this discussion?"

"How much were Bryce and Stevens being paid?"

"I have no idea, but I got the impression they were indebted to Mr. Bradwell somehow, and they were doing what they were told to earn some form of reprieve."

"That would make sense, considering their propensity to gamble with what didn't belong to them," Will said. "They weren't able gamblers either." He reached into his pocket and took out a wad of bills. He leafed through them, extracting a few notes before passing them to her. "Take this. I won it from Bryce on board the *Mercury*. I figure it wasn't his to gamble in the first place."

She took the money. "Thank you, Mr. Leary. You're most kind. This should be enough to at least buy the clothes I'll need for my journey." She stood up and looked around the camp. The light of the day had all but faded to black, and campfires lit the horizon, bathing the tents behind them in an orange glow. They still sat in darkness. Their fire would have to wait. Someone somewhere was playing a banjo, and the faint notes lilted over the wind toward them. "Mr. Bradwell is a rich man and is prepared to make a large investment in me. I don't know how much he's paying my father, but I do know my father's business debts were substantial—well over fifty thousand dollars. If he was willing to pay that much for my safe delivery, I have to assume that he'd be prepared to pay a little more to cover for his own mistake in sending those two rogues to guard me."

"It makes sense, Silas."

Silas didn't answer, just arranged the driftwood they'd found earlier to set a fire. It was blazing before he spoke again.

"We can't be responsible for any accidents that might befall you on the trail."

"I understand that."

"We'll be okay as long as we stick together," Will said. "We'll get you to Dawson, and we'll all be rich by the time next summer comes."

"There is one other thing. What about Mr. Bryce? He's still out there. What if he comes after me in the night?"

"I don't see that happening," Silas said. "Your leaving the bar was a blessing to him—it meant he didn't have to deal with you again. He didn't seem to care what became of you. He has plans to join the criminals and con men here in Skagway. He'll try and make as much money as he can stealing from naive stampeders passing through this hole in the ground over the coming winter and then disappear back to the States. By the time Bradwell finds out that he betrayed him—assuming we make it to Dawson before winter comes—he won't have a chance to do anything. We'll all be stuck in Dawson, frozen in, secluded from the rest of the world."

"He'll just assume you left for Seattle. He probably won't give you a second thought. My guess is we never see or hear from him again," Will said.

"And if we did, we'd protect you. On pain of our own deaths," he added.

"But wouldn't he want to tie up any loose ends?"

"And anger the most powerful man in Dawson even more? If I were him, I would disappear," Will said.

"I heard him say the words 'forget the girl' with my own ears. You're quite safe, Miss Denton," Silas said.

"That's a relief."

"Will, can I speak with you a minute?"

"Of course."

The two men stood up. She watched them as they faded into the encroaching darkness, and she raised a shaking hand in front of her face. She tried to hide the fear within her. It was imperative to make these men think she could handle what was about to come. Who would she travel with if not these men? Some instinct told her she could trust them. Mr. Leary was handsome and sweet and seemed concerned about her welfare. Mr. Oliver was robust and levelheaded. There would be few others like them. Most of the women traveling to Dawson would likely be harlots or wary of taking a young lady along with their groups for their husbands to leer over. She counted the bills Will had returned to her—ninety-seven dollars. That might be enough to gain passage back to Seattle. She suspected the price for the trip back would be rather cheaper than it had been to get here. She crumpled the money in her palm, staring into the fire.

Will knew something of what was about to be said. He'd seen that look before. Silas waited until they were clear of the lines of tents to begin talking. "What's going on with you and this woman? Is there something I don't know?"

"There's nothing you don't know."

"I don't want you making decisions that could affect our chances of making it to Dawson based on any romantic delusions."

"Romantic delusions? Silas, please."

"She's an engaged woman, Will. And not just engaged to anyone. She's engaged to the most powerful man in the town we'll likely be trapped in all winter."

"I know that. I'm not a fool. She's promised us a massive amount of money from her wealthy fiancé if we deliver her to him. I do enjoy her company. I admit that. She is an excellent conversationalist. She will help pass the few moments of downtime we'll enjoy over the next couple of months more pleasantly. You would have agreed to help her for much less, wouldn't you?"

"You still know me," Silas said. "I probably would have taken her up there for a few hundred dollars more than her traveling expenses—at least I would have asked for that. You would have taken her over the trail and all the way up to the Klondike for nothing more than a smile and a thank-you."

"And you still know me."

"I think I do, but you haven't told me much since San Francisco. It's never an opportune time to talk to you. What have you been doing all these years, Will? Your letters were sparse, with little detail. We were worried about you for a long time."

The moon was out in the night sky above them, the stars twinkling around it. The air was fresh and crisp. They passed by a family sitting outside their tent. The father was playing the ukulele and singing a song of how they'd all soon be rich. His wife leaned against him, extending an arm around their adolescent son. Two girls not older than ten sat to his right, clapping along.

Will smiled as he felt a jab of pain inside. "I was surviving, Silas. I didn't want to be in Boston anymore."

"We're your family. Why weren't you prepared to accept that when we were?"

"I appreciate everything you all did for me, but I had to find my own way in the world."

"Why didn't you settle down and marry, get a job and try to prosper?"

"I could ask you the same."

"I have my own house and enough money to live. I just never found the right woman."

"I found several women, but none of them was right. There was someone once—she was older but married. She lived across the street from me in a town in Colorado called Boulder."

"I've never heard of it."

"It's a decent-size town of five thousand people or so. I stopped off there a few years ago on my way out to San Francisco. I had a job and was boarding in a little house. I met her on the street. She was thirty or so at the time. I was maybe twenty-four, but she was beautiful. She had these sad blue eyes that drew me in. Her husband was a mean drunk. He'd come home late at night and beat her. Everyone in the neighborhood knew about it but would still tip their hat to him on the street."

"Of course. No one wants to get involved."

"That didn't seem right to me. One time, I was walking home past her house, and their little son ran out onto the street and then her after him. She had bruises all over her face and blood dripping from her mouth. I heard the husband inside screaming at her. I led her back in and told him to calm down. He went for me, so I put him down. I let him know how it felt. I put as many bruises on him as he put on her." He stopped to clear his throat.

"Just like when we were kids—always the white knight riding to the rescue," Silas said.

"I did a couple of nights in lockup for that, but I could handle it. She came to see me a few days later to say thanks and then came the next day and then the next—always when he was at work and she could get someone to watch the baby. It went on for a while like that until I asked her to leave him and come away with her son. The husband showed up at my boardinghouse the next day, pointing a gun in my face."

"What happened?"

"I guess she told him everything. She must have gotten scared of him or of leaving with me. The sheriff came before he had a chance to kill me, and I left town the next day. I never heard from her again. She's probably still with him. So, yes, Silas, there have been other women, but I never married."

"I just want you to realize that our arrangement with Miss Denton is business."

"Of course. I'll deliver her safely into the arms of the King of the Klondike, and we'll go about making our fortunes with his money in our back pockets."

They made their way back to the tents, where Anna was sitting with her legs tucked up to her chest, her chin on her knees. She jerked her head around as they approached, her breathing slowing as she recognized them.

"We've had time to talk."

"Are we agreed, Mr. Oliver?"

"If you're determined to get to Dawson, I'd feel remiss not taking you. I wouldn't trust anyone else with your care."

"We're agreed, then," she said and shook their hands in turn.

"We leave tomorrow morning," Will said. "We intend to set the quickest pace we possibly can. We've no choice if we're to make it to the Klondike before winter imprisons us down here."

"I'm of the same mind, gentlemen. I look forward to a productive partnership."

It was the same dream—the same faces. The sound of gunshots came like bones cracking. Gore coated the ground like a carpet, and everywhere, the cries of Lakota women and children filled the air like a hideous song. He could see the backs of their heads as they tried to flee. Their bodies flew in the air as artillery landed around them, tossing them up like feathers on the wind, their bloodied corpses falling in awkward heaps on the dirt like discarded meat. The smoke cleared, and the shooting stopped. An eerie silence fell, broken only by the moans of the dying. A pile of bodies came into clear view through the dissipating fog, and the sound of a baby crying invaded his ears. His steps led him to where the bodies lay—the crying child, her mother's dead hands still tangled around her tiny body, reaching for him, her black bitumen eyes beseeching him to take her in his arms. He reached down for the baby when another explosion from behind took his body. Smoke filled his sight, and the crying stopped.

Will wrenched his eyes open, his entire body taut, sweat beading on his forehead. He struggled for air. His chest felt as if it were caught in a vise. His heart was galloping in his chest. The dreams still came even after all these years since he'd left the army. He'd hoped that this place—and this mission—would offer some reprieve. Anna's face appeared in his mind, and his breathing slowed. He clung to the serenity of her beauty, letting it flow over the jagged crevices in his mind.

Silas was beside him, his breathing a gentle hum in the otherwise soundless night. She was in the tent next to theirs. The urge to check on her came to him. Bryce was out there. It was doubtful he'd come after her, but a man capable of murder was unpredictable. Will had known enough of them in his time. He raised himself up on his haunches and inched out of the tent into the cool of the night. It was probably three or four in the morning. The town was silent apart from a couple of saloons in the distance. The moon above radiated enough light to make out the individual peaks of the mountains. They surrounded the town like wraiths, guarding the pathway to riches beyond measure. The entrance to her tent was a few feet away. Will knew that peeking inside would be improper and dismissed that thought from his mind as quickly as it came. Instead, he knelt outside, listening to the low sound of her breathing for a few seconds. Satisfied, he crawled back into his own tent beside his adopted brother and fell asleep once more.

Chapter 5

Sleeping past sunrise would have proved impossible even if they had intended it. The tent city of Skagway awoke almost as one, and soon the hills were a hive of activity. Anna fluttered her eyelids open, taking a few seconds to remember where she was. The fear came first. The pain that came with the memories of her family soon followed. Breakfast had become her meal after they couldn't afford the servants to serve it anymore. Mother had never been one to cook. Her whole life she'd never had to, so Anna had taken the situation in hand. She made breakfast for her sisters every day, at first fresh eggs with fruit, but as time went on, she learned the recipes for chicken in jelly, hashed cold meats, and rice-and-meat croquettes, and would have food on the table for her family every morning. And then, when the money grew even scarcer, she laid out the breakfast cereal, milk, and bowls.

She took several deep breaths, summoning the courage to get up. The noise from outside signified her companions were already awake. She smoothed back her chestnut-brown hair before sticking her head out to bid them good morning. Will greeted her with a smile. She disappeared back inside the tent to finish getting dressed in clothes wholly inappropriate for the journey that lay ahead of them. That likely would be remedied easily enough. There were hundreds of stampeders leaving every day, defeated by the trails. Surely one of them would sell her appropriate clothing in her size.

She emerged a few minutes later. Her new companions were beginning breakfast. She insisted that she take over the meal, and the men stood back. They had myriad other jobs they would have to get through if they were to achieve their goal of getting onto the Chilkoot Trail that day.

The two men packed their supplies onto a large handcart they'd constructed from timbers they'd brought. They loaded many of the supplies onto the handcart, with the balance spread onto a sled and backpacks each man would carry.

"This will get us to the pass—and perhaps the first few miles—but we're going to need to improvise from there," Will said.

"We'll have to cache the supplies and go back for the rest every mile or two," Silas said.

"And here was me thinking this was going to be easy," Will said.

They sat down to the breakfast of bacon and beans that Anna had prepared. The men's table manners were better than she had expected. The profile of the average stampeder wasn't much different from the people she'd surrounded herself with all her life. Bryce and Stevens had been the roughest people she'd met so far. She hoped her future husband wasn't similar in character to the men he'd sent to chaperone her. They finished breakfast in the matter of a few minutes. The specter of Bryce still haunted her, and she suspiciously eyed every man who passed.

"I need to buy some clothes before we leave," she said. "I don't want to wander alone, however."

"I think I can spare a few minutes," Will said. "I'll accompany you."

"No," Silas said. "You stay here and finish packing. I'll go with Miss Denton. Time is of the essence."

"Whatever you say, brother." Will bent over to secure more of their supplies to the handcart.

Silas led her away.

"Let's make for the shoreline," she said. "We'll try to meet up with people leaving today and buy from them."

Silas nodded his approval.

"Where are your companions from the ship—the men you were to travel with?"

"I spoke to them this morning. They weren't quite ready to leave—that's if they ever do. I'm not convinced. We can't afford to wait around. Perhaps we'll see them on the trail. Perhaps not."

"I won't slow you down, you know."

"I don't know anything. I don't know you, but I admire your spirit. Maybe we'll be the ones slowing you down. We'll need each other on the trail, though. The more people I talk to, the more daunting it seems."

They found a couple down on the waterfront, the wife in tears. They had given up. The trail was too much. She was willing to part with her unused skirts and coats for some of the money Will had given Anna the night before. They would be a departure from her usual dress, but then all this was new. It was as if she'd been reborn the moment that steamer had left harbor in Seattle. They walked back together. Silas listened as Anna talked more about the letter her father had received that precipitated her coming here. He spoke little of himself, declaring that they'd have plenty of opportunities to get to know each other over the months of traveling together.

The handcart was packed upon their return.

"I see you got what you went for. Any sign of Bryce?"

"None, thankfully," Anna said.

"I'm sure we've seen the last of him," Silas said. "We'll have to leave it to God to pass judgment on him. No one here is going to."

They were ready in moments. Silas took the handcart alone at first, with Will taking the sled, but a few minutes later, they were exhausted. They would both have to haul the handcart and return for the sled together. Anna had a backpack that cut into her shoulders. It felt like it was trying to drag her to the center of the earth, but she knew this wasn't the time for complaints. It took them almost an hour to move their supplies a mile across town to the neighboring settlement of Dyea.

The Dyea Inlet would lead them to the trailhead for the Chilkoot Trail. Without a formal ferry system, the open market ruled, and they soon found a craft to carry them across for a fee. Several dozen other stampeders were waiting for the same barge, and they had to wait their turn to board. The slate-gray waters of the inlet were calm, barely troubled by a ripple. Anna stood by the captain as they made their way across. The two men leaned against the railing, gathering their strength for what was to come. The captain, a man in his fifties, wore a ragged gray beard that clung to his face in irregular patches. He turned to her as they set off.

"You heading for the Chilkoot Trail?"

"Yes. We're trying to make Dawson before winter comes."

"That's quite a challenge. Not impossible but tough."

"So I've heard."

"There's no shame in turning back—particularly for a little lady like yourself. I've had a few ladies on board lately but none so lovely."

"Thank you, but I've no intention of turning back."

"I've seen a lot of men turn back around—mainly city types who'd never done any hard labor in their lives. Didn't belong up here in the first place, if you ask me."

She looked around the ferry. It was heaped over with so many supplies, it was a wonder it floated at all. Her companions weren't talking. She went to inspect their supplies: flour, bacon, beans, rice, sugar, and a vast assortment of dried fruit. They had an array of condiments, as well as enough tea and coffee to last months. She ran her hand along boxes of soap and a medicine chest. They'd brought pots and pans, candles, picks and axes, shovels, a hatchet, and a box of nails. At the top of the pile, tied down, were two gold pans. Everyone else had at least as much. Some had brought more. One man was transporting a small piano. She thought of her own suitcases of clothes and felt woefully unprepared. She took a deep breath and joined the two men in looking out at the clear water. It began to rain. She didn't reach for the umbrella she'd brought. She just let it run down her face like everyone else.

They followed the hordes as they got off the ferry, making their way through the twin tent town of Dyea. The trail began. Dozens of merchants called out as they passed, touting the best prices on the wares they'd need to conquer the Chilkoot. She asked the men to stop for a minute so she could look for the boots she would need, which cost perhaps ten times what she'd pay in the stores in Chicago. Then she returned to Silas and Will so they could begin the slow process of hauling their supplies to the trailhead once more.

"It seems like whole industries have sprung up to prey on the stampeders," she said. "I wonder where they came from."

Will turned his head. Silas was a few feet behind them and didn't seem to be listening.

"I'd say a lot of them came up the same way we did, with the safer idea of making their fortune from us dreamers. The rest of them were probably here already and are taking the opportunity to make their fortune again—from the likes of us."

"Why wouldn't they make their own way up to Dawson and stake their own claims?"

"Maybe they know something we don't. Maybe what Bryce said is true, and the only fortune to still be made is from the stampeders themselves."

"Do you believe that?"

"I don't know what to believe. I'm just making assumptions based on what I see. I promised Silas I'd go to the goldfields with him, and then I promised you I'd get you there. That's all that matters right now. I hope the creek beds in the Klondike are lined with gold like everyone says, but I can't think about that now. The only thing on my mind is getting there." He adjusted the straps on his shoulders and dug his boots into the muddy ground, pushing onward as the sign for the Chilkoot Trail came into view.

The crowd of stampeders seemed to converge around them. Those whose britches had yet to be sullied by the trail quieted down, as if this were some sacred place. Those who were thick with the mud of the Chilkoot already looked up with dread on their faces. Their eyes were a glimpse into what awaited. Several Indians stood at the side of the trail. She had never seen Indians in the flesh before. Their dark skin was stretched tight as snare drums across their faces. Their dress was varied. Some wore brightly colored jackets, others blue denim half coats. Some were wrapped in blankets of brilliant assorted colors. All wore moccasins on their feet.

"They are the Chilkoots," Silas said. "The local tribe the pass is named after."

She almost asked about the Indians but kept her lips sealed. She remembered how the newspapers back home had detailed the Indian wars years before. She and her classmates in grammar school had recoiled in horror at the stories of Indian brutality toward innocent settlers in the West and cheered the efforts of the brave soldiers who had vanquished them. The Indians she saw now were from different tribes and likely had not seen the likes of the Sioux or the Apaches who had dominated the penny novels she'd read growing up. It was hard to separate them in her mind.

What were they thinking of all this? They had probably never seen many white men just a few years ago, but now the whites were here in droves. They must have thought the white men insane. She wondered whether these people were as bloodthirsty and warlike as those in the lower states, which the stampeders had taken to calling "the outside."

Will helped Silas with the handcart. The gentle patter of rain turned to a downpour. The mud thickened. They slogged on. People dropped their provisions, advanced a mile or two, and then came back to haul more. Will caught up with the sled as Silas and Anna stood to wait for him.

She wondered if the two men had enough confidence in her ability to get their money from Bradwell.

"Perhaps we could spend some money to make our trip somewhat easier. It seems like a lot of others are doing so. I'll make sure Mr. Bradwell covers your expenses," she said, pulling her hat down over her head in a vain attempt to stave off the rain.

"I understand what you're saying, but it's a little early to pay for help," Silas said. "We're still fresh. I don't want to spend all our money. Your future husband might not be quite as generous as we all hope he will be."

"I won't leave you in the lurch. I'll see you get all that's coming to you."

"I have no doubt you'll lobby hard on our behalf, Miss Denton. We just can't take the chance that he doesn't do as you say. The more we carry, the more money we'll have at the end of the journey. We might seek help in a few days."

A mass of men slogged past, a random few with their wives in tow. All were dressed almost identically in brown britches and checked shirts. They ranged in years from late teens up to the age of fifty. Most had packs on their backs. Many pushed carts or drove sleds pulled by ragged barking dogs. Several men had horses or mules, and up ahead, she spied an ox hauling a cart. She moved closer to Will as he struggled behind her. The crowd seemed to thicken the farther they went, and they had to slow their glacial pace further. The going was even, the way flattened by the countless stampeders who had already tramped through. The Dyea River flowed past on one side with impassable mountains leading down to the bank of the other. She could make out snow up in the mountains and knew it wouldn't be long until they would be traipsing through it. Few around her spoke, as if conserving energy for what was to come.

Will gave her a grin, although the weight of the sled was evident on his face. "This could be worse."

"I'm sure we'll breeze through," she said.

Several Indian packers bustled past them, their employers doing their best to keep up.

"This is an old Indian trail. I guess it must be second nature to them."

"I'd never seen an Indian with my own eyes before today—alive, at least," Anna said. "My uncle took me to a show at the fair when I was a child. I was about eight or nine at the time. They had a glass box with the preserved corpse of an Indian chief. The proprietor told of the heroism of the soldiers who'd killed the Indian and what a mighty warrior the chief had been. It was quite horrific. I saw that Indian in my dreams for years."

"And you'd never seen another until today?"

"I've not been to the West. I'm a city dweller. I feel quite naive."

"You've nothing to be afraid of. They're the ones who should be frightened of us. I've never seen an Indian do the things I've seen white men do to each other—or to them."

"I thought . . ."

"Let's cache some of the stuff here," Silas said, pointing over to the side of the trail. "I have a map." He pulled a yellow piece of paper from his pocket. The map was drawn in black pencil, showing the stops along the way and the mountains all around. The trail rose sharply in the middle, leading to the Chilkoot Pass, the highest point, and then maintained a high altitude until almost the end at Bennett Lake. "I'd like to try to go two miles up the trail today if possible."

"Seems ambitious," Will said.

"I'm an ambitious man, brother. You know that."

"Only too well."

They stored their supplies by the side of the trail.

"What's to stop people from taking our provisions?" Anna said.

"Nothing, but what's to stop us from taking other people's?" Will answered.

"I asked the same question to an experienced hand last night. There's an honor system in place here for supplies, and woe betide those who might think to break it."

A dogsled sped past them in the opposite direction.

"It seems they've had enough of the Chilkoot Trail," Will said.

Anna kept what she had on her back as the men loaded up the sled and handcart. They moved off, joining the crowd.

She thought of her family and her home as she went. She kept her eyes trained on the men in front of her, but her mind was thousands of miles away. She was thinking about the day her mother had declared she was pregnant again. Anna had been thirteen; Mary, ten; and Henrietta, who had always thought she'd retain her privileged position as youngest daughter, was nine. Father had never been so excited. Surely he would now have the son he'd always craved—an heir to his then thriving business. The girls spoke of little else during the pregnancy, and though their father had referred to the baby in masculine terms, he had declared himself unsurprised when Mabel was born and certainly couldn't have loved her more. It was years later, when Mabel was seven, that she started to wake in the night with the pains in her chest. The doctors came back with the diagnosis of a disease that Anna had scarcely heard of before.

The trail narrowed, the trees seeming to close in around them. The path worn into the earth wasn't more than a few feet wide, and the two men struggled to move the pull cart over the jagged rocks jutting out of the softening mud. Will moved to the back of the cart to push as Silas pulled, and they went foot by foot, bumping along the trail. Only the Indians, with their cushioned backpacks and hefty walking sticks, seemed to be moving quickly. Anna offered her help but wasn't much use with the heavy weight already on her back. Their progress was best measured in feet. The incline wasn't severe—that would come later—but it was constant. The entire trail seemed to be uphill. It might have been manageable had they been out for an afternoon hike. Perhaps they might have made the two miles Silas had wanted that night with nothing to haul, but as the day faded, the prospect of making it two miles up the trail turned from remote to impossible. All around them, stampeders were dropping their supplies to set up camp for the night.

"I don't think we're going to make it any farther than this tonight," Silas said.

Will stood panting beside him, his arms over the handcart. "How are you feeling?" he asked Anna.

"I'm exhausted," she replied. "I could use a good meal and a nice bath."

"I don't think we can accommodate your bath, but we can feed you. Let's find a spot for our tents, and we'll stow our supplies."

The men did their best to pull the cart off the trail. She was worried it might be blocking the way, but as soon as darkness fell, the stampeders stopped where they stood. Tents popped up on flattened spots along the trail, and fires coughed out smoke from damp wood. She hadn't felt so tired or wet or dirty in her life. Her shoulders ached as she slipped out of her backpack, and her hands shook as she tried to set wood for the campfire. She wanted to be home, to be anywhere but this wretched place. They had brought the kettle along, and she took it upon herself to boil the water for tea, which the men sipped with blissful smiles on their faces. They had bacon and beans again, followed by some dried fruit. The men barely chewed their food before swallowing and were finished in less than a minute.

Will helped her set up her tent. The fires around them extinguished quickly. There were no songs or dances, no guitars, no drinks. Most of the stampeders were asleep within minutes of finishing their hasty dinners. Will didn't talk much as they fixed her tent, merely commenting on what they'd seen that day. She crawled inside alone and collapsed onto her blankets. Roots and rocks jutted up through the dirt, and it took her a few minutes to find a level spot. The men were soon together inside their tent, and the sound of snoring followed in seconds. Sleep did not come easily to her despite the exhaustion that rendered her barely able to move. She was thinking about a place she had never been and a man she'd met only once as a child.

Chapter 6

Dawn came too soon. It was their first full day on the trail. Anna felt like she'd slept minutes, though she knew she'd not woken once during the night. The rain had come again and slid down the sides of her tent as she rose. Her clothes were still damp from the day before, so she reached into her bag for her other dry outfit. Seconds later, her fresh clothes were damp too. Will and Silas sat under a tree, already wet. They'd had the good sense not to bother changing out of yesterday's clothes. She assumed the role of cook once more—not out of any sense of womanly duty but just because she enjoyed it and wanted to feel useful. The men were more than happy to wait as she cooked breakfast. They discussed whether to go back for the rest of their cache sooner or later. They decided to press on to Beaver Pond before going back for the rest. None said it, but they all knew that it would take them another couple of days to move all their supplies to Beaver Pond—less than three miles into a thirty-three-mile trail. It was September 1. They had maybe seven weeks before the rivers froze over, entrapping them at the end of this trail.

Her muscles ached. The rain and cold seemed to permeate her core. It was hard to stop shivering when she sat still. The only cure was to keep moving. They set off minutes after packing, trudging up the soddening path. The trail was silent save for the sounds of boots in mud, wheels churning, and dogs barking in the distance. Conversation seemed a waste of energy. Progress was painful—every step earned. Up ahead, a crowd gathered around a stampeder clutching his ankle, agony etched on his face. The three trudged on, powerless to help the now hopeless stampeder.

Nonessentials lay strewn to the side of the trail, untouched where they were discarded—furniture of all kinds, tables and chairs, china plates, cutlery, extra clothes, worn-out boots, empty cans of food.

Silas was toiling up the slope ahead of them as Will dropped back to walk beside her.

"Usually, there'd be bears in country like this," Will said. Anna turned to him, startled. "You won't see any here—not with all these people. They know better."

"Do you think about your family much?" he said.

"I think of little else. I've no point to reference the new life I'm about to embark upon. I'm meeting a person I don't know. I know you more than the man I'm set to marry."

They trudged along the trail for a few seconds in silence, stampeders a few feet in front and behind. With little room to pass, everyone traveled at the same sluggish pace—slogging together like legs on some giant centipede. The rain was coming again, cold and wet in their faces. Anna didn't move her hand to wipe the droplets off her cheeks. What was the point?

"Tell me about them. Tell me about your family. You've told me about Mabel and her illness. What about the others?" he said. There could be no private conversations here on the trail—not when everyone was so close—but she didn't care anymore. She had heard others speak of wives left behind and children not to be seen for months or years. The countless stories of the bonanza that awaited them upon arriving in Dawson still danced on everyone's lips.

"I have three sisters. Mary is nineteen, Henrietta is eighteen, and little Mabel is nine. Mary is sensible like our mother. She's to be married to a doctor in Chicago next spring."

"You're going to miss the wedding."

"Among many other things. Henrietta is more impulsive, like our father. She's a good person but wasn't always easy to live with. And Mabel, she was our baby. Thirteen years younger. We all raised her. She's the kindest, sweetest person I've ever known."

Will spoke again as the memories flooded through her. "How is she now?"

"Better." She smiled. "They operated earlier this year, took out the tumor, but there's no guarantee it won't come back. I just want Mabel to be able to live an ordinary life, and coming here was the way I could at least try to enable that. Perhaps this expensive new 'radiation therapy' could be the key to that."

"I admire you."

"I think of Mabel when I start to lose faith in my father's decision or my own in not refusing to come here. I think I'd do just about anything to secure a safe and happy future for her, even trudge through the filth in this godforsaken place."

"What does she look like?"

"She's cute as a button, with a forest of brown curls. I miss her every day. I miss each one of my sisters—they're my best friends, and if I have to live my life as their protector, whether near or far from them, I will do it."

"Perhaps I'll strike it rich and give you all the money little Mabel will ever need, plus free you of this Bradwell."

"We can all dream. What brings you here, Mr. Leary?"

Silas was in deep conversation with another stampeder about procuring timber to build their boats once they reached Lake Lindeman at the end of the trail. She was confident that he couldn't hear them.

"I'm here to seek my fortune like every other person except you. I want my piece of the bounty under the Klondike tundra."

They forded a small stream cutting across the trail. Some of the Indians passing through leaped from rock to rock, but she and the others waded through, the water only up to their ankles.

"Are you sure? I don't mean to make presumptions, Mr. Leary, but the more time I spend with you, the more I'm convinced that money isn't something that concerns you overly."

"What gives you that impression?"

"What were you doing in San Francisco when Mr. Oliver found you?"

"Building houses, playing cards. Trying to get by."

"Even though your adopted father runs a profitable chain of drugstores in New England?"

"Did Silas tell you that?"

"Yesterday on the trail. He said his father would have given you any job you wanted."

"Perhaps I didn't want to work there."

"You don't get along with Mr. Oliver?"

"No, it's not that. I want to find my own way is all."

"There's no better place to do that than here, is there?"

"Nowhere better." Anna waited for Will to continue. It took him several minutes to speak again. "A friend of mine in San Francisco wrote to Silas without my knowledge after a drunken night when I espoused my affection for Silas to him." Droplets of rainwater flew off his hat as he shook his head. "I was angry at first. I don't know why. I was angry with a lot of things, I suppose. Silas came to California to see me, and I realized that no one had ever been as loyal or as kind to me in my whole life as he. He's the best friend, the best brother I ever could have had—that's why I agreed to come here, Miss Denton."

The trail grew worse and worse as they went. They took a few moments to climb over two massive boulders blocking the way, as if dropped by a celestial hand trying to ward them off. Will climbed up first and reached down to take Anna's backpack before helping her up and over. He lowered her down to the trail on the other side before jumping down to join her. They put their packs on once more before she began again.

Anna called out to Silas. He stood waiting a few seconds for them to catch up.

"Why did you ask Mr. Leary to come along with you?" she asked as they set into a walking rhythm.

"There's no one I'd rather have asked. No one I could rely on more. I'd trust Will with my life."

"Can we talk about something else, please?" Will asked. "I'm embarrassed by your fawning."

Anna waited a minute to continue. "Even though you hadn't seen him in several years? You came looking for him?"

"It was the perfect excuse to find my brother once more and to pluck him from the wilderness."

"The wilderness of San Francisco, Miss Denton."

"He was alone. I knew that. I saw the opportunity for great fortune. Even if we don't find any gold, we've already found each other once more."

"What about you, Silas?" Will said. "We've established that I'm here because I was lost and you rescued me." Silas didn't rise to his jab. "Miss Denton is fulfilling her noble contract to her family. What about you?"

"I'm here to get rich."

"Why couldn't you have gotten rich at home, working for your father? How many drugstores does he have now? Eleven?"

"Thirteen."

"Why couldn't you stay working for him?"

"He's leaving the business to Ethan when he retires."

"Ethan? Does he want it to fail?"

"Who is Ethan?" Anna asked.

"Ethan is my older brother. He's thirty-four and married with two children."

"Your father's spent the last thirty years building that business to leave it to Ethan? No offense to him—he's a gentleman, but he's no businessman. Nor did he ever want to be. He was a carpenter last time I wrote to him."

"As he is still." Silas's words were flat, his eyes fixed on the trail.

"Why on earth didn't he leave the business to you? You've been working there since you were in high school. You know every inch of those stores." Silas didn't answer. "Why didn't you tell me this?"

"There's little to tell. It's done. I didn't have a chance to tell you. I was too busy trying to convince you to come along with me. Everything happened so quickly."

"But why? What did your father say?"

Silas reached a fist to his mouth and cleared his throat. "He said that I wasn't suitable to run a business he'd spent his life building."

"What? What the hell does that mean? Please excuse my language, Miss Denton."

"It's quite all right, Mr. Leary. I understand."

"What did he mean by that?"

"I didn't ask him to elaborate. I'd appreciate if we didn't talk more on the subject today."

The trail dropped sharply ahead, and Silas stopped. "Do you think you'll manage alone, Miss Denton?"

"I'll do my best."

They set off down the trail once more. The rain came in force again as they reached the top and the wind with it this time. Anna began to shudder with cold, but they kept on. They waded through another stream, almost up to their knees this time. It was the thirteenth time they'd crossed the stream that snaked along the trail on that day alone. She was counting. It seemed as though night—and the short-lived mercy that sleep would bring—would never come.

The sun was beginning to dip in the sky when the clearing of Finnegan's Point came into view. Anna cheered the sight of it almost as if she were returning to her parents' house in Evanston. The camp consisted of twenty tents circled around what counted for a saloon, a blacksmith, and a restaurant. None was made of wood. All were canvas. Scrawny horses were tied near the blacksmith's, and wearied stampeders sat out in the open, cooking over the fires they'd scraped together. The three dropped their supplies in a pile. Silas set about making up their tents as the other two made their way toward the saloon. She would never have frequented such a place before coming here, but any residual sense of etiquette she still had was fast fading. Will held the flap of the tent open for her. It was certainly less grand even than the place in Skagway. Several men stood at a wooden counter, six feet long and two feet wide, that constituted the bar. A man standing behind it in a tall hat slapped a bottle of whiskey down, offering Anna and Will drinks. The bartender poured into two dirty glasses and pushed the bottle across to them. They downed them in seconds. She shuddered as she felt the burn but enjoyed the sense of well-being it brought as it hit her stomach. Whiskey was quite different from the wine she'd had with dinner back home, but then, everything was different now. It seemed natural to drink what everyone drank.

"Can I accompany you to the fine restaurant I spied on the way into town, ma'am?"

"You may, sir. I believe our reservation is imminent."

They walked out together. Silas was talking to some prospectors by the tent he'd half set up.

"How far are we along the trail now?" she asked Will. "Please tell me we're somehow near the end."

"I wish I could. This is five miles from the trailhead. We've got twenty-eight to go, and half of our supplies are two miles back."

"I must say I was hoping for better news, Mr. Leary, but we mustn't grumble. We've got a dinner date to get to."

They made their way across to the restaurant, a spacious tent forty by fifty feet across, which somehow also served as a hotel. Several dozen stampeders sat on the wooden benches inside. She found a spot as he went to the counter. He came back a couple of minutes later.

"It's run by two young ladies from Seattle. One of them is making for Sheep Camp tomorrow with a two-hundred-pound cooking range."

"Their gold rush is right here."

"Not ours, however. I'll be back."

She felt utterly alone as she sat in silence for the two minutes or so that he was gone. No one within two thousand miles would even notice if she walked into the woods and never came back. The world seemed far away—a distant memory. No one in the dining room paid her any mind except for a couple of young stampeders making eyes at her from another table. She was used to averting her gaze and had been doing such since she was a child. Men always seemed to stare wherever she went. Their eyes said more than their words ever did.

She greeted the return of Will—along with Silas now—with relief. They sat down beside her with a tip of their hats, and a few minutes later, a hot meal of beans and bacon, bread and butter, with dried fruit for dessert sat in front of them.

"How do you think we're doing so far?" she asked as she sipped her coffee.

"I'd say about as well as we could have expected."

"Did you see the blacksmith?" Will said.

"He's not there. Someone told me he's drunk, or gone back to Skagway, or can't find his tools, or something. They weren't sure. But he won't be shoeing any of the horses I intend to hire."

"We're hiring horses to pack for us?" she said.

"I think that's the prudent move," Silas answered. "We need to pick up the pace if we're to make Dawson by winter. The packing rate to Sheep Camp, eight miles down the trail, is twelve cents per pound."

"My rudimentary math skills calculate that will cost us a hundred and eighty dollars for the fifteen hundred pounds' worth of supplies we're carrying," Will said.

"He always was the smartest, but does he have to be so annoying about it?" Silas took a sip of coffee before he continued. "There's more, however. I think it's a good idea to procure lumber for the boats we're going to need at the end of the trail. I spoke to a man coming back from Lake Lindeman. He says you can't get it there for love or money. We'd have to cut our own, and that's going to take more time. I found someone willing to sell us lumber, but it's heavy—it weighs almost a hundred and seventy pounds."

"That's almost as much as me. It could well be more than me by the time we get to the end of this trail," Will said.

"Are we agreed?"

"I agree," said Will. "It's a lot of money, but if we can save a few days, it'll be worth it."

"Do you agree with the plan, Anna?"

"Yes—for the same reasons Mr. Leary does. It's vital we don't get bogged down early. I don't want to even contemplate the prospect of being stuck on that frozen lake for the winter."

They finished dinner, and Silas went to finalize the deals for the packhorses and the lumber they'd need for the boats. Will sat outside the tents with her. It was a fine evening, and as the daylight dwindled, the stars emerged from the black, twinkling above them for the first time since they'd taken to the trail. The milky, glacial waters of the Dyea River flowed past a few yards from where they'd set up, and they stared down at the river as they spoke. All around them, the trees turned from green to black.

"I meant to ask, Mr. Leary. Do you have any experience building boats?"

"Not as such, but I'm confident. I've built houses and various other things with my hands many times."

"What about Mr. Oliver?"

"No. He's a manager, an efficient administrator. He's strong and willing, though. We'll get it done between us without too much difficulty."

"I admire your confidence."

"This is tough, but I've seen worse. We'll get to Dawson with any luck. And if we don't, we'll be afforded the opportunity to get to know each other extremely well." He threw a stick into the fire blazing in front of him, its glow dancing across his eyes.

"I hope I'm not an impediment to you."

"Not one bit. We've both been most impressed by your efforts so far. I see no need to look upon you as anything other than our equal. There's no room for notions of a woman's place up here—the trail won't allow it. We've little chance without one another."

She was enjoying the conversation, but exhaustion overcame her, and when Silas returned, she bid her chaperones good night and lay down in her tent. She was asleep in seconds.

The sun, though muted by the thick clouds, was up before six. She peeked out of her tent once she was decent. The men were already awake. She cooked breakfast before they explained that they were going to return for the rest of their supplies, still two miles back on the trail. They gave her the choice of remaining alone or coming back with them. She looked around the camp as she made her decision. The presence of several other female stampeders convinced her that it would be safe to stay and that she should take advantage of her opportunity to rest. Her two companions told her that they'd be back by late afternoon with any luck and left her sitting outside the tent. She sat for a few minutes before retreating inside her tent to a small chest she'd been hauling.

She reached inside for letter paper and a pen. She sat outside the tent and wrote.

> Dear Mother and all,
> I am writing this letter from what seems like the edge of the world. I have no point of reference from my prior life for any of what I've seen or experienced these last two weeks. Everything is new. Everything is alien. The feeling of excitement is palpable among the people here, who have become known as "stampeders." My two chaperones proved unreliable and necessitated finding others. I have joined forces with two young men from Boston. They are noble and honorable types and have treated me as their own thus far. I have promised them financial reward once we reach Dawson. I am certain my future husband will concur with the contract I've made with them.
>
> I miss you all so much. Please tell Mary and Henrietta that I'm bearing up well and little Mabel that we'll be reunited soon. With the help of God, I'll be home in a year or two. Perhaps Mr. Bradwell will be amenable to setting up home in Chicago once the madness of the gold rush ends. I won't know until I meet him.
>
> I miss you always,
> Anna

She began to cry as she folded the letter into the envelope. A lady in a tent nearby came over to offer her condolences and sat with her. The company was welcome. They talked about their plans for an hour or so. She was from Missouri and was traveling with her husband and his three brothers. Anna declined her offer to take up and go with them.

Somehow, she felt safer with Will and Silas than anyone else. The lady sat until her party was packed to depart along the trail and bid her goodbye as they moved out, and she was alone again.

She had lunch in the restaurant again, where she was also able to drop off her letter to be picked up by the mail carrier who would pass through in a few days. After she'd eaten, she settled down by the river to watch the Indians fishing. They went out in small canoes, one paddling, the other ready to strike at the fish with the iron gaff he carried. She watched for a few minutes until the Indian brought the gaff down on the water with a loud splash, before reaching in to land it in the canoe. Each canoe caught several fish, all in this unusual way. Upon bringing the canoes to shore, the Indians went to the restaurant to sell the fresh catch. They weren't seeking to plunder or steal. They were seeking to trade. They seemed honest—contrary to everything she'd previously been led to believe. It was puzzling.

The rain was slicing down when the men returned. She heard their voices through the sound of the downpour and stuck her head out to greet them. They were wet through—their clothes, faces, beards, and boots the color of mud. The skies above were fearsome, and she knew that there would be no more progress made that day. She had been a prisoner in her tent since the rain began several hours before, with nothing but her copy of *Wuthering Heights* to keep her company. It was the one book she'd been able to bring. She'd left several on the beach in Skagway when the scale of the journey in front of them began to become apparent, hoping that she'd find some new reading material once they arrived in Dawson. The only other books she'd seen these last few days were discarded in the mud at the side of the trail.

The men unloaded their backpacks and the handcart as she made tea. They sat under a canopy drinking, trying to hear each other above the cacophony of the driving rain. Silas had arranged packhorses for the next day. They'd be setting out on the eight-mile hike to Sheep Camp in the morning if this infernal weather ever improved.

The next morning, the puddles were deep brown across the camp. The river was swollen, almost bursting its banks, but the rain had stopped—for now, at least. The iron sky portended weather Anna didn't want to contemplate.

The horses belonged to a Montanan named Higgs. He loaded them so heavily with supplies that it was shocking they were able to move at all, let alone climb the uphill trail that they'd face all the way to Sheep Camp. They moved out at a sluggish pace that slowed further as time went on. She walked beside Will as they went. Each still carried a backpack, and Silas pushed the handcart with the boat lumber jutting out in front.

"I've never seen such a sorry-looking collection of flea-bitten nags in my entire life," Will said. "Most of these poor creatures aren't fit for the glue factory, let alone climbing the meanest of trails. Some people seem to think that so long as it's a horse, anything is all right. If it were a piece of machinery, they'd take care of it, but they think a horse can stand anything."

"I've never seen such cruelty in my life," Anna agreed.

He took a few seconds to answer. "I'm not sure we've seen much yet. I'm sure worse is coming—and soon."

Progress was painful. The horses struggled to gain traction on the slippery trail. Several had shoes missing. There were few replacement shoes and fewer nails to secure them in place. The torment the animals endured was unlike anything she had seen before, yet they kept moving. It was early afternoon when the first horse went down. Cans of dried fruit scattered as the horse collided with the sodden ground. Gnarled tree roots cut into her, ripping at her brown coat. She let out a defeated whine and laid her head down, as if to welcome the inevitable. Higgs ran back with a curse as he beheld the pathetic figure lying on her side.

"Oh, Sparkles," he said, shaking his head. "What's the matter, girl?" The horse's left hind leg was broken and hanging at an ungainly angle. There was nothing else to be done. Higgs withdrew a revolver from his pack and held it a few inches above the stricken horse's head. "Goodbye, girl," he said and pulled the trigger.

They took a few minutes to repack the supplies, weighting the other horses, who seemed just as tortured as Sparkles had been before she died. Sparkles's corpse was moved to the side of the trail to rot, and they moved off as the rain began to fall again. Canyon City, a collection of tents in the same vein as Finnegan's Point, came into view as the day waned. The horses lay down in the mud, desperate for any escape from the sufferings of the trail. The men unpacked them for the night, revealing the raw, chafed skin on their backs from the wet blankets. Their legs were a mesh of cuts and bruises from countless rocks, tree roots, and scrub. They were all thin as snakes and exhausted to the point where they could hardly lift their heads.

Several newly constructed wooden buildings stood as a reminder of something of the civilization Anna had once known. She took a walk with both men to the Canyon City Hotel. It was packed with stampeders in for dinner, and they had to wait a few minutes for places to open up on the crowded benches. The lady of the house, who introduced herself as being from Oregon, came to take their order, and a meal of sausages, potatoes, and beans was quick to follow. When the lady came back to take their plates, she stood a moment, looking at Anna.

"Are you with these gentlemen?"

"I am."

"You don't belong here."

"I've made it this far, just the same as everyone else. What gives you the right to make statements such as that?"

"I don't mean any offense, Miss. It's just your face, your eyes, your hands. You've never done a hard day's work in your life, have you?"

"That depends upon what your definition of a 'hard day's work' might be."

Will held up a stern hand. "Thank you for the food, ma'am. We appreciate that. Let me assure you that Miss Denton here has been an asset to our party thus far, and we're proud to be packing with her."

"I apologize if I caused any offense to your friend, sir. It's just . . . I was in her shoes a few months ago. I thought I could conquer the Chilkoot myself, but I turned around and came back. I just wanted to warn you. I didn't come all the way up here to serve in this restaurant, but I got to earn my passage home somehow. I wasn't able for the Golden Stairs, and I've seen hardship all my life. I just hope you know what you're up against."

"The Golden Stairs?" asked Silas. "The passage over the Chilkoot?"

"It's a thirty-degree climb all the way, littered with boulders, covered in snow all year round. The wind and snow in your face with all that weight on your shoulders is more than most can bear. The majority of people turn around and come straight back. What you've seen so far is easy compared to what's coming. You should know that."

"The lady knows what she's getting into and is a lot tougher than she looks."

"Thank you for the advice," Anna said. "We're going to make it the rest of the way—no matter what it might take."

"Good luck," the lady said and shifted away.

The rain kept on, and the trail only got steeper. The horses had somehow survived the night, and the next morning brought the same torment as the day before. Every inch of Anna's body ached, but she drew strength from the horses. She knew her torment was nothing compared to theirs. The trail was still alive with stampeders. They were surrounded all the time. She had become more attuned to the conversations going on around her as time wore on. In between talking to her companions, she had little else to occupy her mind on the trail. She began to notice the different accents and languages, the different races and cultures, all brought here in pursuit of the color. She heard French and German, Italian and Russian. There were almost as many Canadians as Americans and people who'd traveled from Mexico and even from Britain. Late that afternoon, she turned to see Will speaking with another man in a language she'd never heard before.

"Miss Denton," Will said when they caught up to her, "this is Sean Flynn, all the way from Skibbereen in County Cork."

Flynn tipped his hat with a smile. He was about three inches shorter than Will, with an unkempt brown beard and green eyes like emeralds in the mud puddle of his face.

"It's a pleasure to meet such an elegant lady as yourself in a place like this."

His comment elicited a slit-eyed sideward look from Will. She was quite used to such approaches and held out her hand to greet him. She doubted she looked too elegant anyway. Her bathing had been reduced to washing her face in the freezing waters of the Dyea River, and the thought of having a proper bath seemed a luxury beyond measure. She walked with the two Irishmen for a while. Will seemed at ease with his fellow countryman, his accent morphing back to what it might have been. The two men talked about Ireland and what had driven them to the new world. Flynn had been living in Brooklyn when he'd heard about the boundless bounties of the Klondike. He had traveled up with a menagerie of people of different races and ethnic backgrounds. The two were still talking as the train reached Pleasant Camp at the end of another muddy, sodden day. They shared a bottle of whiskey that night that Flynn had brought along for such an occasion, and the next morning, Will woke up white-faced and didn't say a word until lunchtime.

Chapter 7

They arrived at Sheep Camp the next day, thirteen miles along the trail. It was yet another makeshift town scattered among the spruces. It was set along the boulder-lined shores of the river that snaked beside them on the trail. They waded through the frigid river waters, the horses in front, and into the cluster of perhaps a hundred or hundred and fifty tents. Several wooden-built hotels and restaurants stood out among the white tents pockmarking the camp. The rain had been a constant for days. Higgs stopped the horses at a convenient point, and the poor nags got the chance to rest their bruised, bony legs.

Everything was wet. The canvas and rubber covers over the goods could do only so much. Silas and Will stacked the supplies together, cans and other waterproof items covering the more delicate goods beneath. They worked in silence. They had no need to speak. The years they'd spent apart had faded away quickly. They still knew one another, almost as well as when they were boys. But the gaps in time jutted in, obscuring parts of each other's lives they had still to discover.

Will had no great desire to tell Silas about the things he'd done in the army and the years he had been gone. It was bad enough to bear the shame of what he'd witnessed himself. He had no wish to burden him with it.

Late afternoon brought an overdue break from the rain and an opportunity to sit out in the open for the first time in days. Silas left to organize their passage to the next stop: a straight climb to a staging point known as the "Scales." It would be their last stop before the rigors of the Chilkoot Pass and the Golden Stairs. Will looked across at Anna as she tried to clean the dirt from under her fingernails. Her tenacity and determination were greater than those of any woman he'd ever met. He wondered what would have happened if they'd met elsewhere—at a coming-out event or in school. He wondered how he would have tried to woo her. She noticed him laughing and asked what the joke was. He shook his head and blamed his encounter with Flynn the other night. She went back to the futile task of cleaning her nails.

He left her a moment and went to the river. He pooled water in his hands and reached into his pocket for a bar of soap. He lathered his face, focusing on the straggly hairs of his beard. It was longer than it had ever been before. He had no idea how it looked. He hadn't seen his reflection in a week—had deliberately avoided it. He thought about Flynn as he washed his face, neck, and arms. There were other Irish here. There were other Irish everywhere, but Flynn was from the village where Will's mother had spent her childhood. Flynn knew some of Will's cousins, but it wasn't a village he knew. He hardly knew even the one where he'd been born. The images of Ireland in his mind were hazy, like looking through a fogged mirror. It was his family he remembered most, the house they'd lived in—and the day they'd been evicted from it. Where was home? The tenement building they'd died in? That place was nothing more than a frequent setting for his nightmares. The Olivers had tried to make their house his home, but he had felt like a guest, maybe even an interloper.

After ten years of living there, he'd never felt truly one of them and knew that he never would be, so he had joined the army. He had been desperate for an escape and relished the prospect of serving his adopted country against the red-faced menace on the plains and prairies of the West. He'd thought that the army would be the family he no longer had and provide the home he craved, but it wasn't and it didn't. The generals and the newspapers alike praised the indefensible actions his battalion had committed in the name of the Union. His commanding officer, Colonel Forsyth, would never stand trial for the war crimes he'd committed. One of Will's old comrades had told him one drunken night that the colonel had been promoted and had married the daughter of the governor of Ohio. Few of Will's old friends saw things the way he did. Most just went home to their families, willing to forget the atrocities they had perpetrated. He wondered if they slept at night. He wondered that as he stared at the ceiling above his bed each night. There was no home for him among them.

He took off his hat, placing it on the dry dirt beside him, and turned around. Anna sat by her tent alone, and he bent down to cup his hand full of water once more, running wet fingers through his shaggy hair. Satisfied that he was somewhat presentable, he made his way back toward her. Her brown eyes flicked up as he pulled over a crate to sit down.

"There's a hotel here," she said.

"There is?"

"The Palmer House. I took a walk over when you were at the river."

"I didn't realize I was gone long enough."

"You were down there almost an hour. It's nice to see the skin on your face again, I must say."

"I figured I should clean myself up before dinner."

The camp was in a massive gorge, the snow-flecked mountains rising hard and steep around them. Up to his left, he noticed a huge glacier jutting out over the mountain as if it were about to tumble and fall on top of them.

"I want to say, Miss Denton, there's no shame in turning for home from here. Many more experienced than you will have done so. I've met more on the way back than those carrying on."

"You don't think I can make it?"

"I believe you could walk through that mountain if the intention took you."

"Well then, why are you looking to dissuade me? I'll reach Dawson if it's the last thing I do, Mr. Leary."

He was tempted to say that he feared it might just be but was saved by the sight of Silas returning.

"Your brother wants to dissuade me from going any farther."

"No, I don't—"

"He thinks I can't make it."

"I never said any such thing!"

"I got you there!"

Silas laughed. "I should hope Will knows better than to try to talk you out of anything, for that would be an exercise in futility."

"I'm well aware, believe me," Will said.

"There are lodgings here," she said. "It would be wonderful to procure a warm bed or even"—she lowered her voice as if speaking of something clandestine and mysterious—"a bath!"

"I think you might be setting your sights a little high there, Miss Denton," Silas said. "But come with me; there's something I want to show you."

The two stood without a word and followed Silas through the tent town of Sheep Camp. They passed by saloons and restaurants, general stores and pharmacists. All manner of services was available, all charging exorbitant prices. The stores were full of filthy, exhausted stampeders. Many bore the stern look of defeat on their lined faces. The trio reached the tent on the other side of town a few minutes later. Silas gestured for the others to peek inside. A man in black robes sat on a crate at the back of the tent, banging what appeared to be a gavel on a wooden box. Several other men sat facing him. He silenced them as he began to speak.

"It's a courthouse," Silas whispered. A man sitting to the left, with manacles clasped around his wrists, stood accused of stealing a horse.

The judge afforded another man, who appeared to be the defendant's lawyer, the chance to speak on his behalf. He seemed to be making his closing statement. Will wondered how long they'd heard the case. He guessed no longer than a few minutes. The prosecuting lawyer had his say. After a few seconds' deliberation, the judge professed the accused's guilt, to protestations and groans from the left side of the courtroom. He sentenced the man to be taken outside and horsewhipped and then banned from the trail. He was to be taken back to town the next day and, if seen again on the Chilkoot, was to be immediately detained by the US marshal. Will had heard of the US marshal several times but had yet to see him. The guilty man was led out of the tent, past where they were standing, to a chipped wooden post a few yards away. The man leading him out wasted little time. He tied his wrists to the post and stripped him to the waist. A bloodthirsty crowd gathered within seconds, eager to see what followed. Will was less keen for Anna to witness it. He'd seen men take lashings before. It wasn't something any of them needed to see.

"Time for us to leave," he said. The others didn't argue and followed him back toward their tent.

The sun was low in the sky as they treated themselves to dinner in the local hotel once more. It was basic, as everything on the trail was, but well cooked. He never got sick of bacon and beans. The hoteliers announced after the meal that anyone could make room for themselves to sleep on the wooden floor overnight free of charge.

"What do you think?" he asked. "The prospect of sleeping indoors seems like unimaginable luxury to me."

"What about the lady?"

"I don't want to sleep in the tent again any more than you gentlemen."

"It wouldn't be proper," Silas said.

"I don't think the rules of polite society apply here. I won't be performing a cabaret act for the sleeping stampeders. I assume you two will guard my virtue."

"Of course," Will said.

"Well then, it's settled. We'll take this spot, and I'll sleep by the wall."

The sound of the tables being pushed back seemed to take the words out of Silas's mouth. Seconds later, the three of them were helping push back the table they'd been sitting at to reveal the bare boards that would be that night's bed.

"I'll go back to the tents and gather some blankets to lay down on the floor," she said and left.

All around them, weary stampeders took off mud-encrusted boots and hung dirty socks over banisters. The two men took off their tweed coats and threw down their hats to mark out space. A heavy smell of filthy sweat hung in the air like noxious gas.

"Are you sure about this?" Silas said.

"I'm not about to sully Miss Denton's virtue in this place with a hundred filthy prospectors snoring within touching distance. Are you?"

"Of course not." He seemed shocked by the mere suggestion. "I'm not the one to worry about. I've seen the way you two interact together. I've spoken to you before about this."

"And I've listened to you before, brother. She's a comely lady—I'll be first to admit that. But she's a lady first and foremost and not likely to let a smelly cur like myself lay hands on her, particularly in a place like this. Besides, there are other ladies in here."

"Any other unmarried ones?"

"Are you going to perform a survey?"

"It shouldn't matter where we are. We have a business arrangement with Miss Denton and nothing more. I enjoy her company also, though perhaps not so much as you."

"You've developed quite the active imagination these past few years."

"Just make sure you remember why we're here and what our priorities are."

"I think of little else."

She returned with blankets for each of them. Five minutes later, the floor was almost entirely covered with sleeping bodies just inches apart. She slept at their feet, perpendicular to them, against the wall. The lights dimmed to a flicker, and any talking in the room stopped. Dozens lay still, and apart from the sound of snoring, only the howling of the wind outside was to be heard.

Will lay on his back, staring at the ceiling, reveling in the relative luxury of a dry, flat place to lie down. Silas seemed to fall asleep within a minute or so. Will tried not to think about Anna, just a few feet away. He tried to listen out for her, but there was no sound to signify she was even there at all. Clamping his eyes shut, he endeavored to force himself to sleep. He was still awake several minutes later. He raised his torso up to a vertical position. Nothing was stirring in the room. No one else moved. It seemed everyone was asleep.

"Miss Denton." His whisper was so low that he barely heard it himself. "Are you awake?"

No words returned. She was turned away, on her side. "I'm sorry if I implied I didn't think you were up to this journey. I believe you're the strongest and most steadfast woman I've ever met." No answer came. She didn't move. "You might be the most beautiful thing I've ever seen." The words seemed to escape his mouth against his will. He propped himself up on his elbows, beholding the back of her head for a few more seconds, before letting himself drop back to the floor. He was staring up at the ceiling when he heard the whisper.

"Thank you, Mr. Leary," she said.

The snow came overnight. It lay three inches deep when they emerged from the hotel at first light. The mud was covered over, temporarily at least. The trees carried snow like icing, the mountains around them like dollops of cream. The sky was clear now. Will didn't mention the words he'd spoken the previous night. He was glad that the immediacy of the predicaments they faced made it seem absurd to do so.

Several of the stampeders declared that they'd never be able to continue given the new conditions and that the only thing was to cut their losses and turn back. The three companions remained silent as they lined up to leave the hotel in a mournful procession. Each person venturing on knew what was to come and privately questioned their own limits. Each wondered if they would make it and if this was where they'd breathe their last.

"All the more gold for us," Silas said, but no answer was forthcoming.

Silas organized horses to pack for them as far as the Scales. The snow had reminded the stampeders of the oncoming winter, and the packers responded in kind. Their rates went up. The three agreed to spend more money getting to and over the Chilkoot Pass and then to pack themselves from there. To go without help might mean getting stuck—as the rivers froze—and frittering the money away in other ways without the option of reaching Dawson until summer 1898.

Will was alone packing the tent when she came to him.

"Thank you for your kind words last night, Mr. Leary."

"I was under the impression that you were asleep." He walked over and began stripping the tarpaulin from the supplies still to be packed. She followed him.

"I didn't mean to embarrass you," Anna said.

"Didn't you?"

"Well, perhaps a little. I thought you'd be able for it."

He let the tarpaulin fall from his fingers. "You're certainly more than meets the eye, Miss Denton."

"I take that as a compliment, sir."

"As well you should."

Silas walked back to them, ending the conversation as he explained the day's agenda. It was a steep three miles to the Scales, climbing more than fifteen hundred feet.

The valley was strewn with enormous boulders, worn down by eons of glacial movements and rushing waters. The steepening trail doubled the pressure they felt from the weight on their shoulders. It became apparent after a few hours that the handcart would no longer be useful, and the two men were forced to carry the load between them along with the packs on their backs. Will's entire body ached with every step, and even Silas, the strongest man he'd ever known, struggled to deal with the weight and incline. Anna did her best to offer them moral support, but they needed ten more people to make a real difference. The horses began to struggle, and Silas made the decision to unpack them then and there. After a few minutes of shouting, the horse driver offered a partial refund, and the three were left with their masses of supplies in a granite wasteland. Packers passed them on both sides as they rested a few minutes before once more taking up the strain against the relentless mountain. They reached the Scales in the midafternoon. Will was in considerable pain. His legs, shoulders, and thighs were on fire. The two men left Anna with the supplies they'd managed to carry up the first time, and they went back for the rest again, and then another time, until they lay exhausted in the snow next to their wooden boxes, suitcases, and bags.

She had set up the tents upon their return, and they wolfed down the food she'd prepared in seconds. The Chilkoot Pass was within touching distance now, and they could make out the army of stampeders struggling up from the bottom just a few hundred yards from where they lay. The line of people looked like a great black chain, each link moving upward as another joined it from below. There were few animals here; the slope was too steep for them. Only the mountain goats could climb it. The only help they could expect would be from hired packers, mainly Indians, whose prices could scarcely be believed.

Will tried not to look up at the pass but knew that come the next morning, there'd be no ignoring it. Dozens of tents stood around them, and thousands of pounds of supplies piled up around each. The three sat watching the line of people snake up the mountain and then come back down for more supplies. And then do it again and again.

"Most of them must be going up and then back down twenty or thirty times," he said.

"This could take a week," Silas said.

"A fine place to spend a week."

Will tried to ignore the aches and pains overtaking his body as he awoke the next morning. The army of ants was beginning its steady march up the side of the mountain. Anna helped them prepare packs of about fifty pounds each and strapped them to their backs. Silas insisted that she stay behind on the first run. She crossed her arms and scowled but made no verbal protest. They set off. It was only a few hundred yards to the bottom of the chain. They settled in behind a man and his wife conversing in German and grabbed hold of the steel line in place to help them along. They trudged upward, over jagged rocks and stones, forty-five degrees in single file. The conversation around them was soon replaced with groans. The sun was high in the sky, casting a glare down on the patches of snow near the top of the pass. Will kept his eyes down, watching his feet as he went, singing to himself. Up ahead, he saw two men carrying a canoe between them, bent over under its weight. Some stepped out to rest and were unable to rejoin for hours as the relentless march continued up the mountainside. The trail grew steeper as they neared the top, and they found themselves crawling on their hands and knees over snow-tinged boulders. The Indian packers overtook them as they neared the top. They seemed to glide over the rocks and snow.

Their powerful frames were apparently made for rigors white people couldn't bear.

Will felt little elation as he summited the Chilkoot Pass that first time. Dozens of people milled around the flat area at the top before turning around to make their way back down. There was no triumph in knowing that they'd have to turn around and do it all over again multiple times. They cached the supplies they'd carried up together and spread a tarpaulin over them to keep off the inevitable rain and snow. They stuck a flag into the snow beside their goods, as was the custom, and made their way back down. They were able to slide the first hundred feet or so and then climbed down the rest of the way.

Anna had the packs ready when they returned. They stopped off for a warm cup of tea and some dried fruit before setting out again, joining the human chain back up the mountain, their shoulders aflame, their feet barely able to carry them another step. Anna was ready to go upon their return. She had prepared a pack for herself for the third time they ascended that day. Both men knew it was likely to be the last, as the afternoon was well upon them. Will was too tired to argue with her decision to shoulder a pack but insisted she climb between them, with Silas at the head and he behind her. The going was slow but no slower than it had been earlier. She never complained. She slipped and fell over but brushed the snow off her dress and kept on. She crawled most of the last few hundred feet and fell on her side as they finally reached the top.

"We made it." She panted. "Now to do it another fifteen times."

They unloaded the goods and made their way down again to pick up more. The pattern was set. Despite her protests, they allowed her to pack up the pass just once each day. On the fourth day, with almost half of their supplies up the pass already, they had spent more than any of them wanted to on packers. Three sturdy Tlingit Indians carried sixty pounds each up the mountain as Silas and Will followed behind them. It was hard to believe some of the goods people transported. Will saw one company of men hauling pieces of a steamboat up and over the pass to be constructed upon reaching Lake Lindeman. Some musicians dragged a piano up on a sled. One enterprising stampeder transported wooden cages of chickens on his back. And there were still those who turned around upon seeing it. Every day, stampeders came as far as the pass but then no farther. It was a test like no other.

Their heap of supplies at the bottom of the pass dwindled, and by the seventh day, they were packing up their tents and the last of their bags. It was a clear afternoon, and they stood a few seconds, beholding the line of people coming up behind them and the valley below. The beauty of the mountains around them was breathtaking, and for a few seconds, it transported Will away from time and place, from backbreaking labor and the prospect that they weren't done yet. The Klondike and the untold riches that awaited those with the tenacity to make it that far awaited.

Chapter 8

Anna felt changed. Pain was as much a part of her daily existence now as breathing. She hurt all the time. Her skin was lacerated from shrubs and the sharp edges of boulders. Her lips and skin were cracked and chapped from the merciless elements. Her feet were more blister than skin, and her joints ached as if she were a hundred years old. She was thinner than she'd ever been. How would Mr. Bradwell react upon seeing her like this? He was expecting a young, beautiful bride but instead was to be delivered an exhausted hag. But even with all that had happened to her appearance and her body, she felt stronger than she'd ever been. They'd been on the trail more than three weeks. Compliments were sparse when survival was at stake, but she'd received many, even from Silas. She thought back to what her life had been before this place. She was more than that. She knew that now. The evidence was plain as the chapped skin on her face. She had made it this far when so many thousands had not. It seemed that the majority had already turned around and gone home. Only the strongest would make it over the Chilkoot Trail, and she knew now that she was one of them.

Her engagement to Bradwell weighed on her. It was impossible to construct a future in her mind with a man she didn't know. He was older, true, but perhaps he was gentle and kind. Her sadness and worries were greatest when she was alone in her tent at night and in quiet moments on the trail.

Silas and Will were her family now. Yet somehow, she felt as if she didn't fully know Will. It was as if there was some part of him that he kept hidden. Nothing had been said between them—apart from the night in Sheep Camp when she had delighted in embarrassing him for his kind compliments—but an unspoken caring existed between them now. It had gotten them this far, and she knew it would remain all the way to Dawson—when it would end.

Ten days had passed since they'd entered into Canada over the Chilkoot Pass. They had spent those ten days at Happy Camp—certainly a misnomer if ever one existed—where for two days they'd taken shelter from a storm the likes of which she had never seen. Word had come through that Sheep Camp had been washed away. The riverbanks had swelled, and the tents and buildings were gone. Several people were lost. She wondered if the ladies who'd operated the restaurant there had gotten out, but no one knew.

The ferry across Long Lake saved them several days, and now the sight of Lake Lindeman filled her heart with a joy she'd not known since she'd come here.

She forgot herself, jumping into Will's arms, embracing him. She knew how improper it was to do that but was beyond caring. A hundred twenty or more tents dotted the lakeshore, with stampeders bustling among them. They could make out the sawpits from their elevated position and the skeletons of dozens of boats in the process of being built. Lake Lindeman stretched out four miles, narrow and beautiful, with towering snow-peaked mountains around it. The vegetation returned with the drop in elevation and lent a lush appearance to the magnificence of the landscape. She had never seen anything like it before.

It was September 26. It had taken them nearly a month to go over the Chilkoot. The Indians said the lake would freeze in four weeks.

"With any luck, we'll be in Dawson in two weeks," Will said.

"We haven't a moment to waste," Silas said.

Even though the lake was in sight, it still took them most of the rest of the day to pack their supplies down the hill and into the camp. It was late afternoon by the time they had all their boxes, suitcases, and sacks together and piled up beside their tents. Will sat outside the tent, sipping hot coffee Anna had made. Silas was away making arrangements for the next morning.

"Have you any experience in boats, Miss Denton?"

"Not as such. I was out on a yacht on Lake Michigan a few times. I expect this will be quite different."

"That's a fair assumption to make." He put his coffee cup on the ground. Tents were pitched all around them, and the air was filled with the sounds of sawing and hammering nails. Two prospectors engaged in a screaming match forty feet away. One of them blamed the other for incorrectly sawing the wooden boards for the boat they were working on.

Every few minutes, a boat launched. Will stood up and gestured for her to stand with him as a large sailboat was put out on the lake a few hundred yards away. The men inside let out a loud cheer as they dipped their oars in the icy gray water and began to paddle. The boat was about twenty-five feet, the beam in the middle six or seven feet tall, the stern wide and square, with a steering oar behind. Anna noticed most boats had the same look.

"Will our boat be similar to that?"

"Yes. Perhaps a little smaller but of the same ilk."

"I asked you before if you had experience building boats, Mr. Leary. Now I have another question: Do you have any experience sailing them?"

"I will soon, Miss Denton. I will soon."

Nightfall came. Fires cast ghostly orange light on the tents and sent sparks high up into the darkness. It was a fine evening, and some musicians began to play outside their tent a few hundred yards away. One of the prospectors spied the opportunity to make money and set up an impromptu bar outside his own tent, selling whiskey he'd hauled over the Chilkoot at exorbitant prices that no one objected to. Within a few minutes, a large party began. Will called out as he saw Flynn by the fire, and soon, they were speaking their Irish language again, sharing the overpriced whiskey and swapping stories of the trail. Silas stood with Anna by the fire.

"What are you going to do with all this money that you're going to make up in the Klondike?" she asked.

Silas seemed unprepared for the question and spluttered before answering. "It's funny you should ask that. That was the one thing I hadn't planned for."

Several prospectors and their wives had begun to dance to the lively music. "Shall we?" Anna asked. She hooked her arm around his.

"It would be my pleasure, ma'am."

Silas led her out among the others. Scores stood watching the dozen or so couples on the dance floor. Women were always at a premium here. Silas began to spin Anna around, their heels kicking up behind them to the music. She noticed Will standing to the side as they changed arms. He clapped along, calling something to them she couldn't quite make out. Someone shot a gun into the air. More shots followed as bystanders whooped and hollered. The song ended to raucous applause, and Will stepped between them.

"Apologies, Silas, but the lady deserves to dance with a man able to put a step or two together."

"I'll be watching." Silas sounded half-serious. "She's an engaged woman."

"Thank you for always looking out for my virtue," Anna said, "but I don't need a chaperone."

"I understand that *you* don't."

The music began again, and Will took his chance to whisk her away, making sure to move past the other couples and into the middle of the patch serving as the dance floor.

"I might have lied a little—I'm no dancer."

"Neither are most of these people. I had lessons growing up, so I don't have an excuse to be bad."

She directed his hand onto her shoulder and moved with the music. Silas was talking with some other prospectors, Flynn among them. The song ended, and some of the couples left to get drinks or to stand and watch, but Will and Anna stayed on.

"I think I'm getting the hang of this. It's been a while since I've danced with a lady."

"I don't believe that for a second, Mr. Leary."

"It has been a while—weeks, even."

They danced for another twenty minutes or so, until she gestured to him, whispering in his ear. "Can we stop awhile? My legs are aching."

"Thank the Lord. I never thought you would want to stop. I can barely move. I feel like an old man."

"You dance like one too."

He let go and moved to the side. She followed. Silas had disappeared. Will shrugged and went to the bench serving as an impromptu bar.

"Whiskey?"

"Must we?" she answered. "Don't they have anything else?"

"Not here."

He handed her a glass and gave it a clink. He downed it and watched as she sipped hers.

"What do you want, Miss Denton?"

"I want my family to be happy. I want Mabel to grow to adulthood and then to old age."

"No, no, no. What do you want, for yourself?"

"I always wanted to marry a man I'd hardly ever met and move to a town on the edge of the Arctic Circle."

"We all want that. No, seriously."

She took another sip of her drink. "I'm intrigued by this new serious side of your nature, Mr. Leary."

"Call it a moment of weakness."

"I've always wanted to study the law. My uncle I told you about, the one who is a lawyer, used to talk me through the cases he was involved in. I would sit, rapt. I wanted to be a part of that. I still do, though I know there's no chance now."

"Do you think women can perform the same roles in society as men?"

"I don't see why not. I've heard the arguments before—that women are too emotional and that they can't make decisions with a clear mind. I'm sorry to say that men are just as irrational as women. What wars in history have women started? Men? Every single one. Neither sex has the upper hand there. It makes no sense. Why should half of society be stonewalled into the roles of mother, or teacher, or nursemaid? What makes men more apt to use their minds than women? Don't we have the same minds? Haven't you met intelligent, capable women in your life?"

"More than I could count."

She knocked back the remainder of the whiskey in her glass without flinching. "Don't you think they could do the same job as a doctor, lawyer, or any administrative role? I can't vote. I'm not trusted to make adult decisions about the leaders who run the society in which I'm expected to raise children. I have the same rights as the children I'm to raise."

"The suffrage movement is gaining some traction. Some states are for it now."

"I don't live in Colorado, or Idaho, or even the new state of Utah. That's one thing I like about this place; it's harsh and dangerous, but it's fair. It doesn't discriminate against anybody or anything. It's equally unsympathetic to everyone. Either one is strong enough to make it here or one isn't."

"You're obviously strong enough."

"So far. We'll see the rest of the way and when we reach Dawson."

He placed his whiskey glass down on the bar and motioned to the man behind it for two more.

"Take this," he said. "You deserve it."

She accepted the glass. "I'd never had a whiskey in my life before I got here."

"We're experiencing a lot of new things of late."

He knocked back half the whiskey in his glass. Silas was still nowhere to be seen. The crowd around the bar had thickened, and the fire was huge now, perhaps twenty feet tall.

"Have you been down to the lake yet?" She shook her head in response. "Come on—it's a beautiful night. We'll take a look."

"Sounds lovely."

They zigzagged back through the tents three hundred yards toward the lake. Skeletons of half-finished boats lay like enormous fossils on either side of them as they went. They passed stampeders sitting outside their tents raising bottles and singing songs. More shots cut through the night air, and the music seemed to follow them all the way down to the water's edge. The lake was smooth as finished marble, with the barest of ripples sending waves to lick the pebbles by their feet. The clouds had parted, and the moon painted the lake in shimmering silver. A trillion stars blazed above, and the snow on the mountaintops around them shone ghostly white. They stopped at the water's edge, listening to the sound of the night.

"It's incredible," she said. "I don't think I've been able to appreciate the beauty of the nature that we've been battling against these last few weeks. We've seen so much. It's hard to take it in."

"Nature is a beautiful, savage adversary." He finished the whiskey in his hand. "Why aren't you married already?"

"I could ask you the same thing."

"I haven't found the right lady."

"I still haven't found the right man. A man has been found for me."

An old tree trunk lay by the side of the water a few feet away. They shuffled over and sat, two feet apart. A zephyr blew up over the mountains, spreading ripples across the lake, ruffling Anna's hair.

"You think we can do this?" she asked.

"I know we can."

"What's going to happen once we get to Dawson?"

"We'll deliver you to Mr. Bradwell and stake our claim."

"I would so much like to remain in touch once we arrive. You're the closest thing I have to friends here."

"Of course."

"You couldn't have been kinder to me these past few weeks. I'm so grateful to have found you."

"We're lucky to have found you too. You've kept us going. You've given us the motivation to keep on when our spirits might have lagged. You've been as valuable to us as we have to you."

"I'm a better actor than I thought, then," Anna said. "The truth is, I've been petrified since I left my mother and sisters in Seattle. I'd give anything to be back with them. I hate this place, and what do I have to look forward to at the end of it? Marriage to a man more than twice my age who I've barely even met before. Best to get on with it, though, isn't it? There's no place for moaning on the trail, not when we're all trying to survive."

"You've got a glittering career on the stage in front of you if becoming the Queen of the Klondike doesn't work out."

She laughed. They looked at each other and then back out at the expanse of the lake in front of them.

"Where have you been these last few years? Before you reached San Francisco, I mean."

"You're asking me that now? You didn't even know me then."

"I apologize. I didn't mean to pry."

"No, it's quite all right. I was out west. I was in Colorado and Wyoming and California. Other places too."

"Why didn't you go home?"

"I don't know. I was trying to find my way. I was walking around like a blind man without a cane."

She picked up a pebble by her feet and tossed it out into the water, where it landed with a gentle splash. The ripples faded outward into nothing.

"I told you I was in the army."

"Yes."

"I was in the Seventh Cavalry. I was eighteen when I joined—not much more than a kid. I had no idea what the wars were about. I knew what everyone else knew. I read what everyone else read. I thought that the Indians were vicious savages who needed to be brought to heel. I had no idea."

"You had no idea of what?"

"Of the truth. I didn't know that we were the savages. We were the murderers."

"What do you mean?"

"I've seen white men do things Indians would never. I've seen . . ." His voice broke. He spluttered and reached down for his empty whiskey glass.

"You don't have to tell me," she said, moving closer as she offered him some of her whiskey.

"I want to. It's time. I've never spoken of it before."

"I'm here."

"Have you heard of the Battle of Wounded Knee?"

"I remember reading about it some years ago."

"I was there, in South Dakota. The Lakota tribe was the enemy assigned to us. The government had been seizing their lands for years, breaking every treaty we made with them. Their lands were rich, and no treaty was enough to protect them from the prospectors who came. The settlers hunted the bison they relied on almost to extinction. The Lakota had nothing left. A new religion spread among them: the Ghost Dance. It spooked the settlers, and the authorities reacted. We were sent in. We surrounded them—perhaps two hundred men and a hundred fifty women and children. They were to surrender their weapons to us at Wounded Knee Creek." He stood up and patted down his pants as if wiping off some nonexistent dust. He sat back down.

"We went in at daybreak. The snow was thick on the ground, and we had to drag our boots through it. Most of the men had been drinking the night before. I had too. Some had been up most of the night and were still drunk. The men around me staggered through the snow, stinking of whiskey and cigarettes. We set up position a hundred yards or so back from the Lakota. They were a trembling mass in front of us, a great circle of rags, terrified of us. We had been told they were aggressive, that they were bloodthirsty savages."

"That's what I was always led to believe."

"We took the few arms they had, but the officers weren't happy and sent us back for more. We took their knives and arrows and anything they could have used as weapons. Most of the men with me watched the Lakota with rifles raised, fingers curled around the triggers. It wasn't going to take much. One of the Indians began to perform the Ghost Dance. They thought it made them bulletproof. I stayed back as some of the men went in to search them for arms again. One of our men reached in for a rifle that one of the Indians was hiding, and it went off. That's when the firing started. The soldiers around me started shooting into the crowd, aiming at nothing and everything. I saw men, women, and children fall, and then the artillery guns opened up on the ridge above us."

"Women and children?"

"Yes. Some of the Indians were firing back, and I saw men fall around me. The artillery was falling short, and soldiers and Indians alike were torn apart by shellfire, their limbless bodies falling in heaps on the snow. I got down on one knee, looking for targets, but I didn't see any armed Indians to fire at. I got up to follow the men around me. I don't know why—I just followed them. They were running into the mass of women and children, firing indiscriminately, explosions ripping up the ground every few seconds. The officers had lost control. Some men leaped onto horses to pursue those few Lakota who'd managed to run and shot them in the backs as they fled. I was standing still, my rifle by my side, just watching. I remember a soldier ran past me, my best friend at the time, and he was laughing, shooting into the crowd of women and children, the snow red with their blood. The Indians didn't have any cover. They never stood a chance. It didn't last more than a few minutes. When the shooting stopped and the smoke lifted, hundreds of Indians lay in the snow along with a couple dozen soldiers."

"Killed by the Indians?"

"I couldn't say for sure but most likely by fire from the cannons. The artillery men saturated the field—killed anything that moved."

"I never read about that."

"I saw things I could never describe—things no one should have to see. The army gave twenty medals of honor to the men of my regiment for their actions that day. Twenty men received the nation's highest military honor for the massacre of women and children."

"That can't be. Why didn't the papers report it as it happened?"

"Because it didn't fit the narrative they were peddling—that the Indians were savages to be exterminated. People in Chicago, Boston, Philadelphia, and New York don't want to read about that. They want assurances that the government is right and that it's going to protect them. The newspapers called it a massacre but reported the official story—that the Indians opened fire on us, and we retaliated in kind. They blamed the Indians, lauding the officers who sent in the soldiers."

"It's monstrous."

"I got discharged. I couldn't go back home. I didn't know what to do. I just went. I had no idea where I was going."

She was inches away from him, her arm around his shoulders. "There wasn't a thing you could have done. You couldn't have stopped it."

"I did nothing to help those people. I just stood there watching as we tore them to shreds. They were unarmed. It was nothing less than murder."

"It wasn't your fault. You can't burden yourself with the guilt of what happened."

"I can't seem to beat it. I can't . . ." His voice trailed off.

"Some things in life can't be fixed, only carried."

He turned to her, the hairs of his beard almost touching her face. She reached a hand to his face, cupping her palm on the rough surface of his cheek. A voice came from behind them.

"Will," Silas said. "It's best we get to bed. We need to start on the boat in the morning."

"I should go," he said. "I don't want to get put in detention."

They stood together. A wind rose up, blowing cold air from the north, and they hurried back to camp.

Chapter 9

Most had to construct their lumber, cutting down trees upriver and rafting the logs back down to be sawed into usable planks. Sawpits, elevated platforms ten feet or so high, sprang up all over the camp. The logs were laid on top of the sawpits, with one man on top and one below, both working a whipsaw to fashion the logs into boards. Men Silas met spoke of building massive thirty-foot-long skiffs and offered him and his companions a place on board in return for the nails they'd brought. Nails were in high demand, going for more than a dollar a pound. More valuable still was the lumber they'd hauled over the mountains from Sheep Camp. Silas knew he could have gotten any price he wanted for it. None would sell that.

He was happy not to have to endure the rigors of sawing their own lumber. The boards he'd bought at Sheep Camp were higher quality than the spruce logs most were using here, which were soft and quick to break. Spirits around the camp were high, however. Most sang as they worked, feeling that they were close to the goldfields and the fortune that awaited them. He and Will got to work on the boat the morning after the fireside party. Will didn't speak much, and Silas resisted the urge to press him over Anna. That could come later, if the need arose. They were both adults. They would decide what was to happen between them. He knew Will well enough. His history of following advice was spotty at best. Anna was nothing if not honorable and trustworthy, and he was confident that she'd be faithful to the agreement and go to Mr. Bradwell when the time came to do so.

Like everything else in the Klondike, the role of boat designer for hire was available at a price, and he found a Californian to help them. Many who'd come this far were still selling up and going back, even after making it all the way over the pass. The Californian was one of the many who had run out of money and the will to go any farther. He went home the day after going through the motions of showing them exactly how to construct the boat that would float them all the way to Dawson.

After the day was over, they each retired to their tents. Silas waited until Will was asleep and then reached down to the bottom of his pack for his journal. It was difficult to write in it every day—particularly when he required privacy to do so—but he still managed it several times a week. He flipped to the next blank page and took out a pen.

We have just begun construction on the boat that is to safely carry us more than five hundred miles upriver. I'm trying to conceal my fears. We have no experience, and this craft will have to survive ice floes and raging waters. I cannot show my true feelings. Ever. I'm used to that. I need to be strong. We all do. I draw inspiration from Miss Denton every day. She is a truly remarkable lady who keeps our energies focused. We draw strength from her. She has proven to be more than able in caulking the seams of our flat-bottomed craft. Will is a fast learner also and has taken to boatbuilding as he does to most everything—with enthusiasm and vigor. I'm the only one I have doubts over.

Nothing has happened between my two companions. I have no wish to be their chaperone, tut-tutting at their flirtatious glances, but it may be a role I need to assume.

Six inches of snow came on the second day, and they had to work under an awning. Rumor held that the snow was drifting up to twenty feet just a few miles upriver. If there was ever a reminder of the impending winter, the snow provided it. That night, they worked by candlelight until sheer exhaustion drove them to the relative comfort of their tents.

No one mentioned the incident by the lake again. Will and Anna remained friendly as ever but didn't disappear off for any of the midnight trysts that Silas wouldn't have been surprised to encounter. Silas was confident that it had been a one-off and that Will would remember that he, in effect, was working to deliver her to her future husband.

A storm came in when the boat was almost finished. They were confined to their tents for a full two days, enduring the frustration of listening to the howling winds and rain outside. It was October 6 when they got the chance to finish the boat. It had been eleven days since they'd arrived here. Will insisted on christening her *Anna*. It was late in the afternoon, and they agreed to set off the next morning for Dawson. A new life felt within touching distance.

Anna asked Will and Silas to teach her how to shoot. Several times on the trail she had alluded to the fact that most people had guns, and she had no idea how to use one. Dawson was by all accounts a law-abiding town—certainly more so than the free-for-all that Skagway had proved itself to be—but she insisted. They took time for a cup of coffee before leaving the busy tent city of Lake Lindeman and climbing into the hills around it. They found a secluded spot. Most of the trees around the lake had already been taken for lumber, and the spot they found was stripped bare—only the stumps remained. Silas stood back as Will showed Anna the basics of using the pistol he carried. He was an expert, and soon he had her hitting targets they'd fashioned from ten yards away or more.

"I think I'm getting the hang of this," she said as she clipped a target.

"Let me show you another little skill I learned in the army." Will reached into his bag for three throwing knives. He took the knives between thumb and forefinger, aiming at trees five yards away and more. He didn't miss once.

"I'm just as shocked as you are," Silas said to Anna's openmouthed expression. "I had no idea he could do this."

"You want to try?" Will said to Anna.

"No. I'll stick to learning one method of killing people for today."

They stayed out there shooting until the darkness drove them back to their tents. She prepared dinner for them, and they retired to bed, as ready as they would ever be to take on five hundred and fifty miles of rivers and lakes to Dawson City.

"We've been here, in this barren, beautiful land, almost six weeks, and yet it feels like we're just beginning," Anna said the next morning as they loaded up the boat named for her. The excitement was palpable. Silas tried to temper his own with the thought of what was to come.

"The hard part is behind us. We've made it farther than most already, and we're guaranteed reward once we arrive in Dawson," he said.

"What about Miss Denton? What is she to receive?"

"A home," Silas reminded him, though Anna still stood right there. "A family. And the peace of mind that comes with knowing that she looked after her own."

"That's a debate for another time," Will said.

"No, you're quite right, Mr. Oliver. We've all got something tangible waiting for us—notwithstanding the opportunity to strike gold."

"I'd almost forgotten about the gold," Will said. "I'm an expert trekker and boatbuilder."

"And soon you'll be an expert gold digger," Silas said.

"I'll make sure to come visit you two on your claim."

Several other boats were setting off at the same time, and they waited until a large skiff took to the water. The dozen or so people on board shot their guns in the air, whooping and hollering as they set off. Then it was their turn. The logs beneath their boat fell away as it took to the water. Silas climbed in last, pushing off and into the lake. They set their paddles in the water and seconds later were gliding over the quiet chop of the lake, making their way toward the inlet that would take them onward. Not a breath of air disturbed the surface of the lake.

"Best we make hay while the sun shines," Silas said. He churned the water, using the strength in his shoulders to propel the boat. The water was so still that it was as if the boat were suspended on air. No one spoke for an hour or more until the choppy river leading to Bennett Lake came into sight. They had caught up to the larger boat that had launched before them and waved to those on board. Hundreds of stampeders were working onshore at Bennett Lake, almost as many as they'd left behind at Lindeman. A boat was launched onto the river as they passed. More and more people were coming.

"Is there going to be gold for all these people?" she asked.

Neither man answered. Silas didn't want to acknowledge the fact that, even after all this, they could still fail. They kept rowing past the white tents littering the shore of Bennett Lake like seagulls on a beach. The sky darkened above them, and the Klondike wind began to blow again. The waves grew, and soon the sail was taut against the breeze. They lifted the oars and sat back, spray hitting their faces and wetting the tarpaulin covering their supplies stowed in the back. Anna hid down in a gap between the supplies in an attempt to keep dry, but it was no use. The winds thickened, and the mast began flapping back and forth like a blade of grass. They made their way toward a beach where some other boats were sheltering and took to shore.

It was almost evening, and they set up their tents on the smooth sandy beach of the cove. The wind let up as darkness came, and they sat by the fire with the others who'd stopped there for the night. One of the men sitting by the fire—a large man with a thick graying mustache and wrinkled brown skin—wore the uniform of a mail carrier.

"Where are you coming from?" Silas asked him.

"We've come from Circle City in Alaska, all the way upriver. We're making for Lake Lindeman in the morning and then on to Skagway. I'll assume you're making for Dawson."

"You assume rightly. How is it there?"

"It's growing. This time last year, there wasn't much more than nothing there, but it's a town of thousands now."

"How are the people there? I've heard a plethora of rumors."

The mail carrier finished the cup of coffee in his hand. "People do rumors round here better than anywhere else. I've been in Alaska fifteen years now, and it seemed like everyone was going to starve every winter, but it hasn't happened yet. It's cold up there but not so much as a man can't stand it."

"Is there gold?"

"So they say, but that's not my business."

With that, the mail carrier stood up and went to his tent.

The mail carrier was still there when Anna woke in the morning, and she gave him the letter she'd stayed up to pen the night before. Silas wrote to his brother Ethan but not his parents.

"Why didn't you take the chance to send a letter home?" Silas asked Will when they were back out on the water.

"I'm sure you took care of all the details. I couldn't have added anything new. You've seen everything I have."

Silas stopped, letting his oar come up. "You should write to our parents. What are you trying to punish them for?" he said after a few awkward seconds.

"I'm not trying to punish them for anything."

"They're far from perfect, but they love you as their own and would appreciate hearing from you. You may have given up on them, but they haven't given up on you."

Will kept rowing. The lake was almost still, with just a feather of a breeze.

"Silas, we have a long way to go until Dawson. We're going to be in this boat for the next week—"

"I have my problems with them, believe me. I know how they can be, but you need someone in your life, Will."

"You haven't written to them, yet you insist I do."

"I've written to Ethan several times. He'll inform them of our progress." He dipped the oar back into the water. "All I'm saying is that you need someone. They want to hear from you. I know that much. Do it for your own sake."

"I get it. I'll make it right, I promise. You can stop now."

Anna settled back onto the box she had taken to sitting on, huddled against the supplies. The scenery on the river was breathtaking. Mountains rose up on either side, covered in snow now. It lay thick on the banks, blanketing the trees with bright white. The air was sharp, and she covered her face with a scarf that she'd managed to keep dry for a few days. The only mercy of the river was that the trekking and carrying were over. She thought of the poor souls slogging over the Chilkoot in their wake, wondering how she'd ever made it over herself.

A few hours passed on calm waters, a stiff breeze helping them along. Several other boats floated around them. They passed one boat crewed entirely by women, four of them pulling on oars as another lady steered at the back. They stopped to wave to Anna, cheering at the sight of another woman.

"I wonder what five women are doing making their way to the Klondike together," she said.

"I wouldn't want to assume, but my guess would be that they're going to provide the entertainment. There's more than one way to strike gold in Dawson, I'm sure."

"Do you mean to say that those ladies are going to be working as prostitutes, Mr. Leary?"

"I'd say it's quite possible," he said. "They could be musicians or businesspeople of some other variety."

"But that's not what you were implying."

"No, I don't suppose that it was."

A few miles on, they came upon a vast flock of ducks. Thousands of them—flying low over the waters. Will took out his pistol to bag a few for fresh meat. He shot down three in quick succession before Anna asked to try out her newfound skills. She took dead aim, squeezing off six shots before she hit one. She made sure to cook the duck she'd shot that night, presenting it to her companions with a proud smile.

Thin shore ice jutted out twenty feet into the river. It cracked and splintered under the considerable weight of the boat as they pushed onto it, but Anna saw the worry on the men's faces even after they'd cleared it.

"We're going to have to cover more miles in the days we have left," Silas said as they pushed out into the frigid water.

"Will we reach Dawson?" she asked.

Neither man answered as they focused on steering and rowing the boat.

"We're going to do our damnedest to make sure we do," Silas said thirty seconds later.

Mist hung over the river, clinging to the surface like a ghost emerging from the dark water below. An hour passed before it disappeared and the way ahead came into clear view. They navigated through a shallow, muddy lake and then into a larger body of water, which Silas informed them was called Tagish Lake. He was the navigator once more, though it seemed it would have been just as easy to follow the numerous other boats around them. Anna sat huddled back among the supplies as usual.

"We've been lucky thus far. Some inclement weather could sink us in minutes."

The following evening, a familiar group came into view beside an ill-constructed craft that looked like it could be broken into matchsticks at any moment. They had pulled into an icy cove for the night, and Will directed the boat over to join them. Anna recognized Flynn's group on the shore, yet he wasn't to be seen. None spoke, and all shared the same grief upon their faces. She couldn't see what they were staring down at but knew in her heart. Will jumped off first, landing with a crunch on the hardened sand. He greeted several in the crowd, who turned to him with doleful faces. A black man with a gray beard stood aside to reveal Flynn's sodden body, blue at the lips, the skin on his face swollen and purple.

"What happened?" Will said.

"We hit a rock, and he went overboard. By the time we reached him, there wasn't anything we could do."

Will pushed into the group and went still, staring down at Flynn's corpse. He took his hat in his hand. Some of the others in the group moved away to set up tents for the night. Anna went to Will.

"I'm sorry about your friend."

"I hardly knew him. We'd only met on the trail," Will said, but his voice cracked slightly.

"Don't feel ashamed to mourn," Silas said, his hand on Will's shoulder. "You had a connection to him. Your mother—and home."

"I don't know why I'm reacting like this. I've seen death so many times."

The night drew in around them. The others had gone, leaving Flynn where he lay. The bonfire they'd lit glowed against the dark, casting shadows over the corpse. Will crouched beside him.

"We'd best get something to eat," Silas said.

Will stood up, his joints cracking like river ice in the morning. "We have to bury him first."

"Not here. Not now."

"Who'll help me bury this man?" Will shouted over to the party Flynn had traveled with. Their sad eyes flickered to him but then back to the fire. "Silas?"

"How about we have a drink in his honor?" Anna suggested. "We can celebrate him."

"We hardly knew him. Neither did they," Will said, gesturing to Flynn's former companions.

"But you knew where he was from. You knew his people and his traditions and his language and his home. There's no one more fitting than you to celebrate who he was," she said.

"We don't have enough time, nor nearly enough alcohol," Will said. "But we'll do our best."

Despite Will's efforts to dig, the topsoil was solid, so Silas gathered some rocks to weigh down the body. They brought him back out to the river on their boat. It was quiet now, the lapping of the waves against the shore a gentle hush. They held torches lit from the fire, and she took Will's hand as he sang one final Irish ballad. They tipped Flynn's body into the frozen waters of the Klondike.

Next dusk, they came upon a log cabin with the red flag of the Dominion of Canada flying above it. The sign for the Canadian Customs Office was visible in white paint above the cabin, and a few stampeders could be seen making their way in and out. Silas pulled the boat in beside several others, and they made camp. Anna prepared the usual meal of flapjacks and beans; she had become quite adept at preparing something she'd barely heard of weeks before. She took the opportunity to write another letter home as the men went inside to pay Canadian customs duties on the goods they were importing. She found them sitting inside the log cabin with the duty officer. Another old man with a long gray beard offered Silas some tobacco to chew. He accepted it, looking as if he regretted the decision seconds after wedging it in the side of his mouth.

"You'll get through Marsh Lake, then the White Horse Rapids," the old man explained.

"How bad are the White Horse Rapids?" she said.

"Bad enough to take many a man's life—let alone that of a little lady."

Will shifted in his seat, but Anna beat him to it. "I've made it this far, so I think I can demand the same respect as my companions."

"As I was saying," the old man continued, "if you get through Lake Laberge before it freezes, you'll come on Thirty Mile River, and if you make it past that . . ."

"What?" Silas said.

"You'll make Pelly River, but it's gonna close off soon. It's the eleventh of October today, and the river's been snapped tight the twelfth the last two years. You've had all God's blessings on you making it this far, but—mark my words—you won't make Dawson."

"That's your opinion."

"And who are you, missy? Come all the way from San Francisco, have we?"

"Chicago."

The old-timer let out a loud snigger and slapped his knee. "Thanks for that, missy. I needed a good laugh. So many who come through are ill-prepared either with outfits, experience, or plain old common sense." He stopped to light his pipe. "And in Dawson? People ask me how much is flour? How much are eggs? I tell them the same thing: there's no price on what won't be sold. People are going to starve. I've no doubt of that. This country's never been well supplied. I've been here twenty-five years, and I can attest to that. There's not been one year when we didn't lack something. One year, it's wheat, and the next, it's flour. One year, we sat in the dark all winter because of the lack of candles. This is a prospector's country and not fit for the majority of those coming in."

He pointed his pipe at Anna. "These clerks and office worker types might do well for a while, but only those with the grit and determination to succeed through anything will ever prosper in these parts. I have some animal pelts and hides," he said, gesturing to the corner of the room. "They're in high demand in Dawson, but I won't go along with you to sell them, because you're not going to make it."

The ground was white with frost when they woke the next morning. They didn't linger. No one mentioned the conversation with the old man from the night before, but she knew his words had affected each of them. The point of no return had long since passed. They were as likely to be caught in the ice on the way back to Lindeman as they were to Dawson. The only way was onward. There was no room for second thoughts. She knew what their choices would be if the water froze: they could wait the winter out, secluded for six months by the frozen river, or they could make the rest of the way over land. It was hard to know which would be worse.

It was early in the day when they saw the boats huddled on the shore. Silas pulled over to where the other stampeders had stopped to survey the rapids ahead. They jumped onto the riverbank, shaded their eyes from the piercing rays of the late-autumn sun, and peered down. The river swung to the left and then to the right, at which point it unleashed itself into a vicious fury through a quarter mile of white water surrounded by canyons thirty feet high on each side. The water jumped and tossed until it reached a gorge before continuing serenely, as if oblivious to what had just gone. They stood a few minutes watching a boat make its way through, tossing about like a cork. The canopy at the back came undone, and the men aboard rushed to cover it over before they lost all their supplies. Several boxes were dropped in the drink before the boat made it through.

"We can do this," she said.

"We can, but we should move the cargo downriver before we do. I don't want to lose it overboard. It'll take us a while to move it, but I think it's worth the time," Silas answered.

They all agreed and took most of the rest of the day to move their supplies the quarter mile down a well-beaten path past the rapids.

"This is like being back on the Chilkoot Pass again," Will said. "What happy memories!"

"Don't remind me," Silas said.

They were ready in the late afternoon. The weather was fine. The snow had held off that day, and only a breath of wind moved through the air. They would never get a better opportunity. They waited until the boat in front made it through before launching themselves. Anna huddled in the back as Silas took the rudder behind her. Will dug the oar into the freezing water, heaving back and forth toward the whitecaps of the rapids ahead. The noise grew and grew until they couldn't even hear each other shouting. The nose of the boat flew several feet in the air as they hit the rapids, throwing freezing white spray inside, soaking them all.

Anna couldn't see the shore on either side, only the white spray flying and the ends of the boat barreling up and down. They followed the roughest water in an attempt to avoid the rocks. The boat danced through, pitching and reeling like it was on ice. Sheets of water poured in, filling the boat up to their frozen ankles. They jumped from wave to wave, leaving the surface of the water with each one. Silas shouted something, and she looked up at him in time to see a massive upsurge hit the front of the boat, tossing it up and sideways. She saw another wave hitting Silas as he was off balance, and then he was gone—disappeared under the white water. She screamed to Will, who frantically searched the water for him. The boat pitched again as he shouted to her to take the steering oar at the stern. She stood up as he jumped into the seething waters. Within a second, he had disappeared. She was alone, holding on to the oar with every ounce of strength in her. The boat bobbed and jumped again, dancing from side to side, and then the noise dissipated and the way smoothed out. She steered in toward shore, where some others jumped into the water to help her ashore.

"Will! Silas!"

There was nothing. The waters raged. Nothing came to the surface. She turned to look at the stranger who'd boarded the boat to help her. He said something, but she was unable to speak. She couldn't lose them now, not after everything they'd been through. Her legs gave way, and the man went to help her back to her feet. She batted away his attentions, staring at the water. Then she saw them, flailing along, dark figures against the white water as it delivered them down into the calm river below. She called out and saw one of them hold a hand in the air. The man beside her pushed the boat out and rowed to meet them.

"Mr. Leary, Mr. Oliver!" she screamed. "Are you unhurt?"

"We are," Will shouted back as he held on to Silas. "Just get us out of here."

The man helped them up and over the side of the boat until each lay shivering on board, and they made their way to the shore. She helped Will to shore as he coughed and sputtered.

"I thought I'd lost you," she said.

"You can't get rid of us that easily."

The landscape around them was crystallizing with the dropping temperatures, and soon, the river was full of ice chunks big as wagon wheels.

The water froze to the oars, and they had to stop several times a day to hack away at it with axes. The men's mustaches, unkempt and scruffy as they were, became a mass of icicles, and the feeling of warmth became a memory. Anna huddled at the back of the boat under blankets and animal pelts she'd bought from Indians, but it was impossible. She couldn't escape the cold or the old-timer's prophecy. They steered around lumps of ice big enough to crush their boat into tinder and came upon passages so frozen that they barely had enough water to sail through. All hope of reaching Dawson by river seemed lost, and the conversation at dinner changed. They spoke of how they could possibly cart the thousands of pounds of supplies across a hundred miles of frozen forest. None had an easy answer. They sat outside for as long as they could bear, their breath pluming out white in front of them. Sullen-faced stampeders sat with them. Some tried to convince them of the futility of progressing. Several boats were destroyed and transformed into sleds. Instead of leaving by icy water, the other stampeders dragged their goods across the snow.

The morning brought ice floes, grinding and chafing against the shore. The crunching and cracking noises filled their ears. They waited half an hour for an opening in the ice before pushing out into the middle, to be carried along in the current.

"We're close," Silas said. "Let's try and make it as far as we can before we have to resort to packing again."

Anna was only too happy to go along with that idea. No matter how miserable the icy river was, it couldn't compare to packing along unworn, snow-covered trails.

The ice crowded around the boat until it was no longer possible to discern a patch of blue the size of one's face on the surface. Progress slowed to a crawl, but somehow, they kept moving. They woke each morning sure that today would be their last on the water, but the river stayed open just enough for them to slide through as the ice bashed against the sides. There were no other boats around now. It was impossible to know if the others were too far behind them to see or if they had seen sense enough to desist while they were still able. The ice on the boat built up to four inches thick, and they had to stop every hour or two to hack it off.

Hope was all they had left as evening fell on October 30. Somehow, their little boat, battered and scarred as she was, had managed to stay afloat amid the ice floes that made up more than nine-tenths of the river around them. It had been a few days since they'd passed any settlements and almost as long since they'd seen another living soul. They'd come to the decision to make a sled the next morning. They knew they were close now. This was to be their last night on the river. The slicing cold of the north wind was in Anna's face as the men rowed against it. They turned a bend in the river. She stood up. She was the first to see the boats, almost entirely enclosed by ice and the tents lit by warm fires beyond them. Dozens of people were milling about on the shore, and she could see wooden-built structures and even hear the faint lilt of music on the air.

"We're here," she said. "We've made it. This is Dawson."

All three cheered, embracing each other. But in seconds, the men's roars faded to nothing in her mind, and the joy evaporated inside her. They had arrived. She knew what that would mean.

Chapter 10

They had landed in a suburb of Dawson that—the Swedes who'd helped moor their boat informed them—was known as "Lousetown." Thirty or forty log cabins and tents stood back from the river, which was now almost completely frozen over. The town of Dawson loomed a few hundred yards away.

"You were lucky," one of the Swedes, Henrik, said. "You could be the last boat here before winter."

Each tent and log cabin had its own cache, raised off the ground like a wooden cage to protect from the encroaching of floodwaters and the plethora of wandering dogs. The Swedes had room enough in their cage to fit most of the trio's supplies and offered to store them overnight for a small fee. Several Indian women strolled past, carrying firewood and laundry, their children skipping after them.

"This used to be an Indian camp," Henrik told them. "The only Indians left now are wives and half-breed children."

"Where are the men?" Anna asked.

"I don't know. Dead or gone."

"How long have you been here?" Silas asked after they'd finished stowing their goods.

"About two months."

"That makes us veterans here," his friend added.

They thanked the men and, promising to come back later, set off toward Dawson. Anna looked at her worn, wizened hands, the dirt under her chipped fingernails. She hadn't taken a bath in weeks. She must have smelled like the dogs that pervaded this filthy, freezing, alien place. She was in no state to make a first impression. And the rest of her life, there would be no more important first impression than this. The men pressed on along the riverbank toward Dawson, saying little. The snow was ankle-deep. It seemed winter had already settled here.

"It's been quite the journey, Miss Denton," Silas said. "I can certainly say we're going to miss you."

"I can't see Mr. Bradwell, not like this. I have to clean myself up somewhat at least. I can't meet the man who is to be my husband looking and smelling like this."

A clear, cold night had settled over the Klondike River. The moon shone like a jewel. They stopped by the frozen waters.

"We can try to arrange a bath in a local hotel, perhaps?" Will said. "But there's no point in delaying the inevitable. You need to see Bradwell tonight. We need to get paid and be on our way. Our business is now concluded."

She was taken aback. She'd never heard him speak like this before. "I'd appreciate that. I do hope that we can remain in regular contact. I'm going to need all the friends I can muster."

"You'll likely be mixing with a higher class of—"

Silas cut him off. "Of course. We both look forward to continuing our friendship with you."

"Let's get going, shall we?" Will said.

She thought to speak to him, but the maelstrom swirling within her own mind was enough for her to deal with. Her palms were moist, even with the biting cold in the air. She almost wished that this wasn't Dawson, that they had more traveling to do, that they could get back in the boat together and continue.

The lights of the town led them to the mouth of the river and over the bridge into Dawson. The town stretched back several hundred yards. Six wooden buildings stood on the riverbank, and beyond them, the British flag flew over what appeared to be a military building. A sign told newcomers to report to the Mounted Police station to check any weapons. A man with a thick French accent pointed them toward the police station a few buildings down. People milled past them, dressed for the cold in heavy parkas with light fur caps of lynx or beaver. Men walked the streets with packs on their backs. She saw a woman after a minute or two, darting inside one of the saloons a few hundred yards down. They made their way inside the police station, doing their best to shake the snow off their boots. The Mountie, a stout man in his midtwenties with a thick mustache, took the revolvers the men were carrying, though they'd left their rifle back with the supplies in Lousetown.

"Where would a man find Henry Bradwell, if he were looking?" Silas asked.

"What business do you have with Mr. Bradwell?"

"So you know him?" Will said.

"Of course. Everyone in Dawson knows Mr. Bradwell."

"We have something for him."

She understood what they were doing. It was better to be spoken of as a package than admit her true purpose to the whole town.

"You'll find Mr. Bradwell in the Palace Saloon, but he doesn't see people unless he's expecting them. Should I check ahead?"

"No need. He's expecting us. Where could the lady have a hot bath and clean up some?" Silas said.

"The Palace Saloon or one of the others. They're all in a line along Front Street. You can't miss them."

Silent like children, awed by the lights and music, they made their way back out into the cold night air and shuffled down the middle of what seemed like the main street in the town. Wooden-built saloons and stores sat on either side of the street, interspersed with tents and temporary structures. A single cabin sat in the middle of the rough, unpaved road with a sign identifying it as a bakery. Stampeders milled in and out of the stores, which displayed in their windows goods at outrageous prices. A dog walked along beside Anna for a few feet. She had never seen its breed before—gray with thick fur to shield it from the cold. Its bright-blue eyes seemed to pierce the dark.

The sign for the Palace Saloon came into view, and her nerves surfaced again.

"Let's go somewhere else first," Silas said. "We'll get something to eat, and you can get cleaned up. How do you feel?"

"I feel like a child on the first day of school." In reality, she felt like a convicted woman, the date of her execution nigh.

The Dominion Saloon stood fifty feet from where they'd stopped. It was thronged with people, the sound of their conversation and laughter mixing with the music coming from the band playing inside.

"This place looks as good as any other," Silas said, leading the way inside. He didn't seem to notice Will catching her by the arm as she made to follow him.

"I wanted to apologize for my behavior."

"Oh, Mr. Leary, that's quite all right."

"No, it's not. It just seemed that this day would never come. I'm going to miss you."

The light from the saloon danced through his bloodshot, exhausted eyes. She moved closer to him, stopping herself a few inches short.

"There's no need for goodbyes. I'm not going anywhere. Neither are you. It would be ridiculous not to remain in touch—"

"Come on inside." Silas was standing on the step outside the saloon.

Half an hour later, she was luxuriating in a warm bath, her first in what seemed like a lifetime. She closed her eyes, steeling herself to meet her future husband. She had to let go of Silas and, particularly,

Will, no matter how hard that might prove to be. They were the only people she knew here—the only ones she knew she could trust. She was about to deliver herself into the hands of a stranger, but what was the alternative? Go with Will and leave Bradwell behind without even meeting him? Silas would never agree to it. They had made a promise to deliver her, and she knew the type of man Silas was. He would honor his pledge. They had their reward to think about also, and she had her family to consider. She was here for them. No marriage would mean no Klondike gold to save Mabel. That letter from Bradwell back in July had superseded any choices she may have wanted for her own life. She had to do as she was bid, and the first part of that duty was to make herself look pretty for her new husband. She picked up the soap and began to lather the washcloth.

Will's beard was still damp as he emerged from the washroom. The interior of the saloon was plain in comparison to many of those he'd seen back in the United States, but it was livelier than most. Silas was sitting at a table waiting for him. Their food had arrived—bacon, beans, and flapjacks.

"Still the same old food. I hope it's as good as Anna made it."

"The bartender told me that the supply ships didn't make it through the ice in time. Gourmet food is at somewhat of a premium." He pointed to a table of well-dressed men no older than they were. "Those gentlemen paid for the food in gold nuggets. They also bought a round of drinks for the entire bar when you were washing up."

"Well, cheers to them." He lifted his glass to them. They didn't raise their heads from their cards. "So there are rich men here. There's gold to be had."

"I've no doubt that there are many rich men here. Whether there's more gold to be had remains to be seen."

"Lighten up, Silas. We're here. We made it. Now we gather the riches on offer."

"I'm just thinking about what Bryce and Stevens said on the boat from Seattle. Do you remember?"

"Of course. They said the gold was gone, but who believes those two crooks?"

"Maybe not."

They ate in silence for a minute or two. Will let the music and the atmosphere of the place wash over him. She was gone, and it would be better to sever all contact with her.

"Do you think Miss Denton will be all right?" he asked.

"I think she is possibly the strongest person I've ever known, but I'd still like to call in on her every so often. Our promise to her ends with our delivery of her to Bradwell, but we'd be remiss to abandon her here all alone."

"I feel the same way. We don't know this Bradwell."

"My words do come with a caveat, however."

"What do you mean?"

"I mean that you might be best putting the memory of her behind you." Will dropped his fork. "It's for the best. I don't need to explain why to you. You know it's the right choice for her and us both. The last thing we need is an entanglement with the most powerful man in town."

"I think you might be letting your imagination run away with you."

"So indulge me. I'll make sure she's safe."

"And if she's not?"

"Well, we'll deal with that situation should it arise."

"I'm back," Anna said from behind them. Their chairs kicked up tiny puffs of sawdust as they turned. "How do I look?"

He hadn't seen her like this since those first days on the steamer from Seattle. The mud and grime of two months of travel had vanished to reveal her luminous beauty once more. She was wearing a black embroidered dress that they'd hauled all the way up from Skagway. Her brown hair was curled at the front and fell carefree over the sides of her forehead. Her flawless skin was taut over high cheekbones.

"You look wonderful," Silas said.

"Mr. Bradwell will scarcely believe his luck."

"I hope so. I'd very much like one final meal with my protectors before I venture into the unknown."

"We're not going to desert you," Will said. "We'll be around."

"He's right. If things don't go the way they should, or should you ever need us for any reason, don't hesitate to call on us."

"I'm so fortunate to have found you. God was truly smiling down on me when he bestowed you both upon me. Thank you."

"You're quite welcome," Will said, taking her cold hands in his.

"It might be best if you let her hand go," Silas warned. "This is a small town. We don't want to make things any more difficult for her."

He did as he was told and let her hand drop back to her side once again. Anna shrugged, seemingly not knowing quite what to say.

She ordered food, and they sat together for one final hour, swapping stories of their journey. In the end, it was Silas who called time, as always.

"We'd better get you to the Palace."

"No point in delaying the inevitable," she said, although she didn't move.

"It seems fitting—the Palace Saloon—for the King and Queen of the Klondike. It doesn't seem like a coincidence to me," Will said.

"Nor me," Silas said.

The two men were off their seats, having already paid the pricy bill.

"Come along. It's time."

"His eyes are going to pop out of his head when he sees you," Will added. "You'll be the fairest queen this town ever could have hoped for."

"Thank you. You're too kind."

Anna slid off her barstool and led them back out onto the street. She held up the hem of her dress as she strode toward the Palace, just a hundred yards away. The music and laughter grew louder with each step. The bright, garish sign above the door did not match the furnishings inside. The walls were covered in plain red wallpaper with a few pictures of more glamorous locales around the world. Scraggy, unkempt patrons lined up two deep at the bar on the right. The tables for the drinkers were on the left, with two roulette wheels, a craps table, and several poker tables set up behind them. A band played in the corner. A lady dressed in red sequins with a feather in her hair was belting out a song Anna had never heard before. Smoke from countless cigars and pipes swirled above the crowd of men. She spotted three women who didn't look like prostitutes and perhaps seven or eight who did sitting on various prospectors' laps as they toyed with gold nuggets from the bags on the tables in front of them.

"This is home, I suppose," she said.

Will poked through the crowd to gain the bartender's attention with an outstretched hand. "Do you know where I can find Mr. Bradwell? I have someone to see him."

The bartender, a strong-looking man with a protruding belly and a black beard, put down the glass he was cleaning. "Mr. Bradwell is the patron of the establishment. Who wants to see him?"

"I do," Anna said. "I've come from Seattle. My name is Anna Denton."

"Wait here," he said and walked around the bar to a wooden staircase. They watched him as he climbed the stairs before knocking on a door and disappearing inside. Anna felt like insects were eating her from the inside out. The bartender emerged two agonizing minutes later and descended the stairs before making his way through the crowd. "Mr. Bradwell will see you now, Miss Denton."

Will threw an arm in front of her. "I'd be obliged if we could accompany her upstairs."

"I want them with me. I won't go without them."

"As you please," the bartender said. "Knock on the door at the top of the stairs. Mr. Bradwell will see you there."

"Let's go," Silas said, gesturing for her to lead.

The two men walked behind her as she made her way up the stairs. A prospector emerged from one of the rooms, holding hands with a woman dressed in a shiny blue dress that hugged her generous figure. The woman bade the prospector goodbye and surveyed Anna before closing the door again. They came to the top of the stairs. Will stepped in front of her to rap on the door. A voice from inside told them to enter. He opened the door. A tall, thin man with gray hair and a matching mustache stood up from an elegant mahogany desk. He was dressed in a smart charcoal-gray suit, and his deep-set eyes and stony face lit up when he saw her.

"Mr. Bradwell?" she said.

"Yes, yes. You must be Miss Denton." He stepped forward to take her hand. "Who are these gentlemen?"

"I'm Will Leary, and this is my brother, Silas Oliver."

The two men shook his hand in turn.

"Please take a seat," he said, pulling out chairs for each of them. "Would you like a drink?" He went to a crystal decanter sitting on a side table and poured a drink for each of the men. "Would you like some tea, Miss Denton?"

"If it's all the same to you, sir, I'll take a whiskey."

"My kind of woman," Bradwell said.

He poured her a glass, mixing some water in, giving the men theirs neat. He took a seat behind his desk, reached for a drink, and leaned forward.

"I'm so glad to see you. I've been wondering about your arrival for weeks now. I was certain you wouldn't beat the closing of the river. Where are Bryce and Stevens?"

"That's quite the story," Silas said. "Unfortunately, they proved unworthy of your trust."

"Whatever do you mean?"

"It seems they gambled away their return tickets, and we met Miss Denton on the steamer from Seattle. They had a disagreement in Skagway, and Mr. Stevens ended up dead, murdered by Bryce."

"What? How do you know?"

"I saw it with my own eyes," Silas said, his drink in hand. "We had little recourse, as there's no discernible law and order in the town."

"Where is Bryce now?"

"Still in Skagway, as far as we know."

Bradwell turned to Anna. "I'm so sorry, Miss Denton. I can't help but feel responsible. Those men acted on my behalf. What must you think of me for choosing such scoundrels?" No one spoke, so he kept on. "They volunteered. They owed me some money and asked for the job to work it off. They'd worked for me for several months. I deemed them trustworthy enough to undertake what I considered a simple task. Apparently, I made a serious error of judgment. Once again, you have my sincerest apologies."

"We made it in one piece."

"And is that where these kind gentlemen came in?"

"I met Mr. Leary and Mr. Oliver on the boat to Skagway," she said. She could feel her voice quaking in her throat. "They were kind enough to take me along with them over the Chilkoot Trail and down the river."

"You came over the Chilkoot? And all the way up the Yukon? You look like you walked around the corner to get here."

"Miss Denton displayed admirable fortitude," Will said. "At no point did either of us feel she was slowing us down. On the contrary—we wonder if we could have made it here without her."

"Well, here's to Miss Denton and her exceptional courage," Bradwell said, holding his whiskey aloft. They each clinked glasses before taking a sip. "How is your father, Miss Denton?"

"He's well. My family is well. I had several occasions to write to them along the trail, but I've obviously not heard from them since I left."

"Unfortunately, with the river frozen over, we won't be receiving much mail for quite a while here ourselves, possibly not until May or even June."

"June?"

"Winters here are long and harsh. It's a hard country. When did you arrive in? I thought the river was all but impassable by now."

"We arrived just a few hours ago, stowed our supplies, and came into town," Silas said.

"I'm amazed and impressed equally. I didn't think we'd have anyone else come in before next spring."

"There is something else," Anna said.

"Of course."

"I offered Mr. Leary and Mr. Oliver remuneration upon our arrival here to recompense them for taking me on their journey. I had little choice when my other chaperones proved themselves so unreliable."

"I can only apologize again and offer my sincere thanks to you gentlemen. I am forever in your debt and delighted to pay for your services."

"I promised the men five thousand dollars each for getting me here."

"And they shall receive that amount, along with my gratitude and the promise of my friendship. But now it's getting late. I should show Miss Denton to her quarters." He stood up, and the rest followed suit. He shook the men's hands again. "Gentlemen, I should like to invite you to a feast in a few days' time to celebrate the safe arrival of Miss Denton in Dawson. I insist you attend."

"We'd be delighted," Will said.

"In the meantime, if you need help moving your supplies or procuring dogs for a sled or an oven to heat your tent, my man Milton downstairs will assist you."

"You're most kind, sir," Silas said.

"It's the least I could do for delivering this most precious of all packages."

"We're staying in Lousetown tonight," Will said.

"You'll want to be there a day or two at most before you get out to stake yourself a claim. Bonanza and Eldorado Creeks are about thirteen miles away, so you'll need dogs to transport your goods down there. Mr. Milton will supply all you'll need. You can return them when you're done or can buy your own."

"Sounds reasonable. Thanks again, Mr. Bradwell."

"No, Mr. Oliver, thank you. And same to you, Mr. Leary."

Will shook his hand again before turning to Anna, who was standing now too. "We'll see you in a few days for the feast. I think you'll be fine with Mr. Bradwell."

"I think so too."

Bradwell led them to the door and held it open as they walked out and down the stairs. Will waved to her before they went to Milton behind the bar.

"Would you come inside, Miss Denton?" he said and shut the door behind her. She sat down in the same seat again, with the man she had to consider her fiancé behind his desk. "I'm so happy you're here, but I appreciate how you must be feeling. Some old man you haven't seen in years sends your father a letter offering an old-fashioned bride price for your hand. It's not how I'd have had things either, but the simple truth of this land is that there aren't many eligible ladies for a man to marry. I've been working this land for years alone. I've hit my grubstake now, many times over. I want someone to share my success with."

"Why me?"

He laughed to himself and went over to the whiskey decanter, pouring himself another glass. He returned to his seat before he spoke again. "I knew you were there. Your father wrote to me last year, telling me all about his business woes. He and I have been close since we were young. We were in school together—did he ever tell you that?"

"He doesn't talk about the past. I know little of who he was growing up."

"We shared a bed in boarding school for a year. I helped him through some scrapes, and we have kept in touch ever since, although I've not seen him for many years. He told me about his business and of your poor sister's health, and I began to wonder if I could help. He also mentioned that you'd been unable to find a worthy suitor. I know there were men. There must have been men, but to find the right man—isn't that the trick? I was overjoyed to hear back from him after I sent my letter in July. I've looked forward to this moment all these months. You're more beautiful than I could have ever dreamed."

"Thank you, Mr. Bradwell."

"I have money now—more than I could ever spend—but I want a family and a life beyond searching for gold. I don't expect anything from you, but I hope that in time, feelings of respect and friendship will flourish between us."

"Is this your saloon?"

"Yes. It's been in operation for a few months now. The whole town is new. I remember when this was no more than a few tents and a moose pasture. I've seen it grow into what it is today."

"It's only going to get bigger. Thousands behind us didn't get through."

"Yet you did. My amazing Anna."

"Where will I be sleeping, Mr. Bradwell?"

"I have a room set aside for you. Just give me a few minutes to make sure it's clean. We're a small operation here, and we have to make use of all available space."

She didn't want to think of what her bedroom had previously been used for and certainly wasn't going to ask. He had her wait in the room while arrangements were made. He had a man send a sled down to

Lousetown for her belongings, and after she'd spent an hour alone with her thoughts in his office, he came back to her.

"Your room awaits," he said.

He led her past the door the woman had disappeared through earlier. The bar was still packed below, and the music swirled around them, following them into the room. Her bags, still dirty from the trail and water-stained from the river, sat in the middle of the floor. The bed was just behind them, underneath a small window, which had a red velvet curtain drawn over it. The sheets on the bed were freshly made, red to match the drapes. The rug on the finished wooden floor was thick animal fur. Pictures of Parisian ladies adorned the wall, and a long mirror sat in the corner—all lit by an oil lamp sitting on a bedside table.

"You must be tired after your journey. Sleep now. Tomorrow, we will plan the feast to celebrate your arrival, and I will introduce you to the town as my future wife."

"Thank you, Mr. Bradwell."

He closed the door behind him, and she was alone. She went to bed minutes later, wondering how she'd ever sleep with the noise of the saloon below. A few minutes later, she did.

Chapter 11

Bradwell was as good as his word, and the next morning, Will woke to the sound of dogs outside their tent in Lousetown. It had snowed a little overnight, and the panorama of the Klondike River with the town of Dawson in the background was astounding. The mountains around the town were set in white against the clear blue sky, and though it was cold, Will could feel the excitement in the air.

Two of Bradwell's men, who introduced themselves as Carrick and Menard, brought them out of town along a well-worn trail toward the goldfields. The landscape grew increasingly bare as they progressed into the valley. An hour passed before a row of cabins came as the first sign of the creeks. Heaps of dirt lay around with men in parkas and mittens moving back and forth to begin the workday. Some were digging with shovels and pickaxes, hoisting out dirt, while others sawed at logs or hammered nails into planks of wood. A heavy bank of smoke from the night's fires hung over the valley, and the air was thick with the smell of burned wood. They passed more cabins and what seemed like hundreds of men working the frozen land. Carrick announced they were passing Bonanza Creek, where those who'd staked their claims the year before were out working the land, adding to the considerable fortunes they'd already reaped. Bonanza led on to Eldorado, another rich claim. Will stared out at the ragged millionaires covered in dirt, heaving pickaxes and sifting through the soil. They passed a hotel, the Grand Forks, where they could stay while they set up their claim—if they could afford it. The dogs on the sled kept running. They got farther and farther from Bonanza and Eldorado Creeks, but the cabins and claims were ubiquitous. He wondered how there could be this much gold. It didn't seem possible. The dogs came to a halt when they passed the last mine. Only bare, unclaimed land and unbroken snow lay ahead.

"This is the next available claim," Carrick said in his distinctively English accent and hopped off the sled. "Five hundred feet, from that spot on." He pointed to a wooden post hammered into the ground.

"Give us a few minutes to look around," Silas said to the consternation of Bradwell's men, who grumbled about the cold as they sat down to smoke their pipes.

"What do you think?" Will said, looking around the bare, forbidding terrain. "It doesn't seem like much, does it?"

"This is what we came here for."

"We could ask the man working the next claim and the man next to him."

"No harm in that, but what's he going to tell us? If he says his claim struck gold, we still might not. If he tells us his claim's no good, ours still might be. We just have to take what we can get and see what fortune brings us."

They wrote their names on a piece of paper and nailed it onto a post jutting out of the dirt to signify that this claim was theirs. It was claim 97A, which signified that ninety-seven claims, each five hundred feet long, stood between them and Discovery Claim, which itself was seven claims below the riches of Eldorado and Bonanza Creeks.

Carrick and Menard hurried them back onto the sleds and into town. They registered at the claims office, now ready to mine the incredible riches of the Klondike.

Anna woke to the sound of voices downstairs. The undeniable luxury of sleeping in a proper bed with sheets in a heated room did little to stem the wave of loneliness. She tried to reason that Bradwell seemed a kind, decent man, but it wasn't enough. This was the man she was to spend the next twenty years with. *Till death do us part.* She would reserve judgment. She went to her bag and took out the photograph of her family, staring at it for what felt like hours. The closing of the river scared her. No contact with the "outside" until spring. It felt like she was serving the first day of a life sentence. The thought that she would see Will and Silas soon got her out of bed. She put on slippers and a dressing gown before opening the door. Voices interrupted the silence of the morning from the tables downstairs, and as she peered over the balcony, the eyes of several women met hers. Her husband-to-be was nowhere to be seen.

"You must be the new girl," one of them said. "Come downstairs and have some breakfast."

This is to be my life. There's no use in avoiding it. She made her way down the stairs into the empty saloon.

Five women had pushed three tables together to form one, and their half-eaten breakfast plates were still in front of them. She could feel their eyes on her as she descended the stairs. Milton was in the corner, rustling through some papers.

"Come over and join us, honey," one of the ladies said and pushed out a chair.

"Thank you." She took a seat at the end of the table. "I'm Anna Denton from Chicago. I'm a friend of Mr. Bradwell's."

"A friend, huh?" One of the ladies at the end of the table chuckled. "We're all friends of Mr. Bradwell's here."

"Don't mind Gertie," the woman who'd held out the chair said. "I'm Betsy, and this here's Maggie, Delilah, and Katie. The other two girls are still in bed."

"A pleasure to meet you."

Betsy had curly black hair, and her generous bust was almost spilling out of the shiny oriental-style dressing gown she was wearing. She had clear blue eyes, and her features emanated a harsh beauty, much like the other ladies around the table.

"I think I saw you last night coming in with two handsome boys. Who were they?" Betsy said.

"My chaperones. They accompanied me up from Seattle."

"Bully for you! Delilah and Katie were my 'chaperones' from Juneau. Seems like you had the better end of the deal!" Gertie said, and the ladies laughed. Milton went back to his papers. "So you say you're a friend of Mr. Bradwell's? What kind of friend?"

"Gertie, you'll shut your yap if you know what's good for you," came a voice from behind them. Bradwell stood in the morning light, the door to the saloon open behind him.

"Excuse me, Mr. Bradwell. I was just wondering who the new girl was."

"She's not a new girl. This young lady is to be my wife. She's come all the way from Chicago to make a life here with me, so I'd appreciate it if you treated her with the respect she deserves."

"Yes, sir," Gertie said and went back to her breakfast.

"Miss Denton, could I request the pleasure of seeing you upstairs a moment?"

"Of course," she said as she got up. "It was nice to meet you ladies."

"And you, Anna," Betsy said.

She followed behind him as he went to his office upstairs.

"I apologize for not being there when you awoke," he said once they were inside. "I thought you'd want to sleep in, and I had to go out to inspect one of my claims."

"No, not at all. I don't want to interfere in the running of your business, and it's best I get to know the other people who work here."

"I know a lady like you won't have mixed with the likes of the girls downstairs before."

"It's quite all right."

"No, it's not. You're a higher class of person than they. I'll make sure they know that and act accordingly."

"Mr. Bradwell, there's no need."

"I hope you're not disappointed in my business practices?"

She digested the question before she answered. "They seem like friendly ladies, particularly Betsy."

"I want to assure you that I'm providing a service for the men here—fully legal and approved by the local police. These women came here of their own free will, and each earns a healthy wage. It's the best they could have hoped for, really, considering the profession they chose. I treat them better than any other boss they've had—you can ask them."

"I'm sure there won't be cause for that."

"We're not going to be here forever either. I'll have a house built for us once we're married, and we'll have all the space we need for the fine, healthy sons you'll bear me."

She thought of home and her family and handsome, charming men like Will Leary. She thought of walking down the street in fall with the leaves under her feet. She thought of sunny days at the lake and being caught in the warm summer rain.

"Do you think we'll ever move back to the 'outside'?"

"I see you've already picked up the local lingo," he said with a smile. "Perhaps. I have business here, however, and still much gold in the ground. I have responsibilities to my employees. I'm an important man around here."

The King of the Klondike. "I understand."

"I'll have breakfast sent to your room, and you can get dressed."

"No, really, I can eat with—"

"Nonsense. A woman of your breeding shouldn't have to sit with the likes of them. Go along now, and I'll have your food delivered to you. I'll show you around town after breakfast."

She did as she was told and retreated to her room, where she ate and dressed alone. Half an hour later, she heard a knock on the door. Milton had come back for the tray of food he'd delivered. She asked him where Bradwell was, but he replied with only a shrug, closing the door behind him. She lay back on her bed to wait. An hour passed before Bradwell came to her with another apology for his delay. She allowed him to take her hand as they stepped out onto the street. The ladies in the saloon were gone—presumably back to whatever holes Bradwell deemed fit for them.

"I have some people I'd like you to meet," he said as they emerged from the saloon. The streets were a filthy mess of mud and churned snow turned to sludge. The gray sky above matched the shabby storefronts. He led her past dentists and general stores, hotels, furniture suppliers, and a log cabin that served as the post office.

"When will the post office open?"

"Mail sometimes does get through in winter, but it's rare—nothing one can rely on. Only the most experienced sled drivers make it through, and only then when conditions allow. The rest of us are stuck here. Their doors will be shut most days until the coming of the thaw in the spring. Once they do open, every miner for miles around will descend upon them in the hopes of some word from home."

"Do you have family back home?"

"I have a sister in Missouri somewhere."

"Does she have children?"

"Maybe. I haven't heard hide nor hair from her in twenty-five years. She could be pushing up daisies now for all I know."

"And that's where you're from, Missouri?"

"From Monroe County. I was born on a farm. It's probably not there anymore. The old ways are disappearing."

"That's where Mark Twain is from—Monroe County."

"The writer?"

"Yes, are you a fan of his work?"

"I've never been one for wasting my time with books and the like. There's not much call for that up here."

"Your parents sent you away to school with my father?"

"For a year, until the money ran out, and I came back to the farm."

They arrived at a hotel. Her shoes were covered in a film of mud.

"Here we are," he said and pushed open the door for her. The foyer was plain wood, and a young man in a black suit and gray hat greeted her before noticing who she was with.

"Mr. Bradwell," he said. "What a pleasure this is. Mr. Schmidt and Mr. Fox are expecting you."

He nodded and walked behind the younger man to a room at the back. Two men in their fifties stood up, their wives with them. She sat down beside Bradwell at the end of the table. He introduced her as his fiancée. The word seemed out of place. Schmidt and Fox were two of the original prospectors to strike gold in the Klondike, and Bradwell introduced them as friendly rivals might, proclaiming that their claims were almost as successful as his. They wore brand-new expensive suits from the "outside"—undoubtedly hauled over the Chilkoot by Indian packers. She wanted to ask the wives how long they'd been here and what it was like, but they were at the other end of the table. They seemed content to sit back and listen to their husbands' conversation, which was entirely about the goldfields. It seemed they knew every claim and every man who worked it. She ate her lunch—the best steak she'd eaten in years—and stayed quiet. She felt like a child lost in a crowd, searching for a familiar face. The men ordered several bottles of expensive wine. She drank what they gave her and asked for more. The other ladies sipped at their drinks. The waiter came back to fill her glass. The men were embroiled in conversation, ignoring their female company.

"Are you sure, Miss Denton?" Mrs. Schmidt said.

The waiter looked at Anna.

"Thanks for the advice, but I'll take another glass."

He poured the wine.

The afternoon passed. The men moved on to whiskey, never bothering to offer the women anything other than white wine.

It was almost five o'clock when Schmidt addressed her for the first time.

"You know who this man is, don't you?" he said in a thick German accent, pointing at Bradwell. She smiled and nodded—the appropriate response. "This is the smartest prospector who ever walked the earth. This is the sourdough who struck gold without ever having to pan for it himself. Carmack and those Indian savages, they were small-time. It was men like your husband—"

"Future husband, Gustav," Bradwell said.

"It was your man who made this town and who is going to take it into the twentieth century."

Schmidt's wife sat forward to whisper something into his ear, but he dismissed her with a grunt. All eyes were on Anna.

"He has quite the story. I can only say I'm glad to be a part of it."

Bradwell stood up and made a toast to his new bride. She felt like she was thousands of miles away.

The men retired to smoke cigars and drink brandy, leaving the ladies alone. The other ladies hadn't said more than twenty words all afternoon. Hilda Schmidt breathed a sigh of relief as the men shut the door behind them, but it was Prudence Fox who addressed Anna.

"So you're new in town?"

"I haven't been here a day yet. How long have you been here?"

"I've been in the Klondike for almost a year, but we were in Alaska for seven years before that," Prudence said. "We're from Vancouver. We never had children, and I followed my husband up here in his search for gold."

"For richer or poorer!" Hilda said. "We came from Germany to Alaska a few years ago. We had many hard times before our current good fortune. Where are you living?"

"Mr. Bradwell put me up in the Palace last night. I have my own room there."

"With the whores?" Hilda said, looking shocked. "I should think you'll be demanding he move you out of there immediately. That's no place for a lady to be."

"I think you're right, Mrs. Schmidt. I'll speak to him about it tonight. What's life like here, ladies?"

Hilda took a sip of her wine before she began. "It's a vibrant community. It's hard to say; the place is changing all the time."

Prudence shook her head. "It's not New York or San Francisco. It's a small place, but this is the life we wanted. We finally have the riches we've been searching for all these years. I've spent hundreds of nights in tents with the cold wind howling outside. I sleep in a warm room now, under thick, expensive quilts, and in the morning, I have all the clothes I could ever want to choose from. We're people of status here."

"It's better to rule in hell than serve in heaven," Hilda added.

"I'll drink to that," Prudence said.

The window on the cabin was crooked. Silas called Will back over to point out the fault, but he laughed it off. Who was going to see it? No one would care if they didn't. It had been a week since they'd arrived here. A week of plummeting temperatures, of hauling their supplies out to their claim, and of trying to build themselves a cabin to live in. The claim remained untouched, like many of those around them. They had spoken to most of the prospectors nearby, who were open to sharing that they hadn't come across more than a few flakes as of yet. No one was giving up, however, and none had the guarantee of $10,000 from the legendary Henry Bradwell coming to them. Will had thought of Anna often in the week since he'd left her at the Palace Saloon. He and Silas had spent hours analyzing Bradwell's character from the brief interaction they'd had with him. Will always found something to criticize.

He was sawing wood behind their tent when he heard the dogs approaching. He stood up to see Bradwell's man, Carrick, riding toward him on a sled. Carrick called out a command and came to a stop in front of him. He was wiry and thin with a deep scar across his forehead. Will never asked him but placed his English accent from Essex or possibly north London. Will tipped back his fur-lined hood as Carrick got off the sled. They had spent several hours working with both Carrick and Milton in the week since they'd arrived.

"Is Silas around?" Carrick asked.

"He's up on the hill chopping wood."

"Perhaps I should go and see him."

"There's nothing to say to him you can't say to me."

"Mr. Bradwell would like to request the pleasure of your company tonight for the celebration of his engagement."

"I thought it was going to be a few days ago."

"There was a slight delay. You'll find the night to be worth the wait."

"Has he got our money?"

"He's got your money."

"We'd be delighted to attend. Can we hitch a ride back into town with you, perhaps?"

"When will you be ready? I don't have all day to hang around this wasteland."

"I'll get Silas. We'll be ready in two shakes of a lamb's tail."

"Where is he? I'll fetch him, and you can take that time to get changed into something more appropriate for having dinner with the finest people in Dawson."

"You don't like what I'm wearing?" he said, standing back to reveal his snow- and dirt-encrusted coat and tweed slacks.

"I'll go search out your friend."

He left him standing there as he disappeared up the hill.

The sun emerged from the gray above and shone silver on the snow. Silas came back down the hill a few minutes later, his ax slung over his shoulder, laughing with Carrick.

Will studied his face in the mirror before buttoning up his blazer. He hadn't been clean-shaven in years. He looked like a different person. The scar on the side of his face was plainly visible now. Silas was waiting for him at the bar when he emerged from the bathroom in the hotel they had checked into in Dawson for the night.

"What's with the new look? I hardly recognized you."

"I hardly recognize myself. People come here to start over, don't they? New life. New person. I thought I'd try something different, and it's only a new look until it grows back."

Silas finished his drink, and they left. Dinner was at eight in a restaurant on Front Street that Bradwell had booked out for the night. The cream of Klondike society would be in attendance, whatever that meant. She would be there too. She was one of them now.

It was already dark as they stepped out into the slush on Front Street. The omnipresent chill bit at the exposed skin on their faces as they hurried along the unfinished street. A small crowd had gathered outside the restaurant, eager to see the local bigwigs in full formation. Carrick was on the door and waved them through, leaving several disappointed people out in the cold. They hadn't had many occasions to come into town since they'd moved their supplies out to their claim. This restaurant was new to them. One massive table with a pristine white tablecloth spilling off the edges dominated the room. Silver cutlery reflected the warm candlelight. The table was set for twenty or so. Most of the other guests were standing around drinking aperitifs supplied by neatly dressed waiters with white shirts over the aprons tied around their waists. The host and his young fiancée were nowhere to be seen.

"All the richest men in town are here," Silas said so that only Will could hear him. He stopped talking as a young man offered them a drink from a silver tray. "Carrick told me that Bradwell enjoys keeping his enemies close."

"What does that make us?"

"Interested bystanders who stand to get paid."

"Sounds good to me."

He scanned the room once more for her in vain before joining Silas in conversation with a prospector standing beside them, his Indian wife by his side. He introduced himself as George Carmack. Both men recognized the name as soon as he said it.

"So you're the one I have to thank for dragging me all the way up to this godforsaken place I'd never heard of this time last year," Silas said.

Carmack laughed, but his wife remained silent by his side, clutching him. "Yes, I started all this. I'm still working that claim myself. The Klondike has been kind to me."

"It seems in more ways than one," Will said.

"Yes, this is Kate. She's not the talkative type—doesn't feel so welcome at functions like these—but I say screw what anyone else thinks!"

"I'll drink to that," Will said, and they all held up their glasses.

A door opened at the back of the room, and Milton, dressed in a suit and tie, announced the presence of the future Mr. and Mrs. Henry Bradwell. Bradwell walked out, holding Anna by the hand. She looked splendid in a beaded white dress. Her hair was curled tight across her head. Her lips shone ruby red and her eyelashes dusky black. Will almost dropped his drink. He felt Silas looking at him and raised his glass once more, trying to pass the moment.

"She's putting on a brave face," he said.

"Indeed," Silas said and finished his aperitif, handing the empty glass to a hovering waiter.

Bradwell shook hands with several men who approached him, introducing them and their wives to the woman who would be his. Once they'd greeted him, each guest took her hand in turn, kissing her knuckles. They waited until she'd finished introducing herself to the people in front of her before walking over.

"Gentlemen, I'm so happy you're here to celebrate with us," Bradwell said as he shook Silas's massive hand.

"We wouldn't have missed it for all the gold in the Klondike."

"We're honored to celebrate your engagement," Silas added.

"We're going to sit down to dinner in a few minutes, and I know my fiancée would love if you sat at the end of the table with us. I'm just going to say hello to a few more of these old prospectors, and I'll be back to join you. I must say it's funny to see them all cleaned up like this. Usually, you wouldn't have them all gather in the same place on account of the smell it'd cause."

He left them standing there. They watched him begin conversation with a large man in a tuxedo before turning to her.

"Mr. Leary, is that you?"

"It is. I decided to hack away the beard for the night. What do you think of the new look?"

"It suits you, sir. It suits you well. I can see that face of yours now."

"Is that a good thing?"

"How have you been?" Silas asked. "Are you living in the saloon with him?"

"No, I kicked up a fuss after two nights in there. I had to put the pillow over my ears to keep out the sound of fornication. Mr. Bradwell moved me down the street to the Pacific Hotel."

"And where does he live?"

"He moves between a cabin out by some of his claims at Eldorado Creek and the Pacific, but I'm convinced he sleeps in his office most nights."

"I can't believe he let you sleep in that place even one night," Silas said.

"He had no idea when I'd be arriving. He hadn't the necessary arrangements made."

"And how do you find him? Has he been honorable with you so far?"

"Entirely. I haven't seen much of him if truth be told. I didn't see him at all the day before yesterday. He spends a lot of his time monitoring the workers at his claims."

"How are you spending your days, if not with him?" Will asked.

"I've been reading a lot—what books I can find in this town anyway. I went down to the Catholic Church."

"You're not Catholic."

"Father Jones doesn't seem to mind. He's a kind man who's willing to listen."

"I'm sorry we haven't been around."

"You've no need to apologize, Mr. Leary. I know how busy you must be, and you're miles from town. I haven't been without companionship. I've been getting to know some of Mr. Bradwell's other employees."

"You mean the prostitutes?"

"There was a time when you wouldn't have used such language in front of me."

"That was before you spent nights sleeping in a brothel."

"I'll ignore that remark," she said. "I've gotten to know one or two of Mr. Bradwell's female employees—the ones who'll speak to me, that is. Most of them seem scared or intimidated for some reason."

"They're not used to having a real lady about the place."

The sound of a butter knife on glass cut through the air, and a waiter announced that dinner was to be served.

"Make sure you sit close to me," Anna said.

"Of course."

Bradwell took his place at the head of the table with his lady on his right. The two men sat down opposite her as the first course—lentil soup—was served. Will waited until all the guests had been served to slide his spoon underneath the green surface of his soup. He hadn't eaten as well as this in what seemed like years, and he had to hold himself back from draining the bowl directly into his mouth.

It was hard not to stare at Anna across the table, so he turned to Bradwell instead.

"How long have you been in the Yukon, Mr. Bradwell?"

"Since '88," he said, wiping the soup from his thick mustache. "I was never much use in the 'outside.' I worked the family farm in my twenties. I was married, but my young wife died of the consumption."

"I never knew," Anna said.

"I never had occasion to tell. There's not a lot to say. It was a tragedy, but we never had children, and life goes on. I tried my luck in the Colorado goldfields to no avail, but I saw the riches other men reaped. I knew that was the life for me. I came up for the gold rush in Juneau but had little success there. I made some friends, however, and managed to get myself a job working for the Alaska Commercial Company buying mining properties. I soon saw the real way to make money in the gold rushes."

He paused to spoon more soup into his mouth before continuing. "All the best claims in the Klondike, owned by most of the men you see around you here tonight, were gone within days of Mr. Carmack down there announcing he'd struck pay dirt. I was too late to the game, but I had a little money. I met a Russian—a huge man with a scar where a bullet had passed through his cheek—who was in dire need of food. I bought his claim for a sack of flour and a side of bacon. I drew five thousand dollars out of that claim the first day I mined it. I leased it to two other miners, who worked it for me and looked around for other claims to buy. I own forty-three now, and I never get my hands dirty."

"You said that most of the best claims were gone by the time you arrived," Silas said. "Is there still gold out there to be found?"

"By the barrelful."

The door to the street creaked open, and a tall man in black walked in. He took off his hat to reveal the bright-pink skin of his bald head. Bradwell stood up and threw down his napkin as he went to greet him.

"Father Jones," Bradwell said. They exchanged warm handshakes before walking back to the head of the table.

"Hello, Father," Anna said.

"Good evening, Anna. It's wonderful to see you."

Bradwell introduced him to Silas and Will before the old priest retreated to the last empty spot at the table.

Once everyone was settled, Bradwell turned back to Will and Silas. "How is that claim of yours?" he asked.

"We haven't had a chance to work it yet. We're in the process of setting up. Our cabin is currently under construction," Will said.

"How about the men in the area? Have they had any luck? I haven't heard of many good mines around there."

"We'll see once we start digging."

"Here's to fortune, to treasures newfound and yet to be discovered," Bradwell said, holding his wineglass in the air. The others joined him in a toast before returning to finish their soup.

The scent of meat soon laced the air, and each diner was presented with a fine filet with sautéed potatoes on the side. Will looked around the room and shook his head before cutting into the filet, observing it on his silver fork before plunging it into his mouth. Bradwell began discussing his claims again—his workers, the winters here, the river, the other prospectors still to arrive. Anna sat eating her food, never uttering a word.

The waiters came to whisk away the empty plates, each diner satisfied. Dessert came a few minutes later—vanilla pudding or fancy cakes, depending on the diner's preference. Will sat back in the chair after finishing his pudding. He hadn't experienced anything like this since special occasions in the Olivers' house as an adolescent.

He turned to Silas. "I'll be sure to write to your parents as soon as I'm afforded the opportunity."

"No mail until spring. You'll have plenty of time to formulate your thoughts," he said as he scraped the last of his vanilla pudding off the bowl.

Bradwell got up to speak to some of the other guests sitting at the opposite end of the table, bringing Anna along to stand beside him.

"She's got so much to offer, so much to say, but he doesn't seem interested," Will said.

"Watch yourself."

"Has he mentioned anything about our money?"

"Not yet. The opportunity to talk about business will arise after dinner, I'm sure."

A few minutes passed before Bradwell returned to his place at the head of the table to announce drinks on the house at the Palace Saloon, less than a hundred yards down the street. The two men followed the other guests out into the night air. Anna walked with Bradwell as he spoke to a man with round glasses and long gray hair. Specks of snow fell out of the sky like dust, and the diners brushed them off their shoulders as they reached the Palace, which was closed off to the public for the night.

Milton had the glasses of whiskey already poured and lined up on the bar. The saloon was empty except for Bradwell's guests, but the gambling tables were open. Four croupiers had taken their places, and several of the guests made their way over to the tables immediately. Anna took a place at a table with some of the other wives, while Will and Silas stood at the bar drinking whiskey and smoking cigars.

Bradwell soon came over to Will and Silas with the man he'd been talking to on the way from the restaurant. "I'd like you to meet Dr. Johan Krupp," he said. Dr. Krupp adjusted his glasses before shaking hands with each man in turn. "It's always good to know the best physician in town."

"Pleased to meet you, gentlemen," Krupp said in a thick German accent.

Bradwell brought Will and Silas around the bar, introducing them to the rest of the men present, including Fox and Schmidt, the other two biggest landowners and prospectors in town. The conversation was almost exclusively of the color. It seemed that no one wanted to talk about anything else. They were mostly experienced men, none less than forty and certainly none so young as Will and Silas. They didn't talk about spending their money, just of procuring more. They didn't talk about returning to the "outside." They wondered out loud how they'd built their empires here in this far-flung frozen backwater that, like themselves, had been nothing the year before.

It was almost midnight when Will found Bradwell alone at the bar. There hadn't been an occasion to speak to Anna since dinner. She was trapped at the tables. He was stuck at the bar.

"Mr. Bradwell, thank you for our wonderful dinner and everything else."

"I'm the one who owes a debt of gratitude. Anna told me how lucky she was to have found you when she did. I can only wonder what might have occurred if she hadn't. I shudder to think."

"She's tougher than she looks—a formidable character in her own right. We learned that much after only a few hours on the trail with her."

"You're most kind—with your comments also—but a woman like her on the trail? She wouldn't have lasted an hour without two sturdy men like yourselves."

Will sipped his whiskey. "I do hate to bring up the unpleasant matter of money, but do you think you might have the reward we were promised to bring Miss Denton to you?"

Bradwell paused and finished his drink. "Of course, Mr. Leary. Shall we adjourn upstairs?"

"My brother is in the bathroom. Should we wait for him?"

"I'll see him later. We can settle my debt to you in the meantime. Come with me."

Bradwell made off toward the stairs without waiting for a reply. Will set his glass down on the bar before following him. A cheer came from the roulette table. Gold nuggets lay spread over each of the gaming tables. Bradwell took a key from his pocket and unlocked the door to his office before continuing inside. He made his way to the safe in the corner, using his body to shield the combination as he entered it. It opened with a metallic crack, and he reached in to extract a thick wad of bills. He closed it behind him and went to his desk.

"Here it is: five thousand dollars. It seems you've made your fortune without ever having to sink a pickax into the ground."

"I intend to make a good deal more."

Bradwell held the money in the air before pulling it back. "Wait—just an idea—but with the party going on downstairs and all, would you be interested in getting this money as credit for the tables? You could double it or more if you have a good night. The sight of you playing with the cream of Dawson society could do wonders for your reputation also. You can stop at any point, of course, if it seems that Lady Luck isn't on your side."

"Seems like a tempting offer. And if I'm losing, I can cash out at any time?"

"Of course."

"I was never much of a gambler."

"Neither are most of the men down there right now. It's all luck. If your luck's in, you can clean up, but how do you know if your luck's in if you don't play?"

"Good point. I'd never know. Do you play, Mr. Bradwell?"

"I have been known to play from time to time."

"I don't know anything about table games, craps, or roulette. I think I'd be more interested in poker. Do you play?"

"On occasion."

"Do you think any of the other prospectors might be interested? I saw them using gold nuggets at the tables on my way up here."

"A common currency in these parts. I'll see who I can round up. I'll organize your money in chips. They'll be waiting for you downstairs."

"Thank you, Mr. Bradwell. You're very kind."

"Think nothing of it, and as I said . . ."

"If I'm losing, I can just cash out."

"We don't want you losing everything at the tables!"

"Perish the thought."

Silas was at the bar talking to Dr. Krupp when Will returned. He waited for Krupp to leave before taking Silas aside. "I asked Bradwell for the money."

"Did you get it?"

"He offered it to me in credit for the tables instead."

"And you said no. Tell me you said no, Will!" he hissed through clenched teeth.

"I did not say no. This is the chance of a lifetime. I've never been in a room with so many drunken millionaires in my life. I'm not going on the tables. I'm going to sit down with them—with him."

"You're going to play poker with Bradwell?"

"For a while. We'll see what happens."

"This is going to go one of two ways. If you lose, we're back to square one almost, but if you win, we make an enemy of the most powerful man in town."

"He's a gentleman, Silas. Give him some credit. Gentlemen know how to lose. I know what I'm doing."

Will tried to hide his anger at Bradwell—tried to channel it. He ordered another whiskey and knocked it back, reveling in the sense of well-being it lent him. He made his way over to where Anna was sitting with the other wives.

"Hello, ladies. Would it be all right if I were to speak to Miss Denton alone for a minute?"

The women looked at each other without reply, but Anna didn't wait for their consent, standing up to walk with him to the bar.

"I don't like how he treats you," he said when no one else was within earshot.

"What do you mean?"

"He looks down on you. He doesn't include you in conversation. You don't seem like anything more than a trophy on his wall."

"You've been drinking."

"Deny what I said."

"I can't make judgment on someone I don't yet know. I've been here a week. We haven't had the chance to talk as much as I'd like."

"And is this the life you wanted, surrounded by stuffy old men obsessed with gold, smoking cigars, and playing roulette?"

"Who ever said anything about me getting the life I wanted? You think I wanted any of this? Who are you to judge me and to declare what I want?"

"I know you. I know you're about more than this. I know you want to study law like your uncle."

"Any aspirations I might have had toward being a lawyer died with that letter Bradwell sent to my father, and I'd thank you not to bring up our private conversations now. The idea of me ever studying law is nothing more than a pipe dream."

"You're worth more than this."

"What am I worth exactly? Because I can tell you. I'm worth fifty thousand dollars. No more. No less. That's what I was bought and sold for."

"You're worth more than that."

The ladies at the table had stopped talking and were watching Anna and Will.

"An item is only worth what a man is willing to pay for it. The choices made on my behalf were for the good of my family, and I'm willing to honor the contract. Don't make this harder for me, Mr. Leary, because God knows this is hard enough already. I need you and Silas but not this way. Now, if you'll excuse me, the ladies will be wondering what I'm doing talking to you this long."

She went to go back to the table.

"I'm sorry. When is the wedding?"

She stopped and turned back to face him. "We haven't discussed dates yet."

"Congratulations," he said. She walked away.

Milton readied a table in the corner, and the players took their seats. Will sat opposite Bradwell, with Carrick dealing. Carmack, Fox, and Schmidt joined too, each with several stacks of chips six inches high. The buy-in was set at $5,000, but each of the other men played with far more. Two of the men each had a bag of gold nuggets piled beside their chips on the table. Will didn't know if they were there for show, only that he wanted them for his own. Silas had given up trying to talk sense into him and sat a few feet away. Anna still sat with the other ladies, though some who had joined her earlier had departed to their beds for the night. None of the men had left. Was there enough money at the table to buy her back? Could he win enough to buy her freedom and pay her father off at the same time? Bradwell would guard his new toy carefully and would likely jack up the price to many times what he'd paid for her.

Milton dealt the cards. Each player got five, and Milton placed the rest of the deck on the table where everyone could see it. Will studied each man. He'd started playing poker in Kansas City back in '93. It was a simple game about knowing people and yourself. Money was just a way to keep score. He won the first hand. It was a few hundred dollars—small by the standard of what was to come—but the other men thought they were getting to know him now. He bluffed next hand, winning a few dollars more, and then folded next, giving back much of what he'd won. Silas remained silent behind him.

The night wore on. It was almost three in the morning. The women had gone home, Anna among them. Her new fiancé had walked her to the door. The whores were at the table now, sitting on either side of Bradwell, and Schmidt had one on his lap. The other men at the table had been draining whiskey since the game started, but Will hadn't touched a drop in hours, slugging back water from the opaque beer bottle on the table in front of him. He had begun to gather chips. He was up several thousand, and the men around the table were slurring curse words under their breath with each hand he won now. One of the prostitutes, a busty woman with short brown hair, went to sit on Silas's lap. He shifted in his seat as to let her sit down beside him.

"You know him?" she asked Silas.

"We traveled together. Do you mind? I can't see while you're sitting on me."

"Have it your way, handsome. Maybe I'll see you later."

Will's focus was on the game. Bradwell and Schmidt were ready to break. It was only a matter of time before he could go all in and take them down.

"Blinds, please," the dealer called out. Each player tossed a chip into the middle. Fox looked like he was ready for bed, and sure enough, he folded as Schmidt started the betting. Schmidt was in an entirely different place and threw in $1,000. Bradwell followed with enthusiasm he wasn't able to hide. Will did likewise, although the impression he gave the other men was that he'd done it out of a sense of fear or duty. The dealer asked who wanted cards. Schmidt took three, Bradwell two.

Will asked for one. He threw down $3,000, holding himself back just enough, or so he hoped. Schmidt raised another $3,000. Bradwell tried to hide the glee he was feeling as he threw his money down. One of the prostitutes sitting beside him gasped as he raised another $5,000. Schmidt followed him, and Will knew it was time. He pushed all his money into the center of the table.

"I'll raise you eight thousand," he said, looking at each of the men.

"What do you say, Henry? It's only money, isn't it?" Schmidt said. "I'll see you." Schmidt pushed $8,000 worth of chips into the middle. He still had at least $3,000 in front of him, and his bag of nuggets remained unopened.

"It's more than money, Gustav," Bradwell said. "It's more than that." He reached back and pushed all his remaining chips into the middle. "I'll see your eight thousand and raise you another twenty."

"I can't cover that bet."

"Well then, how about this? You throw in your claim, and you come and work for me. You work my claim for me."

Silas grabbed Will by the shoulder, but he shrugged him off. "You're confident I've gold in my claim?"

"I don't think your claim is worth a dime, but I think you and your friend are."

"What would be the price of our labor?"

"Room and board and a ticket home next spring."

"You don't want us here?"

"I don't like the way you look at my fiancée, and I sure as hell don't like the way she looks at you."

"That sounds like a good deal for you but perhaps not so much for me. I can't speak for Silas."

"Let's leave him out, then. Just you, Leary."

"So you'll pay my brother?"

"I'll give him the money for bringing the lady here. You leave this winter, however, on a sled, back to Skagway."

"You think I'd make it?"

"People have. Maybe you'd be one of them."

"I'll tell you what; I'll take that bet, but instead of your money, I'll take one of your claims. Someone told me you've got an unworked claim just off Bonanza Creek."

"I'm in the process of moving some machinery onto it."

"It could be nothing, or it could be rich." He took a sip of water from his beer bottle. "That claim against mine and my word that I'll leave here this week."

"Think about what you're doing," Silas said, but Will didn't turn. He was staring into Bradwell's eyes.

"That seems fair." Bradwell put down his whiskey tumbler. "Carrick, go upstairs and fetch the papers for the unworked claim by Bonanza Creek."

Carrick stood up and went to the staircase. The other games had stopped, and the room was silent but for the sound of his footsteps up the stairs.

"Will, can I speak to you?" Silas said.

"Not now, brother. I'm in the middle of a game. It wouldn't be polite."

Will's cards were facedown on the table. He threw his eyes to them and then to Bradwell's. A tinge of doubt stabbed at him. If he folded now, they'd still have the claim. They'd still have the money Bradwell owed Silas—all that they'd have lost would be the $5,000 Bradwell had given him. If Bradwell's hand was better than his, he'd lose everything. He'd lose Anna forever. Carrick was coming back down the stairs. He had only seconds to decide. Once Carrick threw that piece of paper down on the table, it was done. He picked up his cards, making sure no one else could see them, and placed them facedown on the table again. He leaned back in his chair and stared at Bradwell. Carrick arrived at the table. Bradwell motioned for him to throw down the paper staking the claim, and he dropped it onto the pile of chips.

"Let's see what you've got," Bradwell said.

"No. It's your place. You go first."

He put his cards down on the table. "Full house," he said. "Three jacks, two queens."

Schmidt laughed out loud and clapped his friend on the back.

"Silas, I'm so sorry," Will said as his face broke into a grin. "We're going to have to build another cabin. Four of a kind. Four aces. Thank you, Mr. Bradwell."

Silas roared behind him, and Will let the emotion go at last. He stood up, the feeling of victory coursing through him. Silas threw his arms around him. Will turned back to the table, offering a hand across to Bradwell.

"Thank you for the game, sir. I hope we can remain friends."

"Of course," Bradwell said. He stood up to shake his hand. "This is a day's pay for me. I've forty-two other claims to worry about and the young lady you brought here warming my bed. I do hope you'll be able to attend the wedding."

Will let go of the older man's hand to gather the enormous pile of chips in the center of the table.

Chapter 12

The shadows in his dreams had lightened, the faces of the Indians blurred now. They no longer stared into his eyes, demanding to know why. It was possible now to envision a time when they'd stop coming to him altogether and the pain would end. He'd rarely felt this level of comfort in all the years that had passed since his time in the army, since what he'd witnessed at Wounded Knee. Silas had been right; this experience had been what he'd needed. But there was more to it than that. It was her. The picture of her had replaced the grisly images that had pervaded his dreams. He'd thought of her each of the twenty days that had passed since the banquet. But he hadn't seen her. They'd been to town a few times since, but he'd followed Silas's warnings to stay away for the time being.

Bradwell's anger was apparent, no matter how much he tried to hide behind his semigracious words or outright bravado. They'd cleared the debris from the claim they'd won from him and moved their cabin onto it, piece by piece. The claims around it were rich, bearing thousands in gold a week. It seemed a greater possibility than the one they'd originally taken, which they'd worked for two fruitless weeks before deciding to devote their energies to the claim Will had won in the poker game. He would delight in taking the gold from Bradwell's claim. It would be all the sweeter for that.

Their education in the art of mining had been through conversation with the old-timers, perseverance, and by doing. They'd dug several prospect holes six feet down to where the frost turned the dirt to concrete, and they'd have to let the fires do their work. Much of the woodlands on the hills surrounding the claims had been stripped already, and they spent much of their time trudging miles through the snow to seek out wood or to drag it back. They set the fires each night so that when they came back in the morning, they could dig through a foot or two of melted dirt, clearing it away before setting another fire. They put aside the dirt they'd drawn out to be processed during the warmer months. They heaped it and treated it with the respect a pile of dirt that could be worth thousands of dollars deserved.

It was the third day when Silas came upon the first shavings—just a few dollars' worth, but he celebrated as if they had come upon the mother lode. Will had wanted to celebrate that night—after all, they were rich already. With the money Bradwell had sent to Silas the morning after the poker game and Will's winnings, they had savings in excess of $40,000. It was more than most miners they met had seen in a year of prospecting. It was almost enough to buy Anna Denton. Perhaps if he gave that and some more to her family, she'd leave Bradwell. Silas had deposited it in one of the banks that had recently opened up in Dawson. Will didn't trust banks but had relented after Silas had convinced him of the lack of security in their cabin.

They were ten feet down in several holes now, looking for the pay streak, aiming toward the bedrock, where most of the color would be hiding—if it were there at all.

They settled down in their cabin for dinner. Will doled out their regular meal of flapjacks and beans. Their lifestyle hadn't changed much, despite their newly won fortune. They had come here to dig for gold, and there wasn't much to spend their money on. He handed a plate to Silas and sat opposite him, his food on his lap, when they heard the knock at the door. Silas put his plate aside and went to answer it.

"Mr. Carrick," he said. "What a surprise."

Carrick was working several of Bradwell's claims nearby and brushed fresh snow off his shoulders as he stepped inside. "Hello, Silas. Hello, Leary."

"Carrick," Will said, "you're just in time for dinner. You want some?"

"If you have any to spare."

Will went to the pan and ladled out a portion to Carrick, who pulled up a box to sit on.

"How's the claim?" he asked between mouthfuls.

"We're hopeful. We've laid down some prospect holes," Silas said. "We haven't turned up much yet—just a few shavings."

"You will. It's a good claim. You boys have developed quite the reputation around here already."

"What do you mean?"

"You're the first I've heard of to make their fortune without finding an ounce of gold. The other prospectors stand up and take notice of that kind of thing."

"We're just here to mine the color, same as they are," Will said.

"There's a lot of talk about how you gave Bradwell a black eye. A lot of the miners hold you in high regard for that."

"And you? How do you feel about that?" Will said.

"He's my employer, but I've no huge love for him. It was good to see him come out on the losing end for once. I know he won't miss that money or this claim, but it did rankle him some."

"Has he spoken of it?" Silas asked.

"Not much, but I know the man. He doesn't like to lose. He doesn't like to be shown up in front of his friends either."

"I don't want to make enemies. Should we talk to him? Offer the olive branch?" Silas said.

"I'd stay away for now. He's got that mean look about him. There's no use trying to reason with an injured animal."

"What about Miss Denton? Have you seen her?" Will said as he put his plate to one side.

"That's a major part of your problem right there. I think it's best you give the lady a wide berth too—for everyone's sake."

Silas spooned food into his mouth, staying silent. Will got up and went to the cabinet, taking out a bottle of whiskey—the one luxury their fortune allowed them out here. He didn't wait to ask the men if they wanted some, just poured a couple of fingers into mugs and handed them out. They thanked him as he sat back down.

"Where are you from, Carrick?" Will asked.

"From Surrey originally. Is that a problem?"

"No, Carrick, no problem."

"I feel a little out of my depth here," Silas said, trying to pass it off as a joke.

Carrick didn't seem in the joking mood. "I've met plenty of Irish over here. Some wouldn't give me the time of day."

"I don't hate all English people—just the ones who forced my parents off their land."

Carrick took a sip of whiskey and let out a satisfied gasp. "Well, then I don't suppose we have a problem, because that certainly wasn't anything to do with me."

"Well, all right, then. I'll drink to that."

"Have you been in town much lately?" Silas asked.

"I'm in a few days a week. How about you boys?"

"We've been in a couple of times in the last ten days—just running errands."

"Depositing all Bradwell's money, were we?" Carrick laughed. Neither man answered. "You should come in tomorrow night. Take a break from the slog out here. You could go to a show. Have you seen Arizona Charlie or the Oatley sisters at the Grand Saloon yet? No? Let's arrange a sled in tomorrow evening. You boys can put yourselves up in a hotel. It's not as if you can't afford it. We could have a few drinks. What do you say?"

"Sounds good to us," Silas said.

"All right—it's settled." Carrick drank back the rest of his whiskey and wiped his beard clean.

The crowd at the Grand Theater was as wild as the landscape. Most of the men—for there were almost no women in attendance—seemed already drunk as they flopped down on the hard wooden benches that served as seats. Silas sat in the middle, with Carrick on his left. Will had a beer in his hand and the satisfying feeling of a good dinner in his belly. Carrick had been talking for the last hour about the entertainment they'd be seeing. There were about ten rows of wooden benches, each seating about fifteen drunken prospectors. The small stage was in front of them, elevated a few feet. Like most of the other buildings in Dawson, the interior of the saloon did not match the ornate entrance and sign on the building outside. The plain wooden walls were unfinished and the stage the same. The floor was covered in wood shavings, and the smell of smoke and stale beer filled the air. The shadowy, curtained boxes that loomed above them to the right were different. They were painted red, with intricate golden designs as if the decorator had only made it to them before running out of time or the will to continue. The boxes all sat empty for now as the master of ceremonies came out onto the stage. The whooping came to a crescendo as he tried to speak. He raised his hands, bringing them down with a smile.

"Gentlemen, please," he said. Someone threw a beer at the stage. Suds spattered his pants, but his face didn't change. The crowd quieted. He introduced the first act, and the crowd cheered as Arizona Charlie waddled out onstage in full cowboy getup, with his wife dressed in silver sequins with a foot-long feather in her hair. Several bawdy whistles came up from the audience. A Mountie stood silently at the back of the room, his pistol on his hip. Apart from Arizona Charlie, he was the only armed man in there. Charlie set his wife on one side of the stage while he delivered an array of prepared jokes that had the prospectors rolling in the aisles. He then drew his pistol and shot glass balls from his wife's hands from ten paces. Will cheered along with the rest of them. Figures appeared in one of the boxes, drawing his eye. He recognized Schmidt and his wife as they sat down. Arizona Charlie stepped back another couple of paces, this time with his weapon holstered, but Will felt himself drawn to the boxes once more. Bradwell stepped out, waving down as the king to his adoring subjects. He reached back through the curtain to take Anna's hand. Radiant in a blue dress and matching hat, she took her seat. Bradwell called across to Schmidt in the other box, seeming to share a joke. Even Arizona Charlie stopped a few seconds to pay homage to the king, bowing before he continued his act.

"There's your boss," Silas said to Carrick. "He doesn't seem affected overly by his recent losses."

"He's here a couple of nights a week—along with his new trophy," Carrick said. "I try to avoid him as much as possible."

Silas and Carrick watched the stage, but Will watched the box above. Bradwell sat beside Anna in an elegant tweed suit with a contented smile under his gray mustache. She was rigid, straight as a board. He doubted she'd be able to pick him out. It would be almost impossible to spot him amid the throng of wide-brimmed hats. Arizona Charlie finished his act and accepted the generous applause before making way for Lottie and Polly Oatley. The prospector sitting beside Will raised a handkerchief to his eyes as the ladies sang of home and lost loves. Anna didn't move, the champagne glass in her hand untouched.

The Oatley sisters finished their set, and a kick line dancing the cancan emerged from the side of the stage to whip the previously quiet prospectors back into a frenzy. The music was almost drowned out by the sounds of the hollering from the crowd. And when Will glanced upward again, they were gone—Anna and Bradwell both.

"Forget her," he said out loud, although no one heard but him. "Enjoy the show." He finished his beer, cradling the glass in his hand. The cancan ended, and the kick line disappeared, much to the consternation of the crowd. They began booing and calling them back. The master of ceremonies returned to soothe the mob once more, but there was no quieting them this time, and the booing continued unabated. The master of ceremonies held out his hands.

"It's not usually as rowdy as this," Carrick said. "Perhaps the whiskey was half-price before the performance."

Two stagehands pushed a piano onto the stage, and Bradwell emerged behind it. Much of the crowd was stunned into reverential silence. Those who didn't know who Bradwell was were soon informed by those who did.

"Thank you, gentlemen," Bradwell said.

"This has certainly never happened before," Carrick said.

"I hope you're enjoying the show," Bradwell continued to a resurgence of whoops and catcalls. "Most of you know me, but for those of you who don't, my name is Henry Bradwell, and I'm one of you. I'm just like you. The only differences between you and me are timing and luck, and I hope every one of you has the luck and timing that I've enjoyed these past few years. The gold is there. Don't ever doubt it." The crowd let out a huge cheer, which he soon quashed. "I have a special treat tonight. They let me do these things because I own half the place," he said to a chorus of laughter. "As some of you know, I'm soon to be married, but not many of you know how talented my wife-to-be is. Come on out, Anna."

She walked out with a smile as tight as a scar. Some of the men began to whistle and call out. "Now, now, she's my fiancée. Please conduct yourselves appropriately." His tone commanded respect, and the men stopped. She took a seat at the piano. He took a piece of paper out of his pocket. "This piece is called . . . What is it?" he said, scratching his head. "It's 'Sonata No. 17 in D minor' by Ludwig van . . . It's some pretty piano by Beethoven." The men cheered.

She looked out into the crowd and then down at the piano. Not a person spoke. She waited a few seconds and then began. The notes swelled from the piano, filling the air, swirling around every man in the room until all thoughts of kick lines and dance-hall girls and even her own beauty were dismissed by the sheer power and urgency of the music. Men stared on like children as she worked the keys, her concentration absolute. She played on and on, the minutes disappearing like smoke in the wind. Bradwell was still standing beside her, apparently unaware of how long the piece was, yet every man in the theater remained rapt. Will saw the dance-hall girls at the side of the stage standing, watching. It was perhaps seven or eight minutes into the piece when Bradwell tapped her on the shoulder, and she nodded to him, bringing the music to an abrupt halt.

"I think she could have gone on all night," he said, but his words were lost in the applause that exploded from the benches. Will rose to his feet. Silas and many others joined him. She stood, a contented smile on her face, and took a bow before Bradwell led her offstage.

The stagehands came to wheel away the piano, and the benches were withdrawn. It was the last act of the night. Will sat staring, transfixed, until a stagehand tapped him on the shoulder, asking him to move. The dance floor was revealed, and the dance-hall girls came back to mingle with the crowd. A four-piece band appeared on the stage and immediately began to play. A circle of prospectors surrounded each of the girls, every man holding up the tickets they'd purchased in advance for the pleasure of dancing with one.

A caller bellowed instructions from the stage. "Come on, boys, let's get this going. You know who's first. Everyone who bought a ticket will get a turn." The crowds receded to the bar at the back of the room, leaving each of the ladies with her first dance partner. The miners stomped around the dance floor a few times, their women in tow, before the caller signaled an end to the dance, and the next ticket holders stepped up.

"Will you be partaking?" Will asked.

"I have a ticket," Carrick said, reaching into his pocket. "Cost me a dollar—it'd better be worth it." He gulped down his beer.

Carrick waited his turn, and the three men stood at the crowded bar watching as each lady danced with dozens of eager suitors who they barely made eye contact with as they trotted around the floor.

Will finished his drink. "I need some air. I'm growing weary of watching people who can't dance all night. I'll be back in a while."

"We'll be here," Silas said.

He made his way through the crowd and out onto the street.

"I didn't realize you'd be so long up there," Bradwell said as he pulled Anna along by the hand. "I told Schmidt we'd meet him and his wife for drinks after the show."

"It's a twenty-five-minute piece," she said. "I don't think I was onstage for ten."

"Well, it seemed to go down quite well, and the miners know who you are now. They'll know to steer clear. You'd shudder to see how they act around unmarried women—like a bunch of voracious animals."

"There aren't many women here, and those who are here have a tendency to charge for their services."

He tugged on her arm as they stepped out into the deathly freeze of the night. She tucked her chin down into her fur coat as they went. The moon was full over the town, illuminating drunken miners stumbling out of saloons that would serve alcohol until dawn and beyond. Sunday was the only day of rest, where no labor of any kind was permitted. Father Jones had told her that men had been fined for chopping wood on Sundays or even for fishing. Sunday was the Lord's Day—set aside for rest. They passed by the church.

"Are you going again on Sunday?"

"I think so," she answered, her voice muffled by her coat.

"You're not even Catholic."

"They don't seem to care. Why should you?"

"I don't."

"Would you consider coming along?"

"I don't know. I'm a busy man. But perhaps you're right, seeing as I did construct the place. It could be beneficial if I attended once in a while."

A Mountie tipped his hat to them on the street, the gold buttons on his scarlet jacket gleaming in the moonlight. Despite the drunkenness, gambling, and legalized prostitution, she felt safe in this town. The omnipresence of the Mounties saw to that. In church, more miners were talking about sending for their wives and children once spring broke.

They reached the hotel where Schmidt and his wife were waiting for them. Schmidt's wife greeted them with her usual icy smile before claiming to be tired and persuading her husband to leave with her. Ten minutes after arriving, Anna and Bradwell were alone once more, sitting on opposite sides of the table. She was staring into her wineglass, watching the ripples as she shook the stem.

"Will you come to my bed tonight?"

Her insides froze. The smile she hid her feelings with must have seemed like a crease in the rigid skin of her face. "I'm not sure we're ready for that yet, Mr. Bradwell."

"Call me Henry."

His first name felt foreign in her mouth, like a new language. "All right, Henry."

"If not tonight, when?"

"We should wait until the night of our wedding. That would be the more proper thing to do."

"Yet you won't set a date."

"We've only just met. I've been living here a month. There's so much to adjust to, so many new people."

He gripped the tumbler in his hand with white knuckles. "My patience is growing thin. My deal with your father was that I'd send the money to him once we wed."

"Yet the winter prevents you from doing that. Nothing is coming or going from this town until May at the earliest. You said that yourself. So you can't send the money until that time, no matter what should occur in the interim."

"So you're going to hold the winter against me?"

"Of course not, Henry . . ."

"You're going to hold me to ransom for the next six months until I can send the money to your father?"

"No, of course not."

"Well then, will you set a wedding date?"

She found herself cringing away from him. His face had tightened, and his cheeks were flushed red. He brought the whiskey tumbler to his mouth, finishing it off.

"I just need a little time."

"How much time?"

Several people were looking over at them. His eyes were black pinpricks, focused only on her. The waiter approached the table but turned away.

"A few weeks. I'll give you a decision soon—I promise."

"Is this because of him?"

"Who?"

"Don't play dumb with me. You know well whom I'm referring to. That Irish fool who brought you here—Leary."

"I should hope you're not implying that anything untoward happened between Mr. Leary and myself," she said, her voice almost breaking. "He's never been anything less than a consummate gentleman and would never lower himself to use language like that in front of a lady."

"I saw it the minute you walked into my office with him. Do you think I'm blind? I saw the way you two were with each other, like two silly kids."

"Why did you invite him to our engagement banquet?"

"To confirm my suspicions and to run him out of this town."

"You don't seem to have been successful in that regard."

He snatched her wrist before she could take it away. "We're leaving now." He threw far too much money down onto the table without releasing the iron grip he had on her. He pulled her outside, dragged her around the side of the building, and poked a finger into her chest. "Don't you ever dare to speak to me like that in public again! What are you here without me? You're nothing. And you never will be."

He ran fingers through his thin gray hair, seeming to relent. "Anna, all I want is for you to be my wife. I apologize if I'm jealous for what I see between you and the Irishman. I just need your assurance that nothing ever happened."

"You have it," she said, her voice quavering in the dark. "Nothing has ever happened between us."

"You will come to my bed. I'll give you one week to decide when." He disappeared back toward the Palace without another word.

She watched him as he went. She stood there until the cold penetrated her to the point where she had to move. She walked back toward the hotel where Bradwell had put her. She was caught in a vise. The decency in Bradwell was there to see. He was good to the ladies who worked for him when so many would have been cruel and coarse. He was generous to the people of the town. He had funded the church himself. Surely she could still fulfill the promise to her father and be the dutiful wife Bradwell wanted her to be.

She hadn't realized how things must have seemed between Will and her, but those were false impressions. Will was sweet, funny, brave, and handsome, but there was no romance between them. There never could be. She couldn't allow her emotions to sway the decisions that had to be made and the promises that had to be kept. Will had his path in the Klondike, and she had hers. Hers was the dutiful wife and mother. Happiness would follow; she just had to be patient. She was sure that Bradwell would calm down and be more patient and attentive once they were married or once the children came. The fact that she felt no attraction to him was immaterial. She would do as women had for generations. The love that her mother felt for her father was rare, almost an anomaly. Anna's role was to obey, to produce children. She would have the satisfaction of saving her family, and surely that would be enough to keep her content through the years of a loveless, stale union with a man thirty years her senior? She knew she had to go to him before it was too late. He was angry. She couldn't let that anger turn to resentment. Bradwell resented Will and Silas already, and that was dangerous in a town like this. She had heard him cursing them behind closed doors, shouting at Milton and Carrick that they'd made a fool of him. She had to convince Bradwell that she was here to be his wife for her sake as well as theirs.

She turned around and strode back toward the Palace. Her heart was beating hard in her chest, her hands shaking as she pushed the saloon door open. The blare of music, conversation, and laughter hit her as soon as she walked inside, and the smoke hung low over the room like a fog. She glanced around the crowded saloon. The tables were lively with prospectors losing the gold they'd toiled to gather, and the bar was thick with others drowning their sorrows. Gertie and Katie were working a couple of prospectors who looked like they had money to spend, but the other girls were nowhere to be seen. She knew where Bradwell would be if he wasn't downstairs on the floor or at the bar. The door to his office was ajar a few inches.

She rehearsed what she was going to say as she made her way up the stairs. She put her hand on the door and heard a strange shuffling noise coming from inside. She pushed it open just far enough to stick her head through.

Anna felt her blood turn to dust. Bradwell had his back to the door and his pants around his ankles. He was bent over the desk with Betsy's legs wrapped around him, grunting as he thrust into her. She met Anna's eyes but didn't speak, and Anna backed out of the doorway.

She turned around and descended the stairs back to the saloon floor. She kept her eyes to the ground and pushed through the burgeoning crowd and out onto the street. She had no idea where to go but began walking anyway. She didn't want anyone to see her like this.

"Miss Denton?" came the voice from behind her. Will stood alone. "Anna, where are you going?"

Chapter 13

She turned to walk away, aware of every drunken prospector on the street as she pulled her scarf over her face. Will followed beside her, asking questions she couldn't answer—not here. Bradwell had eyes everywhere. Everyone was looking to curry favor with the King of the Klondike. Will and Silas seemed to be the only people not in his debt—who didn't care what he thought of them. Will knew the risks too, and he kept two paces behind her. The cold city streets were almost deserted, but one person who knew them would be enough. She turned to him.

"We can't be seen here together. I can't be responsible for getting you killed."

"To hell with Bradwell and his men! Why are you so upset? Tell me what he did to you."

She saw the sign for her hotel a few hundred yards away. There was no other safe place.

"We can't talk here. Go to my room in the Pacific Hotel. It's upstairs—number 104." She reached into her pocket for the brass key. "Take this. I'll follow you in a few minutes. Make sure no one sees you go inside."

"I'm an expert at that."

"Go. I'll take a walk around the block and clear my head."

He disappeared into the dark of the Dawson night. She stood still for a few seconds and made her way along Front Street, along the frozen

Klondike River. A stray dog moved to follow her, loping along by her side as she passed through dully lit tents, their occupants visible as shadows against the canvas. The river was quiet, a thick bed of ice covering it from bank to bank. The mountains stretched up to the cloudy sky beyond. The photograph of her family she kept in a frame beside her bed came to her, and she imagined Will sitting on her bed examining it. The tears had dried now, frozen by the Arctic air. She stood by the river for five minutes or so, staring at the gray ice that imprisoned them all there.

The front desk at the Pacific Hotel was empty—as she'd hoped—as she entered the small wooden-built hotel she'd been living in these past few weeks. Mr. Bailey never worked the desk past midnight. She looked up at the first-floor balcony. Will had seemingly slipped past unnoticed.

She moved up the stairs, aware of every creaking step as she went. None of the doors opened. They never did. She turned the handle on the door to her room. He had lit a candle and was sitting on the chair by the dresser. She closed the door behind her.

"Mr. Leary. What must you think of me—inviting you to my hotel room like this?"

"When are you going to call me Will?"

She took her coat and hat, hanging them on a stand by the door. She made her way over to the bed and sat down, aware of his gaze upon her every move.

"All right, Will," she said.

"I saw you tonight, you know."

"Where?"

"In the theater at the Grand Saloon. I saw you play. It was the most magnificent thing. Your talent is astonishing."

"Piano lessons three days a week do pay off, I suppose," she said. "I didn't see you there. I was trying not to look at the faces in the crowd—just at the keys on the piano."

"Did Bradwell put you up to it?"

"He wanted to present me to the prospectors—as a warning to stay away or to show off his new trophy, perhaps. I was the one who insisted on playing the piano. I would have been embarrassed to just walk out onstage to be paraded in front of a group of baying men like a piece of meat."

"You have the respect of each one of those baying louts now. I can assure you of that."

"Thank you." She reached for a handkerchief, using it to dab the wetness from her eyes. "Would you like some water?" she asked.

"Yes, please."

She took a jug of water from the shelf beside her bed and poured it. She handed the glass to him, feeling the warmth of his touch as he took it.

"So why are you upset? What did he do?"

She dug deep inside herself, drawing the words up like water from a poisoned well. "I walked in on him, engaged in a carnal act with one of the ladies from the saloon."

"What? Who?"

"Does it matter?"

"Hardly. I'm sorry."

"It's shocking, but there's little to be done about it."

"Did he see you?"

"No, but she did."

"What are you going to do?"

"I don't know. I promised my father. Mabel needs that money." She took a sip of water before placing the glass back down on her bedside table. "He expects me to marry him soon."

"And what do you want to do?"

"My wants are nothing to be taken into account."

"I could repeat the question."

"Please don't stir these feelings up inside me, Mr. Leary . . ."

"Will."

"Don't do that to me."

"Then why don't you do it? Why don't you marry Bradwell?"

She ran her fingers over the velvet drapes. "I have to."

"No, you don't. You don't have to do anything."

"What are you talking about?"

"Your family will survive without that money. There are plenty of other ways to make money here. Our new claim is going to produce enough gold—"

"I gave my word. I gave my word to my father."

"I could send some money to your family once the river ice recedes. I have more money than I know what to do with."

"You think I'm some whore to be bought and sold, to be passed from man to man, to be purchased by the highest bidder?"

"Of course not. I want to help you."

"I'm engaged to him. Perhaps you should leave now, Mr. Leary. It's not proper for us to be alone together," she said as she got off the bed. She moved to the door, clasping her fingers around the handle.

"You can't possibly consider marrying him," Will said.

"He was frustrated. I'm sure any such behavior would stop once we were married. I can see the good in him. He's given back so much to the people of this town."

"Let me help you."

"It's not as simple as that. It's too dangerous. He hates you. He'd kill you if he knew you were here. He's untouchable. He meets with Rousseau, the captain of the Mounties, for lunch once a week. He'll crush you if you defy him."

"You think I'm scared of him?" Will said. He moved to sit on the bed. She went to him.

"I think you should be." She spread her arms around him, her head tight under his chin. She had never done anything like this before—with any man. "I think there was a time when I could have done this—when I could have fulfilled my duty and married him. But that was before Bryce and Stevens gambled away our tickets—before I met you. This all would have been so much easier if I'd never met you," she said, the tears solid and thick on her cheeks. "I never knew I could have my judgment clouded like this. I never knew a man could stir these feelings inside me."

He moved his mouth to hers. She closed her eyes as she felt their lips meet and moved her hand to the stubble on his face. They both stood at once, their movements languid and slow. He drew back and took her face in his hands.

"We can't do this," she said. "If he finds out . . ."

Her words were lost as he moved in to kiss her once more. This kiss was rougher, more rugged, and she felt his hands down her back, tugging at the ties on her dress. Every other thought melted away as her lips parted to welcome his kiss. She heard herself moan as he drew away from her and began breathing heavily. The loss of control in his eyes excited her, and she moved to undo the buttons on the front of her dress as he took off his jacket. The realization that she had wanted to do this since she first met him quickened her movements, and she pushed the dress to the floor, revealing her white undergarments. She turned around again as he untied the strings on the back of her undergarments, and then she moved to kiss him. Now just in her brassiere and drawers, she bent to rip down his pants, and he was naked in front of her. She unclasped her brassiere and felt first his hands, then his mouth on her breasts before they moved onto the bed. She pulled down her drawers and lay on top of him, wordless and kissing him, his hands over her back, her hair wild and sprawling in his face.

They kissed for a few minutes, his hands and mouth over her until he turned her onto her back. He leaned down to kiss her as he brought his hips in line with hers. The pain made her flinch at first, and he moved to stop before she put her hand up to his face, urging him to continue. The rhythm was slow at first, like waves lapping the lakeshore, but he soon quickened, and she heard herself call out without knowing it. He arched his back as she abandoned herself to the sheer pleasure surging through her. It was like nothing before. Who knew how long it was before it ended, but when it did, he collapsed down beside her, both their bodies wet with sweat. She kissed him again and rested her head on his chest.

Silas finished his beer, placing it down on the bar. Carrick was on the dance floor with one of the young girls he'd paid. He hadn't questioned why Silas didn't want to join, seemingly content to let him be. The caller shouted out as the music ended. The lady let go of Carrick and walked away without a goodbye. The next ticket holder immediately accosted her, and Carrick made his way back to Silas, a sly smile on his face.

"Anyone would think she didn't care about me," he said.

"I'm sure you were the highlight of her night."

"What time is it anyway?"

"It must be after two in the morning."

Will had been gone awhile, but Silas wasn't about to go searching for him. He knew how to look after himself.

"No sign of Will?"

"He never came back. Perhaps he found a lady friend."

"Paying for it more likely."

"I don't know. He was never the type who had to pay."

"What about you?"

He laughed. "It depends on the night, my friend. Some nights are good; other nights—not so much."

"Ain't that the truth?"

"So how long have you been working for Bradwell?"

"A year or so. I was in Forty Mile in summer '96. I was wandering around Canada for a few years after I left England in '91. I heard about the discoveries here and came upriver the next day. I took a claim on Bonanza and started working it."

"It didn't work out?"

"It's not that the claim didn't work out—more that I didn't."

"What are you talking about?"

"The claim was good. It still is. Bradwell's drawn more than fifty thousand out of it as far as I can tell."

"Bradwell?"

"You're beginning to see how things work around here now, aren't you?"

"What happened?"

"I had some debts from my life before I struck it rich, and he offered to pay them for me. I was to pay him back from the gold I drew from my claim."

"But you didn't?"

"I gambled all my gold away. Bradwell offered to lease my claim from me for five years, keeping all that he found, of course. He offered me a job working my own claim but for him. I've been doing his bidding ever since."

"Why? He took your claim."

"My creditors would have done far worse to me if they'd gotten ahold of me first. Some of us aren't cut out to be millionaires, I suppose. It galls me to see how much money he's making that should have been mine, though. The gold in my claim is a drop in the ocean to him, but it would have been everything to me."

"You resent him for that?"

"Wouldn't you?"

"Is my brother in danger?"

"I don't think so. That's not Bradwell's style. He's not Leary's biggest fan, but would he hurt him because he beat him at cards? No."

"What's he like?"

"Bradwell?"

"Yes."

"I have no love for him. I wouldn't cross him. Somehow, I don't think anyone here knows the real Henry Bradwell. He never talks about the past. It's as if his memory only goes back to when he first struck gold. I don't know much about him, and I don't ask. It's easier not to."

"He's getting married to my friend."

"She's never going to have to worry about money a day in her life."

"There's more to it than that."

Carrick ignored what Silas had said, reaching into his pocket. "Wait a minute," he said. He turned out the pockets in his britches. He'd no more than a few coins left. "Looks like I'm out of money."

"I have some."

"You want to keep drinking?"

"Yes."

"I live close by—not more than five minutes. I have some money there. I could go back and get it."

"I don't mind lending you a little."

"I'd be more comfortable with my own. You want to come along? I'll only be a few minutes."

"Sure."

They pushed their way through the crowd, which was almost as thick as it had been at the beginning of the night. The air outside was frigid, and they tucked up the lapels of their coats as they walked. Silas followed beside Carrick, but they didn't talk. Carrick led him through a maze of half-finished buildings and tents until they came to a wooden cabin, identical to the dozens around it. He pushed the door open and lit a candle in the corner, illuminating the interior with golden light. The cabin was neat and tidy with a bed on the wall in the corner.

"You want a drink?"

"Sounds fine."

Carrick went to the cupboard and took out a half-drunk bottle of whiskey and two mugs. He gestured for him to sit down on a wooden chair he'd pulled out before he lit the stove in the corner. The cabin warmed up to the point where Silas was able to take off his coat in less than a minute. Carrick sat down opposite him and raised his mug. They both drank back. Silas fought the burn in his stomach for a few seconds before he began to talk.

"You've always been alone here?"

"Yes. I came here alone, and I'm sure I'll leave the same way."

"You've no wife or girlfriend back home or down in the outside waiting for you?"

"No, there's no one. What about you?"

"Same," Silas said, taking another drink.

"I've been prospecting for years; there was never the time nor the place for a woman in my life. You were working in a drugstore for years in Boston, no? Living the button-down life? What's your excuse?"

"I've no excuse. I never found a woman worth my interest, is all."

"Surely there was someone? A big, good-looking guy like yourself."

"Bessie Taylor."

"Bessie who?"

"Bessie Taylor." He raised his cup into the air. "She was the one I was meant to marry. She would have said yes too. I know she would have. Her parents met mine, and she was just waiting for me to propose."

"You could be home right now, married with kids. What age were you?"

"Twenty-one."

"What happened?"

"I just lost interest. Bessie was a sweet girl but nothing fascinating. She didn't have that . . ." He snapped his fingers. "It's hard to say, but whatever I was looking for, she didn't have it."

"Sounds familiar. I was always more interested in gold—it doesn't moan nearly as much." Carrick reached for the bottle. "You want some more?" Silas held out his cup as a response, and Carrick poured a few fingers in. It was beginning to snow outside, and Silas stood up to look out the window. Carrick went to the window and stood peering through the frosted glass beside him.

"It's a beautiful sight. I never get sick of it."

"Except when you're out in it," Carrick said.

He moved a hand to Carrick's rough cheek. He went to say something, but Silas shook his head, reaching in to kiss him. Carrick put his arms around Silas's waist and pulled him in. They moved toward the bed and started to undress.

Chapter 14

Silas descended thirty feet to the bottom of the mine shaft in the claim Bradwell had owned a few weeks prior, a candle illuminating the walls around him. The frost held the soil tight, but Silas had put wooden supports in nonetheless, and he bent down as he passed the one holding the center of the tunnel. A spade and a pickax lay at the end of the shaft from where he'd left them the day before, and he set down the candle he was carrying as he got to work. Last night's fire had done its work, and he cleared away the ashes and debris it had left, shoveling them into a wheelbarrow. He heard Will coming down the shaft and saw the dark outline of his body as it interrupted the dim passage of light from the surface.

Will took the wheelbarrow without a word and turned back toward the light. Silas dug into the thawed earth, shifting the soil behind him in neat piles. Will returned a few minutes later to remove what he had put aside and then again a few minutes after. Silas felt the muscles in his shoulders working like a machine in perfect synchronization as he plunged the shovel into the dark earth again and again, coming up with great clods of soil to lay behind him.

It had been three weeks since they'd gone into town to see the show with Carrick, and he had seen Carrick only in passing since—a few waves from far away, whereas once he would have come over. He'd left Carrick's cabin that night while the other man was still sleeping. Silas knew what was coming in the morning. He'd seen it too many times. So he'd sneaked out under cover of darkness, making his way back to the empty hotel room he'd meant to share with Will that night. He'd been awake when Will came in before dawn but had stayed silent and thought better of asking questions. Will told him the next day that he'd been with a lady in one of the brothels in town. He said he'd liked her so much that he wanted to make his way into town again that week, and he'd been five or maybe six times since.

Silas never asked her name or even where she worked. He didn't want to force Will to lie. A dark feeling of inevitability had come across him, but there was nothing to be done now. Will was a grown man, and Silas trusted Anna's judgment.

"Anything?" Will said from over his shoulder.

He hadn't heard him coming with the sound of the pickax.

"Not today. Not yet."

"We'll get there. I know it," he said and dug his shovel into the fresh pile of earth to haul it away. Will had been different these past few weeks. It was hard to put a finger on it, but it was unmistakable. A light seemed reignited inside him, and the hardships of the Klondike were suddenly nothing more than challenges to be overcome. He disappeared into the darkness of the mine shaft.

Silas thought about Carrick. It was hard not to. Still, he didn't even know if he wanted anything more from the man. Perhaps Carrick was angry with him for leaving the next morning without so much as a goodbye. Surely he understood the risks. It was impossible to believe this type of thing had never happened to him before.

"Nothing to be done now," Silas said and shook his head, plunging the pickax into the dirt once more. He shifted the soil aside and drove the pickax in harder and harder, feeling the impact through the wooden handle.

"Watch that you don't break it—or your arms—brother," Will said.

Silas was panting. "Did you deposit that gold we drew yesterday when you were in town?"

"Of course. We got ninety-seven dollars—not bad for a day's work."

"Better than a month's salary for most people back home."

"The mother lode is waiting, my brother. I can feel it."

Silas had to adjust the plane of his swings not to hit Will. There was just enough room for the two men to work. Sometimes they worked together without a word between them for hours. Silas asked the question burning a hole in his mind.

"Have you seen Miss Denton?"

"What?"

"On your trips into town. Have you seen her?"

"No, I haven't."

"Because one of the miners on the next claim . . . Bilson, you know him?"

"The old man from Alberta?"

"Yes. He told me that she and Bradwell have set a date for the wedding. I don't think we'll be receiving an invite, do you?"

"I hadn't heard."

Silas stopped, turned the pickax upside down, and leaned on the end. "You hadn't heard?"

"Oh, I do remember hearing now. The wedding's set for April."

"May, I thought."

"Oh yes, you're right."

"You've lost interest in Miss Denton all of a sudden, have you?"

He resumed shoveling. "No use chasing unicorns, Silas. Not when we're already doing that every day down here."

"I almost might believe you if I didn't know you better, brother. And what unicorns are we chasing? We've made four hundred dollars in this mine in the last three weeks. That's a year's salary."

"You're right, Silas. It must get tiring."

"What?"

"Being right all the time."

"It's a responsibility I bear gracefully." He started into the soil again.

"The bedrock must be close," Will said. "We'll see how much this claim is going to pay out soon."

"Even if we don't strike gold here, that doesn't mean the whole claim's bare. We could be in the wrong spot."

"You mean we're not going to be millionaires today?"

"I wouldn't bet on it."

"I couldn't even if I wanted to, being banned from the gaming tables in every saloon in Dawson."

"That's probably a good thing."

"Too little, too late for them."

They continued for an hour or so, clearing out the soil from last night's fire before they brought down more firewood and set that in place. They lit the dried moss and twigs they'd stashed away in the corner of their cabin and set wood on top. The smoke from the fire followed them up the shaft, and the air felt clean and refreshing. The snow-covered landscape was alive with activity. Bradwell owned several of the mines around them, yet they hadn't seen him in weeks—not since the night in town. Perhaps things had settled down. Maybe Will was telling the truth and he had lost interest in Anna. *No way. I know him too well to think that.*

They sat down on the hill. It was as cold as it always was, but the sun was out, and they wrapped themselves in the expensive animal-fur parkas they'd bought in town a few weeks before. The ubiquitous white tents dotted the valley in front of them, and prospectors wandered around, laden with wood or tools or both. Black smoke billowed into the white sky from several holes across the valley. The landscape had a ghostly quality to it—bare as it was, stripped of all trees and vegetation, the snow stained brown and black where the miners had been. They sat together eating their flapjacks and beans and watching the frenzy of activity that was the daily currency here.

"Is that Carrick?" Will said.

A tall man, similar in build, was strolling toward a claim several hundred yards away. Silas squinted to make out the man's face, feeling the nerves flutter inside him like a kid. He berated himself silently before he said, "No, it's not him."

Will resumed eating. "It's been a while since we've seen him. I thought you two were friends. Did something happen that night we were in town?"

"Not as far as I remember. We were drunk as skunks, though. I don't remember much toward the end."

"Oh. It's strange that he hasn't called over for so long. I was curious."

"Yes. Perhaps he's been busy."

"You should try to speak to him again. You two got along so well. We all need friends, especially out here."

"You're all the friend I can handle," Silas said and raised himself to his feet.

They waited another hour for the smoke to clear before they made their way back into the mine, rags over their faces. The smoke cleared, and they removed the masks. Will took the shovel and stood beside Silas, digging down until he heard the sound of something solid.

"It doesn't feel like frozen soil," he said.

Silas picked up a shovel, and they worked together to draw back the soil, their energy renewed, their limbs tireless. The candle was almost burned out beside them, and Silas held it up as he peered down at the dirt. He replaced it, and they kept going, shoveling and scraping until a table of something that looked like rock came into view. Silas got down on his hands and knees and cleared away the dirt with his hands, and the unmistakable glint of gold winked at him in the half-light.

"Get the candle."

Will held the candle inches above the ground to reveal a thick seam of gold four or five inches thick, snaking through the dirt.

"It's the mother lode!" Silas screamed. "We've done it! We're rich!"

"Holy sweet baby Jesus and mother of Mary! Look at all that gold."

Will dropped the candle.

"Congratulations!" Captain Rousseau, the ranking Mountie officer in Dawson, said as he held his glass in the air.

"Thank you," Anna said. She took a sip of the fine champagne in her glass and returned to her caviar.

"We've decided to wait until the worst of the winter is over but not so long as to greet the spring itself," Bradwell said.

"When is it?" Rousseau said in his French-Canadian accent.

"May fifteenth."

"Why so long?" the Mountie said, grinning beneath his impressive mustache.

"We've so much to arrange," she said. "That doesn't seem like any time to me."

"I wanted it sooner, but you know the way women are about their wedding day. She's been dreaming about this all her life. It's going to be perfect—a perfect day," Bradwell said, placing his hand over hers. It felt like a salamander on her skin. "We've decided that Father Jones should officiate, and we're going to have the reception in the Palace. It's going to be the biggest party this town has ever seen."

"I just hope I get an invite."

"Of course." He slapped Rousseau on the back. "We wouldn't dream of having it without you."

Anna sat back in her chair, her part in the charade played. It was exhausting, and the guilt at lying to so many people was gnawing at her.

The two men continued talking, the remnants of their lunch on the fine china plates in front of them. They were laughing about something, but she wasn't listening anymore. What if they could read her mind? What would Bradwell do to her if he knew? The two men clinked their glasses together, though she didn't know to what they were toasting. So many toasts. So many congratulations. So many lies.

She stood up. "I must go. I have an appointment, gentlemen."

"With whom?" Bradwell said. He put his whiskey tumbler back onto the table. The two men waited.

"Father Jones. I need to arrange some things for the church."

"In the middle of lunch? It can wait."

She sat back in her chair. There had been no appointment. The lies came easily now. She'd told more lies in the last three weeks than she had the rest of her adult life. This lunch seemed like it could be a long one. She was all too familiar with how these afternoons went. She'd have to wait.

Two hours passed. The sun had already set when they emerged from the restaurant. Bradwell had that loose tone in his voice. It was cold and dark, and he put his arm around her shoulder. She didn't speak. She had settled into a pattern of speaking only when necessary. He never protested.

"Are you still going to see Father Jones?"

"Yes, I'll walk over to the church now."

"Tell the old man I said hello and that he'll see me in church one of these days before the wedding." The church was three hundred yards away through the snowy, sludge-covered streets. "I'll walk you over there. I have some business to attend to."

"Very good."

They carried on in silence through the encroaching twilight, curtains twitching in the buildings they passed. He stopped her, putting both hands on her shoulders.

"Will you come to my bed tonight?"

"Oh, Henry, I don't know . . ."

"You promised—just as I did the same when you asked for a longer engagement. You promised me a night to tide me over."

"Do we have to discuss it here and now? On the street outside the church?"

"Yes, I think we do. I've been more than patient with you. Perhaps you've still got your Irish friend on your mind?"

"No, of course not."

"Well then, what is it?"

"I just never thought . . ."

"You never thought what?"

"I never thought I'd be engaging in such behavior before I was married."

"Anna, please," he said, wrapping his arms around her. "There's nothing sordid or dirty about what I'm suggesting. We're to be man and wife. This is going to be an important part of our lives, and this was the deal we made. Otherwise, we'll have the wedding on New Year's Eve as I first wanted. Take your choice."

She closed her eyes. "All right." The darkness of the night seemed to engulf her.

"Tonight?"

"Tonight."

"Wonderful. I'll arrange for dinner in the Pacific, and afterward, we'll retire to my room. Until later, my love."

The wooden doors of the church creaked as she pushed them open, the sound of her sobs echoing through the empty wooden building. She stumbled to the back pew, and Father Jones appeared as if from nowhere.

"What is the matter, Anna?"

"So much, Father. I don't know . . . I can't even recognize myself in the mirror anymore."

"Whatever are you talking about?" The old priest sat beside her. She leaned into him, the fabric of his shirt against her cheek.

"Will you take my confession, Father?"

"You're not Catholic, my child."

"Please, Father. I need absolution. Some comfort."

"Of course. God forgives all."

"I have so many sins to confess."

The old priest made the sign of the cross in the air in front of her and sat back. "Go ahead, my child. What would you like to tell me?"

It was hard to believe the words that were forming in her throat. "I fornicated with a man who's not my husband."

Father Jones looked paralyzed. "With another man, not Mr. Bradwell?"

"Yes. Several times. I think about him every moment of every day. I don't want to marry Mr. Bradwell, but my family promised me to him. I'm so confused, Father."

"Who is this man?"

"It's the man who escorted me here, Mr. Leary. I'm afraid what Mr. Bradwell will do to him if he finds out."

"Mr. Bradwell's a good man. He donated thirty thousand dollars to this church. He built this place. None of this would be possible if it weren't for his generosity."

"He's given a lot, I know."

"He does so much for so many. You probably don't know the lengths of his philanthropy."

"He doesn't discuss any of his business dealings with me. I think he considers me below the likes of that kind of conversation."

"These aren't modern times, my dear, and this isn't a modern place. You need to be careful. Your husband-to-be is a powerful man."

"What am I to do, Father? I love another man. I've only just realized it. I can't marry Mr. Bradwell while I feel like this."

"You've let your juvenile impulses sway your better judgment. It's not love. It can't be."

"You think I should marry Mr. Bradwell?"

"Of course. He'll give you the stability and foundation for a good life this Leary never could. You need to dismiss this affair as a grave mistake. Don't tell another living soul and move on. The Lord will forgive you, just as Mary Magdalene was forgiven. I just fear that Mr. Bradwell won't be so understanding if he finds out."

"I have no intention of telling anyone else. I knew that I could trust you."

"Of course."

"The simple truth is that I don't have the feelings for Mr. Bradwell that this other man inspires within me, and I know I never will."

"You're submitting to the base instincts that the Devil has placed inside you to distract you from what's right and proper. These temptations are to be controlled. We can't let them control us. Can you imagine what society would be if we were to let such urges go unchecked? We'd be no better than the beasts of the field."

"But I love Will. He's good and noble—"

The priest held a finger in the air. "You need to cut off all relations with that young man. I'm sure he's a good man, and his intentions may even be true, but you're betrothed to another. I know it's not easy, but this is the Devil's doing, Anna. You need to resist his trickery."

"I'm sure you're right, Father. I don't know what I was thinking." It was easier to go along with what he said. How could a man who'd never been with someone else understand how she felt? Apparently, judgment would be the price she'd have to pay for the absolution she'd thought she craved as she came here. She would follow her heart. This meeting wouldn't change that.

"Just make sure Mr. Bradwell doesn't find out. For Mr. Leary's sake as well as your own."

There was nothing to be done. Nothing at all. The look in the priest's eye told her everything she needed to know. Bradwell would kill him.

Will leaned down to inspect the snow-covered stones. There was a message underneath. She'd left three on top of one another. That was the signal.

My cousin is in town on the 21st and 22nd. He'll be gambling on those nights after 10:00 p.m.

He'd bought a cabin in Lousetown. She would be there tonight. It was the 22nd. He'd missed her the previous evening, but his heart warmed at the thought of seeing her for the first time in a week. Tuesdays and Wednesdays were their nights. Bradwell stayed at the hotel in Grand Forks, close to his claims, on Tuesdays and rarely bothered her the night after. Will worked all week with the thought of their nights together wrapped around him like a warm cloak. She was with him all the time. He replaced the stones and made his way around the side of the warehouse and onto the street. The gold they'd taken the last few days was heavy in his backpack, and he trudged through the frozen mud as the wind sliced at the exposed skin on his face. He joined the line of prospectors in the bank, most of who were depositing a pittance compared to the riches he carried. The bank had previously been a windowless storage warehouse, and the smell of rotten fish hung heavily in the air.

"You're that Irish kid who struck the mother lode over at Bonanza?" said the old man in line in front of him. His wrinkled face told the story of years of toil.

"I see my reputation precedes me. Will Leary," he said, offering a handshake.

The old man took it. "I'm told you stuck it to Bradwell too. Hearing that about made my day. Lot of folks round here think the same. He ran me off my claim last spring, and now I'm stuck scraping dust and shavings."

"I'm sorry to hear that."

"Not as sorry as I am, but anyone who pokes Bradwell in the eye is a friend of mine."

"Much obliged," he said, but the thought of his burgeoning reputation made him uneasy. Prospectors whispered wherever he went now.

He reached the front of the line. He dumped the bag full of nuggets on the counter, and it added up to almost $6,000.

He ate dinner alone, lingering at the table as long as he could afterward to waste time. People knew him here too. Everyone knew who the new lucky prospectors were. He had become one of the exclusive sect, separated from the rest of the insanely hopeful by the weight of the color. He and Silas were among those who could toss money around like confetti, spending hundreds on drinks for people they'd never met and thousands on impressing showgirls who wouldn't have looked at them weeks before. He was one of them now, without the ostentation. He didn't need that. The truth of the Klondike was that it was no different from the outside; a few got rich while the vast majority slogged in agony for the bare necessities. Most of the stampeders who made it here never even staked a claim, just wandered around looking for employment from those who had struck it rich. Hundreds of them, with little else to do but wait for spring and escape from the frozen jail cell that was Dawson.

He sipped his coffee, put the cup down on the plain wooden table, and thought of the way the fire in the cabin danced in her eyes. He watched the clock in the corner of the saloon, remaining quiet by the edge of the bar. He hadn't dared go back to the Palace since his win there, but plenty of other saloons in town blared music and served whiskey. There were other places to drink and waste time. He put the cup down on the bar and held it empty in his hand. He left twenty minutes earlier than he needed to, stepping out onto the street with his scarf over his face. He ducked behind a building and waited a minute or two before reemerging and walking the wrong way. He stopped at the side of the street, aware of every man passing him on both sides, and turned to walk toward Lousetown. The frozen river was silent as he walked along it, and the moon above cast down ribbons of luminous gray, illuminating the hills around the town. Fifteen minutes later, he was at the cabin, and he pushed the door open and made for the stove in the corner. He'd remembered to stock it in advance last time he was here with her, and he had only to light the tinder inside to get it going. It warmed the cabin quickly, and he placed his coat on the back of a chair facing the door.

He heard her before he saw her. He was standing up and ready as the door pushed open.

"Anna," he said. Her movements were languid and slow, and she barely made eye contact as she closed the door behind her. "What's the matter? Is everything all right?" She threw her arms around him. Her body felt almost limp against his. "Anna?"

"I came here last night. You weren't here."

"I'm sorry. I couldn't make it into town. It was too risky."

"I didn't stay." She took off her coat and brushed past him to sit on the bed. He went to join her, but this was different. She was different. "We can't do this anymore—it's too dangerous."

"I know how dangerous it is, but—"

"Let me rephrase that for you, then: I won't do this anymore." She put a hand on his chest as he leaned into her. She got up and paced to the window. "I can't be responsible for what might happen if Bradwell finds out about us. I can't shirk this overwhelming guilt I'm feeling. It's like a millstone around my neck. I can barely hold my head up anymore."

"You're not married yet. What have you to be guilty about?"

"The constant deceit that is the daily currency of my life now."

"It's a necessary evil. We've no other choice. We're trapped here until spring, but as soon as the river breaks, we're leaving, and we'll never have to be wary of Bradwell or anyone else again."

"And what about Silas? What does he do when we leave?"

"I have news for you."

"Answer the question!"

"If you'll let me speak," Will said. "He'll likely be happy to leave with us."

"Have you told him about us yet?"

"No, I haven't, but—"

"I asked you to tell him. He deserves to know. This . . . sordid thing that we're engaging in—"

"What's sordid? There's nothing shameful about what we do."

"I'm engaged to another man, Will, and that man happens to be the unquestioned king of this tiny world we're inhabiting. We're risking everything and not just of ours. We're risking a terrible retribution that could affect Silas also, and I can't live with that. I can't put him at risk any longer."

The wind howled outside, rattling the window frame. "I understand what you're saying, but if we stick to our original plan—"

"We can't. I can't continue to see you like this, not until May. It's too risky."

He went to her and took her in his arms. He helped her out of her coat and hung it up. "If you'll let me speak," he said. "We struck the mother lode."

"What?"

"I deposited more than six thousand dollars in the bank earlier today, and we've only just begun. It's there, glinting in the dirt at the bottom of our claim, just waiting for us to come and get it."

"How much?"

"We don't know yet. More than we'd ever need, most likely. Some of the miners around us have already taken out hundreds of thousands. There's no reason to believe that our claim won't yield the same."

"Congratulations," she said. Her voice was flat. She went to the bed and sat down.

"This is what we came for. Can't you be happier for us?"

"I'm delighted for you, my darling, and for Silas too."

He sat next to her and went to kiss her, but she turned her head. "What's the matter, Anna? You still haven't told me. There's more to this. We've spoken of the danger and guilt before. What did Bradwell do? Are we in immediate peril?"

"Perhaps. We're always going to be in jeopardy as long as we keep this up."

"I will do whatever it takes to be with you. The river will break. Silas will be rich enough by then that he'll never have to work again, and I'm positive he'll be just as eager as we are to get out of this frozen backwater."

"Bradwell took me to his bed."

"What?" He felt hollow.

"Part of the agreement I made with him to defer the engagement was that I'd give myself to him sometime between then and now. He threatened to put the wedding forward to New Year's Eve. He mentioned your name. I got scared. I thought he'd hurt you. I thought it best." Her voice faded to nothing. He felt his legs drop from under him as he came down beside her on the bed. She leaned her head on his shoulder, her tears wetting the fabric of his shirt.

"He forced you?"

"It was part of our agreement." She drew away from him, rocking back and forth on the bed. "I did it for us. I did it to give us the time to formulate our plan to leave. I did it for you."

"I'll kill him."

"No, Will, don't even say that. He'll destroy us if we go against him. We'll stick to our original plan of leaving together, but meeting like this has to stop. It's the only way. We can give back the money for Mabel and forget all about Henry Bradwell and this place."

The pain came again. The ache behind his eyes returned, and he could see the faces of the Indians at Wounded Knee in front of him once more, could see their eyes as small dead things, black holes in the snow-encrusted whites of their faces. "I can't continue as if nothing happened. I can't do that."

"You will because you have to. Rousseau is Bradwell's best friend. Everyone in town owes him something. Rousseau would hang you if you went against Bradwell, and then where would I be?"

"Stuck with nothing and no one."

"Exactly. Nothing changes except this. We can't see each other anymore, but that doesn't mean we won't be in each other's hearts."

He felt the darkness. It was all he could do to answer her. "I love you, Anna Denton."

"And I love you, Will. We have to be patient. I can see the rest of our lives together, stretching out in front of us. We'll get away once the river breaks, with Silas and everything else we need."

He could feel the finality of this moment. This was the last time they'd do this here—the last time they'd do it for a long time anywhere. They lay there for thirty minutes or so just holding each other before he summoned the energy to break the silence.

"Does anyone know about us? Have you told any of the girls in the Palace or a friend I haven't met?"

"I told Father Jones, but we can trust him. I wanted to confess my sins. He's a priest—a good man. He won't breathe a word. Betsy knows some also."

"Bradwell's prostitute?"

"She has no love for him. She's using him and every other man, saving her money. I speak to her every day. She's the closest thing I have to a friend here."

"Are you sure you can trust her?"

"I am. If you ever need to get a message to me, go to her. She's loyal to me, not him. She's a remarkable lady—one of the strongest people I've ever met."

"You would know. I must say I'm surprised, but I trust your judgment."

"I'm right about her. I know her."

"You're also right about Silas. He deserves to know about us—to protect himself against whatever may come."

They lay on the rickety bed in the cabin for another hour before she dragged herself to her feet.

"If Bradwell touches you again, I swear . . ."

"It's not going to come to that. I've done what I had to. It won't happen again."

"How can you even bear to be around him, now that he's done that to you?"

"I'll bear it, with the thought of the reward to come. We've no choice. There's no escape. Even if I left Dawson, he'd find us. There's nowhere we could go for a hundred miles in every frozen direction that he wouldn't."

"I can't not see you."

"Of course you can."

"How are you so strong?"

"Because I have no choice."

He followed her to the door. They kissed as if it would be their last time before she departed into the cold black of the night.

Chapter 15

1898 came, and the dark cloak of winter spread further over the Klondike. The prospectors rose in darkness with the novelty of a few hours of dull light before the sun faded out once more. The talk in town was that half the stampeders were on the brink of starvation, living off beans every meal. Dozens had fallen to dysentery or "Canadian blackleg," as the locals called scurvy. Salt was worth its weight in gold, and nails were going for twenty-eight dollars a pound. The only horses in Dawson were slaughtered for dog rations, as no one had the food to spare to keep them alive. Spring seemed like a distant dream. Though Will and Silas had enough food in their supplies to keep them going, they grew tired of their meager diet. They had long conversations in the mine about the sumptuous meals they'd have once the river broke. Their imaginations almost satiated their growling stomachs as they dug into the mine face. The gold kept coming. They were richer than they had ever hoped but had nothing to spend the money on.

It was five o'clock on January 31. Will sat on the bench he'd fashioned by the entrance to their mine shaft as the dim light of the sun faded out for another day. He was thinking of her again. Though he hadn't seen her these last five weeks, she remained with him. Silas emerged from the mine and flopped down beside him, filthy shovel in hand. He breathed out plumes of white condensation in the frigid air.

"We talk all the time about what we're going to do when we leave but never when," Will said.

Silas rubbed his hands together and reached into the pocket of his coat for gloves. "No, I don't suppose we do. What are you thinking?"

"I'm thinking I'd like to be sitting at some café on the street in southern California right now, spending some of this money."

"That sounds fantastic. I think about the 'outside' most of the time. Remember what it was like to be hot? And clean?"

"Just about. I think if we stay up here much past spring, we might forget altogether."

"You want to leave this spring, with this mine producing the way it is? Another year here, and no one we love will ever have to work again."

"We'll have enough money for that by spring."

"You haven't been into Dawson much lately. No more times with that lady of the night you were telling me about?"

Will picked up a stone from the ground beside him and pitched it down the hill. "There's something I need to tell you."

"What? You're planning a wedding?"

"Not quite. It wasn't a prostitute I was seeing—it was Anna Denton."

Silas stood up and threw the shovel. It clattered off some rocks as it careered down the hill. "How did I know you were going to say that? I knew you were going to say that."

"Yet you never said anything."

"You're a big boy. I thought you'd have the good sense not to endanger our lives for a woman. I just hope that Bradwell hasn't found out."

"I stopped seeing her before Christmas. We figured it was getting too dangerous."

"I presume that was Anna's decision?"

"Yes, but—"

"I knew it. What the hell were you thinking? You know whom she's engaged to. You know what he'd do to you if he found out."

"I was more afraid of what he'd do to you."

"What's this got to do with me?"

"You're my brother. I was afraid he'd hurt you too, as some manner of revenge. So I agreed, and we've not seen one another since."

"Why do I think we haven't heard the end of this?"

Will laughed. Silas didn't. "That's the reason I want to leave once spring comes. Bradwell won't be able to stop us once the escape route of the river opens up. We'll just sail away."

"With his wife? You're going to sail away with his wife?"

"We're going to leave before the wedding, with the fortune we've amassed here, and we want you to come."

"What if the river doesn't break by May fifteenth? What if it's still frozen?"

"Then we'll delay the wedding somehow. We've thought this entire situation through."

"How exactly will you do that?"

"Anna will fake ill. We'll deal with that situation if and when it should occur."

"You really feel that strongly about her?"

"I do. I feel better about everything because of her. She's the key to my happiness. I'm sure of that. I love her."

"I've noticed how much happier you've been lately. I didn't want to ask why. I was probably afraid of the answer. She's still engaged to Bradwell, though."

"She doesn't love him. She never will."

"You really think you can get away with this?"

"I do. We'll have plenty of money by then. We can lease the mine or get someone to work it for us. This is going to work."

"I admire your confidence but not so much your willingness to gamble everything we've earned, as well as both our lives."

"I'm sorry. I didn't want to drag you into this. I can't leave you here to face Bradwell alone when we leave. I won't do that."

"So you want me to flee back downriver with you—Henry Bradwell screaming after us?"

"With the bags of gold we've made here and all the cash we can carry."

"You make it sound fun. Did you ever consider that I might not want to leave when you made all these plans on my behalf? Did you ever wonder how I'd be affected by your actions?"

"Every day. I'll call the whole thing off if you say so."

He shook his head and sat down beside Will again. "We have Anna to consider in all this too. I don't want to leave her here with him any more than you do."

A figure emerged from the darkness, trudging up the hill toward them. He was alone, and Will wondered if he could have heard their conversation before dismissing it as impossible. It was Carrick. The tall Englishman pulled down his scarf.

"Carrick," Will said.

"Hello," Silas said.

"Hello, gentlemen. It's been a while."

"Where have you been these last few weeks?" Will said. "I saw you were working the claims nearby a few weeks ago, but you've been a stranger."

"My apologies. I've been busy, and I'm not here on a social call either. The old man wants to see you."

"About what?" Silas said, tension plain in his voice.

"Just a business proposition," Carrick said. "He's forgotten all about you cleaning him out back in November at the card table."

"You make it sound like I cheated."

"No one's suggesting anything like that. I certainly had no problem with what you did. I enjoyed seeing that look on his face when you laid your cards down as much as anyone. The old man said he wants bygones to be bygones. A few thousand bucks doesn't mean much to him."

"Must be nice, eh?"

"Word is that you fellas will be in the same position soon."

"So what does he want?" Silas asked.

"Don't ask me. He doesn't tell me anything anymore. I have the feeling I'll be looking for a new employer soon. I certainly hope so anyway."

"I'm sorry to hear that. When is this meeting to take place?" Silas said.

"Would tonight suit?"

"What if we say no?" Will said.

"You've nothing to fear. Just give him a chance to say his piece. What's the worst that could happen? Even if he did try something—which he won't—Dawson is crawling with Mounties. You're not worth getting into legal trouble to a man who thinks as much of himself as Bradwell does."

"We'll hear him out," Silas said, looking at his brother.

"I'll let the old man know. You can make your own way in?"

"Of course."

The Palace was heaving when they walked in. Will looked for Anna, but, of course, she was nowhere to be seen. He put his hat under his arm as they approached the bar. A new bartender flicked lazy eyes up at them as Silas asked about the meeting. He gave them drinks and told them to wait as he ran to Milton, who was sitting in the corner. Milton shook each of their hands, then disappeared upstairs for ten minutes. The tables Will was now barred from playing at were full on the other side of the saloon, two deep with stampeders determined to win back the money they had wasted getting here.

"I feel like we're returning to the scene of a crime," Will said when he was sure no one else could hear. Silas downed his whiskey without comment.

"Mr. Bradwell will see you now, boys," Milton said from behind them. "He's in his office." The two men followed behind him, snaking through the crowd to the stairs. He pushed open the door to the office. Bradwell sat behind his desk, both hands on the leather surface in front of him. Carrick stood beside him. He nodded to each of them. Two seats sat ready for them. Bradwell stood up as they approached, and he walked around to shake their hands.

"Thank you for coming at such short notice, gentlemen," he said as he returned to his seat. They sat down across from him, with Milton remaining by the door.

"Would you like a drink? Carrick, can you fetch our guests some of that fine scotch?"

He went to a crystal decanter on the side table and poured glasses for all three men.

"Thank you for the whiskey," Silas said. "What can we do for you, sir?"

"First of all, I'd like to bury the hatchet, as it were."

"We've no quarrel with you."

"I'm glad to hear that. Some of the prospectors around town—some of those less successful than you or I—have cast Mr. Leary in the role of the hero after he cleaned me out and won my claim."

"That was a fair game and in your saloon," Will said.

"Of course it was. Let's not quibble over a few thousand dollars, shall we? It demeans us all." He took a sip and placed the tumbler back down on his immaculately clean desk.

"How is Miss Denton?" Silas asked.

"My beautiful bride to be?" He beamed. "She's wonderful as ever. You know women; there's nothing more important to them than their wedding day. She's been dreaming about this since she was a girl, and I intend to make all of those dreams come true."

"Congratulations," Will said.

The floorboards creaked as Carrick shifted his weight.

"Thank you. I'll pass on your regards to my wonderful Anna."

"It's a beautiful story, and I'm sure you'll have many happy years together," Will said. "But I don't think you brought us here to discuss wedding plans."

"I didn't, Mr. Leary. I have a proposition for you." He clasped his hands together and leaned forward. "I'd like to buy back my claim."

"That's a producing claim. You're talking about an expensive proposition," Silas said.

"I heard you've done well, but now it's time to cash in. Just imagine it: you'd never have to go down into a dark hole in the ground again."

"We like dark holes," Will said.

"We'd need to know how much you'd be willing to offer before considering it."

"How about forty thousand?"

"We've already taken that much out, and we're not hard up anyway," Will said.

"It's worth more. Far more," said Silas.

"How about fifty thousand?"

"I'm beginning to love that mine," Will said. "It's like a second home to me now."

"How about sixty thousand dollars?"

"That is a tempting offer," Silas said.

"You'd have more money than you could spend in a lifetime, and I'd have my claim back. It was the first one I ever lost. My claims are like children to me. Losing one hurt."

"I'm sorry to hear that, Mr. Bradwell, but I think we'd be fools to sell for less than a hundred and fifty thousand," Will said.

"I could do eighty thousand." Bradwell took another sip from his glass. "That's more than anyone's paid for a claim here."

"I'm inclined to agree with my brother. The potential in the claim is boundless. I don't think we could reasonably consider your offer at that price."

"How about ninety? You'd be robbing me blind at that price. Don't be fools."

"I think we're in agreement," Silas said. Will nodded to him. "I don't think any amount of time is going to change our minds."

Bradwell stood up. "You're making a huge mistake. Ninety-nine out of a hundred prospectors will never see nearly that much money in a lifetime. You could return to the outside as soon as the rivers break. You'd be rich men."

"We've made our decision, sir."

"Have it your way. My men will accompany you downstairs to the bar. They'll make the arrangements with the various bartenders."

"Thank you, Mr. Bradwell," Silas said.

"Now, if you'll excuse me, gentlemen, I have a young lady to see."

He shook each of their hands again as they stood up and hurried out of the office and down the stairs.

"You didn't want to take the easy payoff?" Carrick said.

"It's probably worth a lot more than that," Silas said. "And if it's not, I want to be the one who finds out."

"Do you really enjoy going down dark holes?" Milton said as Will walked past him.

"Not especially. That was a line for the occasion."

"It was a good one."

The evening passed. Silas found comfort in the fact that Carrick didn't seem to bear any ill will. Perhaps he'd stayed away all that time out of a sense of shock or awkwardness. Men often reacted that way. Few remained true to the feelings that had spurred them into the situation in the first place. Few were willing to face up to the truth that lay inside them.

Carrick, Silas, Milton, and Will were at the packed bar, the crowd flowing around them. They stood their ground, drinking Bradwell's most expensive whiskey on the house. It was an hour before Silas asked the question.

"So what was that all about? Surely Bradwell didn't expect us to sell."

"He doesn't consult with us. We're told to jump, and we ask how high," Milton said.

"I don't think that was so much about the mine as our Irish friend here," Carrick said.

"I know that," Will said.

"He wants you out of here. I'm pretty sure he was going to put a clause in the deal that you had to stay in Grand Forks until spring. It was more about getting rid of you."

"He's still hung up on that?" Silas said. "We've not seen Anna for months, have we?"

"Months."

"He's paranoid," Milton said. "He's old enough to be her father. And then he sees you stroll in."

"He's nothing to fear from me," Will said.

Milton lit a cigar, offering one to each man. Silas and Carrick accepted, and soon the air was thick with smoke. Another hour passed. The whiskey began to take effect.

"Let's go somewhere we can talk. There are too many ears in here," Milton said. He led them out into the wash of cold air outside. They walked without talking for a few seconds before scuttling into another bar.

Milton was slurring his words as he spoke now.

"I'm done working for that crook. By the time this rush is over, he'll be the richest man in the goddamn world, and we won't have a dime."

"You sound like a man who needs a change," Silas said.

"You're damn right. I didn't come all the way up here to break my back to make someone else rich."

"All the good claims are gone. The new arrivals are chasing a fool's errand now," Carrick said.

"Not all the claims are gone," Milton said.

"No? Do you know something we don't?" Silas asked.

"We've been talking. We might have a proposition for you. We could use some help. We need someone who's not afraid to stand up to that cantankerous old bastard," Milton said.

"Are you sure we should tell them?" Carrick said.

"Can we cut the cabaret?" Will said.

"All right," Milton said, his voice low. "We've heard there might be a new rush."

"Where?"

"East. Thirty or forty miles out—just as much as in Eldorado or Bonanza. Maybe even more."

"Where did you hear about this?"

"An old friend of mine came in from there a few days ago. He said it was strewn with the color—all over the dried-up riverbeds. All you have to do is reach down and gather it up. We could do with two good men to help us out—two good men who aren't going to tell Bradwell that we've gone behind his back. He'd string us up if he knew we were holding out on him."

"You want us to go out east with you in the middle of winter? It's too dangerous."

"We have horses."

"Where did you get them?"

"From the Indians, and we have a tracker too. We'll be out there a few nights, but we can stake our claims and come in. We can go back out in spring or else sooner. But mark my words: this is the new rush. We have to get out there before someone else does."

"Where's your friend who discovered these new goldfields?" Silas said.

"He's going back out with us."

"When?"

"In a few days."

"What do you say? We could be the new kings of the Klondike. We could buy and sell Bradwell five times over among us! Are you in?"

"What do you think, Silas?"

"And it's proven? The gold's there?"

"It's all over the place. We just have to go out there and take it," Carrick said.

"Surely it's worth a look, brother," Will said.

"I think so," Silas said. "I have one question, though—why us? If Bradwell knew you were colluding with us, he'd string you up."

"That's why," Milton said. "He'd have us banished from town whether we went with you or anyone else. You're good miners—you've proven that much—and I know for darn sure you've no love for the old man. We chose you because we know you won't go to him. You want to get one over him just as much as we do."

They set the trip for the day after the next and then toasted their good fortune with the finest scotch in the house.

Will and Silas made their way back to their claim the next day, spending most of the precious daylight hours nursing the hangovers they'd cultivated the night before. The mine remained untouched that day. Will got up for some fresh air, watching the five-o'clock sunset. When he arrived back at the cabin, Silas was preparing dinner for them, and the smell of bacon and beans hung in the air. Silas was a better cook, but they still took equal turns. A few minutes later, they were sitting down at the small table they shared, mugs of coffee steaming, wolfing down the food.

"What do you think of this trip we're to make tomorrow?" Will said.

"I'm dubious, but we came up here to find gold and make our fortunes. This could be our chance to return to the outside as legends."

"I feel the same. At worst, we'll have wasted a few days' mining time."

"At worst, we'll die out there. That's rough, unexplored territory."

"We've been through worse. I don't think anything could equal the travails we went through just getting here."

"I agree. Maybe we should have taken the money, though."

"Ninety thousand is a lot."

"It's hard to comprehend turning it down."

"I think I would have taken the money from anyone but him."

"Tell me something I don't know. I think he wanted to face you down or to extend the olive branch. Either way, it looks like we've established a cease-fire with the King of the Klondike."

"I don't think he'll be quite so happy if we strike gold in the wilderness east."

"Or when you steal his fiancée?"

"Yes, there's that also."

Will scraped the last of his beans off the plate as Silas stood up to clear away his dishes. "This is the last time we'll ever share accommodations like this," he said. "It'll be all luxury from here."

"I shouldn't think we'll ever live together again after we leave the Klondike, whenever that happens."

"We've done well here, my friend."

"Yes, we have, brother."

Will went to the sideboard. Dark had fallen outside, and the only sound was that of the howling wind. An unopened bottle of whiskey sat on the shelf. He reached in for it, then thought better of it and shut the cabinet door, returning to the table to drink coffee with Silas. The stool creaked as he sat down. The aroma of coffee climbed into his throat, and he blew on the cup before taking a sip.

"Do you remember when we were on the trail, and I asked you about your father's business?"

Silas placed the coffee mug down on the table. "I do."

"You said you wouldn't speak of the reason why he left it to Ethan, even though you're clearly the more capable businessman."

"What makes you think I'd want to speak of it now?"

"We're alone. We've found success. You don't need your father anymore. You don't have to tell me, but I've been thinking of what you said lately."

"Obviously."

"What did you mean when you said he didn't think you were suitable?"

Silas shifted in his seat and stood up. "You want a real drink?"

"Perhaps we shouldn't with the journey we have ahead of us tomorrow."

"Since when were you the sensible one?"

"The Klondike has done strange things to me."

"And love. Love's done worse."

Silas took out the bottle and came back to the table. "Consider this a return to your Irish roots," he said as he poured a little into each of their coffee cups.

"Sláinte," Will said, and they clicked cups. "You never answered my question."

Silas took a long drink from his mug and returned it to the table. "It's not something I relish reliving. I always presumed the business would be mine."

"It's a mistake, pure and simple. I'd speak to your father myself if I saw the need, but that isn't there now—not with all the money we've made. Is it?"

"I still would have liked to see where I could have taken the business. I wanted to expand the stores throughout New England, even down to New York and Philadelphia. I met with the old man and went through my plans last year. He seemed enthusiastic at first."

"What changed?"

"You're not going to let me get away with this, are you?" Silas asked. Will drank from his cup. "Father expressed concern that I never married. He started talking about Bessie Taylor again."

"Bessie Taylor? He's rehashing that ancient history? He always used to talk about her."

"She's married now—to a doctor. They have a whole gaggle of children. He said that should have been me and asked why I never showed any interest in marriage or even courting a woman. It developed into a fight. I didn't see what my personal life had to do with my ability to run a business I knew and that Ethan had little interest in. I stormed out. I thought Mother would be on my side, but she sat down with me and expressed the same concerns. What was a handsome twenty-eight-year-old man with a good career doing in life to not attract a wife?"

"What did you tell her?"

"I told her . . ." He took another drink from his now almost cold coffee. "I told her I wasn't interested in women as more than friends." His eyes were forthright and stern, as if he were reliving that conversation right here and now.

"What happened then?"

"She cried. She cried as if I'd told her I had a fatal disease. She told Father. He fired me the next day and gave the business to Ethan."

"I'm so sorry. But he financed this trip, didn't he? He gave you this chance."

"He gave me nothing. I financed the trip myself. I sold my house and everything I owned. My siblings were in the dark. My parents never told them. I came looking for you. You were my last hope."

"You found me, brother."

"I thought I could escape here, with you, and that we could find whatever it was we were searching for here in the Klondike."

"You were right. We have found it. I found Anna. She's all I want now. I have you to thank for that. I owe you everything."

"I'm happy to hear that. It felt good that you needed me. It felt good to bring you back."

"Have you written to them? Do they even know you're here?"

"I spoke to Ethan before I left. I told him that I'd had a falling-out with Father and was getting away for a while. He knows I came to find you and then we'd come here, but I've not written since."

"You must. We'll make this trip out to the wilderness, and we'll pen the letters together once we get back. It doesn't matter that we can't send them. We can mail them once the rivers break."

"We can take them ourselves once the rivers break."

"Exactly. Your parents will forgive you. Just give them time."

"How can they forgive me when I've not done anything wrong? How can being faithful to the person I am be wrong?"

Several hours passed before Will declared that he was exhausted and still feeling the effects of the previous night. He went to bed. Silas sat at the table alone, staring out into the dark beyond the panes of glass he had placed in the window. He relived every word and syllable of the conversation with Will. Did he feel relieved? Will hadn't seemed surprised. A part of him had always thought Will knew. There would be no one easier to tell, but he felt like he knew how to phrase it now. If people were ever to know his secret, he would know how to say the words.

He remembered the disgust in his mother's eyes when he'd told her and the way she'd backed away from him on the couch as if the mere act of sitting beside him had suddenly become abhorrent to her. That look on her face had haunted him ever since. It remained tattooed in his mind no matter how hard he tried to scrub it away. He had seen her only once since, when she had clung to his father's side, tears streaming down her face as if she were watching him die in front of her that very moment. Perhaps to her, he was dead.

Silas took another shot of whiskey, aware of being drunk now and wary of the potentially dangerous journey they'd be embarking on the next morning. Carrick seemed over his previous shock. Perhaps there might be something between them, but likely not. Carrick had probably dismissed it as a drunken tryst, something to distract him from his whores for a few hours. Silas knew that if he ever broached the subject again with Carrick, it would need to be with due discretion. Having a reputation like that could be fatal in these parts.

He reached under his mattress for his journal. He flipped past his meditations on Skagway, Stevens's murder, and the Chilkoot. He ran his eyes over his own words about Dawson, the engagement party, and Will fleecing Bradwell at the poker table. He came to a blank page and began to write, the words seeming to pour out of him.

I've always fit the definition of a robust, strong, and able man, in all ways but one. I remember with vivid colors my first occasion of feelings of love toward another young man. It was Mark Atkins, a boy I went to school with, who awakened within me what many seem to despise so much. I can still recall his dark, raven-colored hair and his sparkling brown eyes. I was fifteen at the time and he just a year older. We were children, dealing with all the familiar fumbling nervousness all adolescents do but with one important difference—even at that age, we knew we'd be shunned, or worse, if anyone found out about us. I didn't understand why. I still don't.

He's married with two children now, running a dry-goods business in Boston. Somehow he was able to set aside his true nature to pursue his life in what society deems to be the correct manner. And so was I, to a large extent. The difference between us is that I never found a woman to hide behind, to use for the sole purpose of denying my true nature to the world. Nor was I willing to ensnare some poor unsuspecting woman into a loveless sham marriage.

I wonder about Carrick. How does he feel? Have his experiences been the same as mine? I'm sure he'd come out with the familiar lines of our experience being down to the dearth of women, but I know that to be a lie. I know by the way Carrick held me that night in his cabin that it was neither an accident nor the first time he'd taken a man to his bed. I saw the shame in his eyes that first time we met afterward. It was all too familiar. I hope he somehow finds peace. I hope I do too. Perhaps I can here, at last.

He read over his words. Just seeing them seemed to soothe the fire raging inside him. Having anything as personal as this written down was dangerous, but he could destroy it later. He needed to let the words live for a few days or weeks. Just so he could return to them when he felt the pressure building inside again. He didn't want to stop. There would be no better time to write the letter to his parents he'd been sounding out in his own head his entire adult life. He wrote.

> Father and Mother,
> I don't know if this is a letter you'll even read, but I'll write it in the hopes that you could still find a place for me in your hearts. I never meant to hurt you or anyone else. I never sought to bring shame to the family or to publicize a secret I've kept with me my whole life. I've always felt this way, as long as I can remember.
>
> I've tried to control my nature—and even to suppress it—but to no avail. I've been through those times, had those sleepless nights, ashamed of the feelings within my heart, but in the end, I realized my only path to happiness was to accept myself. I realized who I am. I'm the son you carried for nine months and the child you reared with love and affection. I'm the person I always was. I love you both, as I always have. I love Ethan and Elizabeth, my sweet sister, and

all their beautiful children. Father, I'm still the boy you taught to fish and who you would bring into the drugstore with you and who would sit on the counter sucking on a lollipop. Mother, I'm still the boy you'd read stories to at bedtime and who you would dance with in the parlor every night after dinner as Elizabeth played her violin.

I found Will in San Francisco. He accepts me, as I knew he would. He doesn't see me as some reprehensible degenerate or someone to be pitied. He sees me as his brother. For the first time in my life, I'm comfortable with who I am. The Klondike is the perfect place for me to begin my new life, even if I don't stay. Everyone here is escaping something—except me, perhaps, because there's nowhere one can go to escape oneself. I'm a successful, happy man. I love you with every inch of my being and long for the day we can be together again.

Your son,
Silas

Chapter 16

Silas reached under his bed and checked for what he'd written the night before. He read his words again. He was shocked by his own candor and was considering whether to destroy the pages of his journal then and there when Will began to stir a few feet away. He tucked the letter in his journal and stowed it back underneath his mattress as his brother opened his eyes.

The weather outside was as they'd hoped: calm and clear. Silas lit a candle almost melted down to the nub by his bed. The fires in the mines around them colored the landscape in orange blotches of light, the smoke barely visible as it rose into the inky night sky. Will seemed recovered from his ails of the previous day as he dragged himself out of bed and over to the washbasin.

"How did you sleep last night?"

"I slept in patches, a few hours here and there," Silas said. "I'm sure I've no need to mention how unwise it would be to divulge what we spoke of last night to anyone."

"Of course not, brother. We'll discuss that again in a few days, but we've enough to occupy our minds for the next while. We'll have little time to think of anything else."

"Did you dream of her last night?" Silas asked.

"Only as an apparition. I couldn't touch or feel her. It's hard to explain."

"I only ask because I heard you call out in your sleep. I thought you might be having a nightmare again."

"That was a different dream."

Will took the trouble to shave and was just finishing as they heard the sound of the horses. It was 9:45, and sunup was approaching. Travel would be close to impossible during the dark that pervaded at this time of the year, so they would need to be ready as soon as the dawn came. Silas was packed and greeted the rest of the party waiting outside. Carrick was on his horse, the saddlebags loaded, with Milton on a gray mare beside him. Silas didn't know the other two men on horseback behind them, and at the back, the Indian tracker sat on a sleek brown mare. He was covered head to foot in moose and caribou fur, his face stoic as granite.

"I didn't realize we were going to have extra men along," Silas said.

"They're just here to bring the horses," Carrick said.

The two men got off the horses and tied them to a post outside the cabin. They left without a word and wandered down the hill.

"Do they know . . . ?"

"They think we're taking a ride into the country to trade some pelts with the local Indians. They have no idea. Bradwell doesn't know them. They won't mention it to him because they never speak to him. Believe me—we're as concerned with secrecy as you are."

"More so," Milton said.

Satisfied, Silas returned inside the cabin. Will was clean-shaven and ready. The sun was rising as he packed the saddlebags on the horse set aside for him. Silas went back for his luggage, looking to where he'd hidden the journal under his bed. He went back out. The horses were tied and packed up. Will mounted his horse. He was wearing his pistol on his hip.

"Wait a minute," Silas said.

"The sun's up. We don't have any time to waste," Carrick growled, but Silas ignored him and went into the cabin. Guns were strictly controlled in Dawson, and there was little need for them on the claims, but Silas reached under his bed for his revolver, checked it was loaded, and slipped it down the back of his pants. The men were already moving along the trail, only Will waiting for him as he emerged into the light of the morning.

"Let's go, brother," Will said, and Silas mounted his horse.

They rode east, the Indian tracker at their head, keeping the frozen Klondike River in the distance on their left. Soon, all sign of man disappeared, and they entered the forests beyond anything they knew. The dim light of wintertime barely permeated the tree cover, and they rode in near darkness even though it was the middle of the day. The weather remained fine, with little snow to obscure the way or little wind to blow in their faces. Silas stayed behind Carrick with Will behind him and Milton at the back. They rode in single file. The miles were hard-earned. The paths were rough and uneven—much like the trails they'd suffered getting to the Klondike. Silas thought of his parents as he went but not as he'd seen them last. He didn't think of the indignation they'd expressed to him. He remembered his times with them as a child, times when he would fish in fall and swim in the lake in summer. He thought of his nephews and nieces and how he'd done those same things with them, and he wondered what they had thought when he'd suddenly stopped calling over. He determined there, on that frozen trail in the Yukon wilderness, that he would return to them, that he would see their faces once more. Some things were worth fighting for.

Darkness fell too soon, and they stopped to make camp. Silas, Milton, and Carrick pitched tents in a clearing they found in the snow as Will and the Indian tracker worked on the fire together. The tracker spoke English but only when necessary, and he worked in silence as they gathered the wood and set the fire. Each man had brought enough food for five days and cooked their meals over the fire as the others waited, circled around it.

Silas was aware of Carrick, taking care not to look over at him unless he spoke. The desire to know why he'd ignored Silas since their night together remained a curiosity he couldn't quite repress, and he got up a few minutes after Carrick excused himself to the woods alone beyond the fire. Silas met him as he was coming back to camp, shivering under the blanket wrapped around him. The other men were fifteen yards away through the thicket.

"We haven't had a chance to discuss what happened—in your cabin that night."

"I'd really rather not," Carrick growled. "It was a mistake."

"I'm happy to leave it in the past. I'm not trying to overreach in any regard."

"Well then, we're of the same mind. I'd rather not mention it. There are so few women out here . . ."

"I understand."

"I'm not of that mind."

"Of course not."

Carrick made his way back toward the fire, and Silas stood alone for several seconds before moving off.

The men slept late. There was little point in rising before the sun, but all were once again ready as soon as it peeked out over the horizon to bathe the forest in light. Questions were surfacing in Will's mind. The cold seemed to be permeating every cell in his body. He was beginning to wonder if this was such a good idea after all. Perhaps they would have been better off staying on their claim and maintaining a low profile until the rivers broke, but it was too late for second thoughts now.

"How far are we?" Silas asked as they sat around the fresh fire at breakfast.

"About a day," the tracker said without looking up from his metal plate of food. "The mountains." He pointed over the trees toward the massive mountain range that loomed in the distance. "We go just before the mountains."

The tracker set out in front. The mountains drew closer, their white-gray peaks looming like giants edging toward the group. Conversation was minimal. Will resisted the temptation to ask how close they were and whether there was any gold at all. They continued on, the horses treading between rocks and fallen trees. The terrain became steeper as they entered the mountain range. The trail wound up the side of the mountain, and they climbed higher. They slowed to a crawl as they inched along a mountain trail, only just wide enough for the horses. The tops of the trees, encrusted with snow and ice, were twenty feet below them. Will held on to the reins with white knuckles.

A word from Carrick to the tracker at the front brought the train to a halt. Will raised his head. Carrick turned around, the glint of something silver in his hand.

"Now!" Carrick shouted and raised the gun in his hand, pointing it at Silas's horse. "You filthy bastard, I've been waiting for this." He pulled the trigger. Silas's answer was lost in the roar of the gun. His horse's leg crumpled, and both Silas and the horse toppled off the ridge. Will reached for his gun but heard the thunder of Milton's revolver behind him, and before he could turn, he was plummeting into the green-white abyss below. He heard the air whistling through his ears, cold and vicious, and then he was in the trees, the razor-sharp branches jutting into him, tearing at his skin. The horse's body descended in front of him, breaking branches as it went. He reached out for a branch, checking his fall a second before his hands gave way and he descended again onto the snowy ground below. He came down on his shoulder and heard a howl escape his mouth, the agony burning all the way along his left side. His legs flailed in the air as he tumbled down a hill, the sound of his own bones cracking in his ears, and then he came to a stop. A stormy haze settled between his ears as he blinked his eyes open and shut. The pain came first, followed by thoughts of Silas and Anna and then Bradwell. The horse gasped and then went quiet. He heard groaning from a few feet away.

"Silas," he said, his voice crackling like wet twigs in a fire. The answer came as a moan, and he turned his head to see Silas, ten feet away. They were in an opening, a circle of trees around them, and above them, Milton and Carrick were coming. Will struggled onto his elbows, dragging himself over to his friend. Silas reached an arm toward him, his beard covered in blood, his eyes cloudy and gray. Will took his hand as he reached him, holding it to his own chest. The pain from his side shot through him. Silas's hands were icy cold, his clothes ragged and torn.

"Will," he said, his voice low, "I can't feel my legs."

"I'm going to get you out of here. We're going to get out."

"No," he whispered. "You go. They're going to be coming for us."

"I won't leave you."

He coughed, a spurt of red coming up to stain his lips. "Send the letter."

"What?"

"The letter under my bed. It's in my journal. Send it to them."

"Send it to whom?"

"My parents." He let his head fall back on the snow. "It's who I am, Will—who I've always been."

"I always knew, brother, and I never loved you less. Don't leave me, please."

"Go," Silas whispered. "Get Anna. Get out of . . ."

Silas's eyes faded, and his fractured breath stopped. He went still. Will picked up his head, cradling it in his arm for a few seconds. He laid Silas's head back on the snow and reached to close his eyes. Silas had brought him home the day of his parents' funerals. He remembered waiting on the porch when Silas disappeared inside. He was bewildered and alone. He had nowhere else to go. No one else offered to take him in. Only Silas. Silas gave him everything. Everything he was today he owed to Silas, and they had killed him. Red-hot anger rippled through him.

The weight of his grief rendered him motionless for a few seconds, but he knew they were coming for him. The Indian tracker had helped them plan this. They'd soon be down to finish the job. He felt for the gun on his side. He reached down to hug Silas's lifeless body.

Then he raised himself to his feet. He used his good arm to wipe away the encrusted snow, blood, and tears stuck to his face. The sound of the horses coming down the trail was getting closer. He saw the Indians at Wounded Knee in front of his eyes, beckoning him with dead fingers, their frozen limbs jutting out at horrific inhuman angles. He put out a leg, expecting to be greeted by a torrent of pain, expecting it to give way, expecting to fall in the snow to wait for the inevitable, but he took a step and then another and made it to the tree line.

His left side was ablaze with agony, his arm useless as a rag doll's. He gritted his teeth behind swollen lips. His vision dimmed, his eyes unsure, and he felt himself rock back on his heels, using a tree behind him to maintain his balance. The sound of the horses grew louder. He looked back at his own horse, lying dead a few yards from Silas. He ran back to it as best he could, meandering from side to side until he fell against its still-warm corpse. His left hand useless, he ripped the glove from his right with his teeth and reached into the saddlebag for food and water. He pulled out a bag of dried fruit and a water canteen and slung it over his shoulder, grimacing at the pain. He rushed back toward the tree line and took one last look at his brother. Then he ran, the sound of his own breath booming in his ears as he rushed through the trees. He heard Carrick's livid voice behind him, echoing off the mountainside.

"We need both bodies. Where's Leary?"

Will stumbled through the dense forest, a foot deep in snow. Every step sent waves of pain through him. He could still hear the muffled voices of Silas's murderers behind him and knew he had only seconds before they came after him. *One injured man against three—I've no chance.* The Indian tracker would follow his trail. He didn't have the time or the energy to cover it, but he had to try—for her and for Silas. He would use every fragment of his anger to drive himself forward. He raised his leg out of the snow, plunging it back in a few inches in front, using the trees for balance with his one good hand. The trees blurred against the light until it was hard to tell one from another. He tripped over a fallen branch and fell down a precipice he hadn't seen in front of him, shrieking as he came down on his side. He looked up, trying to emerge from the daze he'd fallen into. He'd come over a small rock face, six or seven feet high. He moved his feet to make sure his legs still functioned and got up to run again. He was on a hill now, running back down, away from the mountain towering behind him. He tripped again but got back up. He felt the gun smacking against his hip as he went. Surely there could be no escape. Surely the gun was his only hope now. It had been years since he'd used it on anything other than targets, but now the lust for revenge hung over him like a black mist. This could be his only chance to make them pay for what they'd done to Silas. If he just took Carrick down, that would be enough. He reached for the revolver with a shaking hand. It felt heavy, and he had to rest it on a branch to keep the barrel straight. He rubbed at his eyes, but his vision didn't clear. He longed to lie down in the snow, to rest. *This is useless.* He couldn't see straight. They'd cut him down as soon as he fired the first shot. His only hope was to run, but where? He had no idea where he was.

He replaced the gun in his holster and began to move again. A patch of light emerged at the end of his sight. It expanded and filled the horizon as the tree line ended, and he came to a small cliff twenty feet high, leading down to a snow-covered pasture with more trees beyond. His rope was back with his horse. The snow at the bottom of the incline looked a few feet deep, and he thought about jumping before dismissing the thought as suicidal. He paced along the edge of the cliff, searching for a place to climb down. Two vital minutes passed before he found a likely spot with just enough arm holds. He got onto his knees and lowered himself off the edge. His feet had found holds in the rock face when he heard footsteps and saw the barrel of a gun pointed at his face. Will froze as he looked up at the Indian tracker. He looked down to see where his body would fall. He thought of Silas, dead in the snow. The click of the Indian's revolver echoed through his ears, and he closed his eyes to wait for the rush of the bullet.

"I'm sorry for what happened to your brother," the Indian said. "I am Four Bears of the Han people. I did not know what those men were planning."

Four Bears had uncocked his pistol, and it was sitting in the holster on his hip.

"What? I don't understand."

"Go now. I'll tell them you escaped. They need both bodies to steal your claim. It has to look like an accident. There's a Han village a day north of here. Go now. Tell them I sent you. There's a storm coming. We can't search much longer."

"Thank you."

He lowered himself down, gripping as hard as he could to the rock face with his right arm as his left dangled by his side. Four Bears stood to watch him descend, and just for a moment, Will thought he would draw his pistol to finish the job, but he turned and headed back.

Will reached the bottom of the cliff, plunging into snow up to his waist. The pain and the cold were almost more than he could bear, but he struggled toward the tree line once more.

He peered up at the foreboding gray of the sky above him. Four Bears was right; there was a storm coming. Night was approaching. It wouldn't be more than an hour or two. Carrick and Milton would have to turn around and make camp. He pushed into the trees, leaving the cliff behind him, scanning the ground for shelter. His legs kept slogging through the snow, but progress was slow. It took him another twenty minutes to go two hundred yards, and the exhaustion of his chase was turning his legs to jelly. The urge to stop and rest was overpowering. He shouted out loud to himself to keep on, to keep moving. The day faded. The shadows of evening merged to form darkness that swallowed everything. The temperature dropped even further, and he started to feel his body stiffening. Every step was a miracle now. He knew that death would come soon.

Will's eyes adjusted to the dim light, and soon he could see the shapes of trees and rocks in front of him. The shaking of his limbs made moving even more difficult, and he searched with increasing desperation for somewhere to escape the ubiquitous bite of the night air. His eyes spotted a dark patch in a group of rocks ahead, and he made for it with renewed energy. The entrance was six feet wide, but he had to bend down to enter. He drew his pistol as he plunged inside. The bottom of the cave was made of dry twigs, and he shuffled along as his eyes struggled to adjust to the pitch-black. The sound of something else breathing stopped him dead. *The bears are asleep. They will be for months—unless I wake them.* He forced his body still and lay down on the twigs, aware of every tiny sound he made. He knew that the bears were ready to wake up at any sign of danger and would tear him apart if they perceived him as a threat. It was hard to tell how close he was to them in the absolute dark of the cave, but judging by the sounds of their breathing, he couldn't have been more than six feet away. He lay down on the dry ground in the relative warmth of the cave. The exhaustion he felt made him forget his fears, and he was asleep in seconds.

The light of morning illuminated the dull interior of the cave, and he flicked his eyes open. His body convulsed with pain, and he turned over to see a pile of black fur three feet from where he lay. It was a family of bears—at least three still sleeping almost on top of him. He stilled his body and raised himself to his haunches, biting down on his swollen lip to stifle his cries. His gun was on the ground by where he'd slept, and he reached down for it before sneaking out and into the daylight. The storm had broken during the night, and the sky was its usual slate gray. Fresh snow lay on the ground, obscuring the tracks he'd made coming in here. He looked back into the cave. The bears remained unmoved. Only the gentle sound of their breaths differentiated them from the silence of the cave.

He remembered what Four Bears had said. It was probably twenty miles back to the nearest claim and another twenty to Dawson. Making the Han encampment was his only hope. The morning sun did little to warm the freezing air. He tried to bounce from foot to foot for warmth, only serving to aggravate his broken ribs or shoulder or arm. He ate some of the dried fruit he'd scavenged from his horse as he went, and the water was still unfrozen. He had to stop himself from drinking all of it. The pain was with him every minute. It had become part of him. He used the memories of Anna to control it. He remembered the nights they'd spent in the cabin when nothing else in the world mattered and the conversations they'd had about their future together. There was still so much to live for.

He thought of Silas as he walked alone through the frozen forest. Carrick knew. Will remembered what the man had snarled at Silas before he shot his horse. Somehow, he knew what Silas had been trying to hide. Had they spent a night together? That must have been it. There was no other explanation. It must have been the night when he'd gone to Anna. Was he afraid Silas would talk? Silas would never have told anyone—Carrick must have known that. He wasn't disgusted with Silas; he was disgusted with himself. Killing Silas wasn't going to fix that. But this wasn't Carrick and Milton's doing alone. Bradwell was behind this. This was about their claim. It had all been lies—the gold, the plans to go behind the old man's back, and the discontent Carrick and Milton had spoken of. Will wondered what Bradwell had promised them—a working claim of their own, maybe? They had shot the horses to make it look like an accident so Bradwell could take the claim back. Bullet-ridden bodies would have been hard to explain, but dying in a fall in the mountains in winter was not a rare occurrence here. Bradwell would be able to wrangle the claim back for nothing. But Will knew it wasn't about the money.

He walked all day, stopping only to shave ice from low-hanging twigs to put under his swollen tongue. The forest dissipated, and the frozen mass of the river came into view. It must have been four o'clock. The light of day was ebbing away. The Han weren't there. The riverbank was deserted. His legs gave way under him. It was all he could do to sit up. He allowed himself three minutes to sit there, taking the time to eat the last of his dried fruit and drink some water. He cried out as he raised himself to his feet and made his way along the riverbank.

Anna was all he could think of now. The possibility of a future with her—the fear of her future with Bradwell—kept his legs moving even as the darkness came. There would be no surviving this night unless he could find the Han camp. Even if he found shelter, he doubted if he'd have the energy to rouse himself in the morning. He kept on. He had no choice. The ragged sound of his breath was a constant now. He knew he hadn't long. He fell on one knee, his entire body screaming to let it rest, to fall on the snow and let oblivion take him. He saw Silas. He saw him as if he were there with him, reaching out a hand.

"Get up," he heard him say. "You've still so much to do. She needs you."

He forced himself upright again, dragging his feet through the snow as the light of a campfire came into view. He turned the bend in the river; three hundred yards from where he stood, five lodges covered in animal furs sat circled around a blazing campfire. He tried to call out, but it came as more of a whimper. His legs folded underneath him.

"I can't make it."

"You can make it. You will," Silas said. "Now get up!"

He forced himself upright. The wind swirled around him, almost pushing him forward toward the tents on the riverbank.

Anna sat in her room alone, reading one of the few books she'd managed to find in the local grocery store. This was the last she'd not read. She threw it down on the bed, for what would she do once it was finished? She heard a knock on the door. Revulsion flooded through her at the thought it might be her future husband.

"Who is it?"

"Betsy," came the voice through the door. Anna invited her in, but she refused. "I can't. I just came over here to fetch you. Milton and Carrick were out in the wilds these last few days, and they have news they say concerns you."

"What is it? What's going on?"

"I just know what they told me, which is to get you. They look like they've been through all manner of hell, though."

She took five minutes to ready herself as Betsy waited, and then she followed her to the Palace. Anna's palms were wet with sweat despite the cold. It was night. It seemed like it was always night.

"We never did speak about what I saw that night in Mr. Bradwell's office," Anna said. Will's surprise that she'd put her trust in Betsy had given her a sliver of doubt. She needed to make sure she could trust her, and clearing the air seemed like the logical first step.

"No. I'm sorry you had to see that. I didn't want to do it, not when you're meant to be marrying him."

"Is that a common occurrence?"

"You should ask him that."

"But I'm asking you."

"It's been going on awhile—since before you came. I'm sure he'll be putting all that behind him after the wedding. A good woman can change even the worst of men."

"Is that what he is, 'the worst of men'?"

"He's been good to the girls and me; I just hope he's good to you. I appreciate the friend you've been to me."

Anna took a few seconds to answer. She reached out and touched Betsy on the hand and felt the other woman's fingers curl around hers. "And I appreciate you. I know you had no choice." They walked on.

They arrived at the Palace. It was full of dinner customers. Thirty or forty people sat at the tables eating overpriced, basic food. None complained. The band was tuning their instruments in the corner of the room. The night's revelry would soon begin. Betsy led her up the stairs to the office, where Milton and Carrick were standing by the desk, their clothes and beards encrusted with snow and filth. Bradwell was seated behind it. He had a grave look on his face. Betsy closed the door behind her as she left.

"I'm sorry to drag you over like this, my darling, but we have news you should hear. It's only right we tell you first," he said. He stood up and went to her. His chair fell to the floor, but he didn't move to pick it up. He took her hand as Carrick began to speak. She resisted the temptation to pull it away.

"We took a trip out to the wilderness with your friends Leary and Oliver. Mr. Bradwell heard about a new strike out there and sent us out to look. We thought they'd be interested. They jumped at the chance."

"I know how much you cared about them. I was trying to make peace," Bradwell said. "I didn't want to tell you in case they didn't find anything."

She stood frozen to the spot. Somehow, she knew what he was about to say.

"We were out a few days ago when the weather turned. We had to give up looking and turned around to make it back, but there was a terrible accident," Carrick said.

"What? What happened? Where are they?"

"They didn't make it. They fell off a cliff ledge."

"They died trying to save one another," Bradwell added.

"We have Oliver's body, but we never found Leary's. He's still out there somewhere."

"I'm sorry, Anna," Bradwell said.

"What happened?"

"I saw it with my own eyes. I saw Oliver's horse slip from that mountain trail. It was the most horrible thing I've ever witnessed," Milton said. "And then the Irishman fell. He was trying to rescue his friend. They both went down before we could reach them."

"You have Silas's body but not Will's?"

"Leary?" Carrick said. "We weren't able to retrieve his body, but I saw him fall. He's dead. I'm sure of it. He could never have survived out there, even if he didn't die from the fall."

"We'll give your friend a full funeral—the grandest this town has ever seen," Bradwell said.

"How were you able to retrieve Silas's body but not Will's?"

"The weather was worsening. They knew the risks. They went of their own free will," Carrick said.

"You saw them die? You're lying."

"What are you talking about?" Carrick said. "I realize you must be distressed, Miss Denton, but—"

"You—you did this." She pushed herself away from Bradwell.

"You're upset. I know how close you grew to them on the trail."

"You couldn't kill them here or in the creeks. The Mounties would never have allowed that. So you lured them out with some false promise."

"You're being ridiculous. You need to calm down."

"So what happens to their claim?"

"Let's not talk about this now, my love."

"It goes back to the Miners Association to decide—the same association you happen to be chairman of."

Bradwell stood back. "Gentlemen, you should get cleaned off and rest after your horrible ordeal." The two men nodded and left without another word.

He went to his crystal decanter as the door closed. "You need a drink, my dear," he said, pouring each of them a glass. He went to pass it to her, and she smacked it out of his hand.

"You did this! You murdered them!" She raked at him, leaving three red gashes across his cheek.

"You bitch." He punched her in the face. Her lip exploded in a shock of crimson, and she fell back onto the floor. "Now, see what you made me do? You're being insane. Calm down."

"I'll never marry you," she said, stemming the blood flowing from her lip. "You can keep your money. My father would have never sanctioned this marriage if he knew who you really are."

"Oh, wouldn't he? Money can make people act in the most peculiar ways, Miss Denton. I don't think your father would change his mind even if he were standing here right now."

"It doesn't matter, because he'll never see a dime of that money. I'll die before I marry you."

"And what about Mabel? How will she afford her medicine?"

"I can make the money myself."

"How, exactly?"

"That's not your concern. You're not listening to me. I said I'll never marry you," Anna said as she raised herself off the floor.

Bradwell took a sip of his drink and raised his hand to feel the gashes she had ripped in his cheek. He flinched as he ran his finger along them. "Oh, but you will, my dear. You'll marry me or else I'll leave you here with nothing and no other option but to join those whores working the floor for me down there."

"I can leave here whenever I want."

"You could try and leave when the river breaks in May, I suppose, but how will you live until then?"

"I can work."

He laughed. "As what—a dancer at the Grand? You'd be popular there, but you forget who owns half the place. I can make sure that anyone who employs you is run out of town. But let's not even consider that. Suppose you do survive until spring—some miner takes you in as his personal whore or something—what then? How do you get back to the outside? Are you going to trek back over the trail alone? How will you get down the river? I mean, there are ferries, but you can't afford them. You're nothing here without me." He took another sip of whiskey. "So what other options do you have? I'll grant you one—you can work for me. You'll make me a lot of money. Every miner for a hundred miles would line up for hours to have a piece of the likes of you. They'll think they've died and gone to heaven. You'll be on your back day and night."

"Father Jones will take me in. He's a good man—"

"Oh yes, our venerable local priest. I suppose I should just tell you this now that we're getting everything off our chests. You're right—I did send Carrick and Milton out with the express intention of murdering your friends. You worked it out. The Mounties never will, though, not when we've got two witnesses telling them it was an accident. Congratulations, though. Well done. Less admirable, however, is the affair that you were carrying on with Leary."

"What? What are you talking about?"

"Oh, don't play dumb with me, Anna. It demeans us both. Your priest friend told me all about it."

"What?"

"Yes, I've known for a while now. I've known what a ridiculous little whore you are." She backed away as he advanced toward her. "I've known about your secret rendezvous with that Irish degenerate. Perhaps you can think about him when you have all those filthy prospectors on top of you? That might make it easier."

"Father Jones told you?"

"Who do you think built that church? Who do you think covered up the incident with that Indian boy last summer? Captain Rousseau would have thrown him out of town for that. I own him, just like I own you."

"Why won't you just let me go? I don't care about my father and his business. He can go to hell. I'll get the money for my sister somehow."

"And let you win? Let you defy me? I didn't break my back all these years to have some jumped-up little bitch run me around in circles. You will bend to my will one way or the other."

"You're going to burn in hell."

"Better to rule in hell and all that, my dear," he said, finishing his whiskey. "I'm offering you a choice. We can go ahead with the wedding, or you work for me on your back. I can forgive you over time for your reprehensible behavior, but I can't in all good faith send the bride price now—not after what you've done. I'll explain as much to your father and the reasons why in the letter I send him in the spring."

He turned to put the glass down, and she exploded at him, punching and scratching his face, blood and skin under her fingernails until he grabbed both her arms and threw her back on the floor. He pinned her with his knees, raining punches on her. The pain came at first, but soon she felt only the thunder of fists on numb skin. He got off her, but she found herself unable to move. She felt arms on her, carrying her and then laying her down. Voices and then Dr. Krupp's face came into view, his putrid breath on her. She felt the pinch in her arm and then a sensation like nothing she'd ever known. In seconds, she was floating, her body numbed and somehow in a perfect state of bliss.

Chapter 17

Dreams emerged and disappeared just as quickly. His parents. Ireland. Anna. Silas appeared again, sitting in the corner of the lodge, his head bent at the angle of the slanted roof, watching. Will opened his eyes. It was hard to know if he was still dreaming or awake. The Indians from Wounded Knee seemed to have come back, crowding around him. One of them reached down to take his left arm and placed his foot under Will's armpit and pulled. He screamed in agony, begging the man to stop. A sound like a body falling on concrete filled his ears, and the man let go. Will fell back down on the caribou-fur bed, and a woman reached in to wipe the sweat beading on his forehead. The pain in his shoulder felt different now. It felt clean. The pain was still there, just lessened. His eyes felt heavy, and though he wanted to speak, he succumbed to sleep once more as the wind rose outside, howling like the wolves that prowled the forests all around them.

The same woman who'd wiped the sweat from his feverish brow was there as he woke up. She said something in her language, placing a gentle hand on his chest as he tried to get up. He felt as if someone had cut a hole in the top of his head and filled it with sand. He fell back onto the fur pelt and used his good arm to drag the blanket made from the same animal over his body. The woman disappeared through the flap at the front of the tent. He was alone for a few seconds—surprised to see that Silas had gone. She came back a few seconds later, chattering as she bent down to enter with a man following behind her that he swore he recognized.

"You're awake," Four Bears said.

"How long was I asleep?"

"Two days. You must eat now."

"I have to get back to Dawson." He contorted in pain as he tried to get up.

The woman used the same hand to force him back down.

"No. The storm is coming again—this time much worse than before. You must eat. Then we talk," Four Bears said.

Another woman entered with a wooden plate of meat, and Will filled his mouth in seconds, attacking the meal like a ravenous animal. The food seemed only to awaken the hunger that had lain dormant inside him. He finished the entire plate in less than a minute, washing it down with icy water. Four Bears sat in the corner waiting and began to speak as Will handed the plate back.

"Those men brought great dishonor upon me. I did not know of their plan to murder you and your brother."

"Where are they now?"

"I left them at the first claims we came upon, and the miners there directed them back to the town. They know nothing of your escape."

"Where's Silas, my brother?"

"They brought his body with them, bent over my horse."

"You told me that they wanted both bodies to steal my claim. Did they tell you anything?"

"They told me nothing, but I know the ways of such men. You have a claim, don't you? You spoke about it at the campfire."

"We have a successful mine."

"You have drawn much of the yellow metal from the ground? Scarring the land for something that has no use?"

"We have. It's worth a lot of money—something that I have no use for here and now."

"The foolish ways of the white man have destroyed my people and the lands we once thrived on. Few of us remain, even after the brief time the white man has been here."

"Yet you spared my life, and your people took me in."

"The ways of those other men were dishonorable. The Han do not deal with enemies like that. We are hospitable and extend kindness even to those we don't know."

"Thank you, Four Bears. Thanks to you too," he said to the woman, "and to everyone in the camp."

"There are but ten of us here, and we must move soon. We follow the hunt and go where the moose and caribou go. But not until the storm passes."

"Can you get me back to my cabin? It's on Bonanza Creek."

"You must rest now. We'll wait a few days, and then you move with us."

"Can you get a letter to Dawson for me? I have to tell Anna Denton I'm still alive. I have to get her out of there."

"When the storm ends. We will stay here until then. You rest now."

Four Bears raised himself up and left. Will saw through the flap of the tent that the snow was coming in earnest now, and he turned over on his side. Silas came to him again.

The doctor had come again in the night. Anna could feel the point on her arm where he'd injected her. It was swollen and stuck out from her skin as a red blotch. The mirror was in the corner. It had been two days since she'd looked at herself. She hadn't thought about looking. Somehow, everything had felt wonderful in that time. She'd been content to be in this room alone, lying on this bed, bereft of pain. The drugs had even blunted her anger. She lay back on the bed, her mind garbled and incoherent. Thoughts came and went, disappearing into the haze.

She turned her head as Bradwell walked in. She could see the red gashes she'd left on his cheek. He sat down on the bed beside her, placing a hand on her hip as she turned onto her side to face him. Even that felt fine. Everything did. Somehow, the world was beautiful.

"I wanted a wife," he said. "I was prepared to pay good money. You came from a prestigious family. I knew you were beautiful. But they sent me a whore."

"No . . . ," Anna said, but her voice came as a whisper that he might not even have heard.

"But I'm a generous man, and I'll give you one more chance. I've moved the wedding forward to the week after next. The bruises on your face should be sufficiently healed by then. I won't be embarrassed by your ridiculous appearance on my wedding day."

"No, I don't want to," she managed.

"If you try to run, I'll find you and put you to work as the whore you're meant to be. And if you embarrass me in front of my friends next week, I'll have some men pay your family a visit in Evanston. They're not beyond my reach, even there. No one is beyond the reach of a man of my means." He coughed, reaching up to touch the scratches she'd left on his face. "I'm a good man, Anna. You've driven me to this. None of this needed to happen. None of it would have if you'd kept your end of the bargain. Those men would still be alive. I hope you're happy." He stood up.

"I'll explain everything again if you don't understand," Bradwell continued. "It's plain that you're under the influence of the drugs I had Dr. Krupp give you." He went to the bed and jerked Anna's face toward him, pinching her chin between his thumb and index finger. "Oh, you are beautiful, even with those bruises you brought on yourself. You'll see in time that everything I've done was for the best. You'll grow to accept your life here. The mistakes of the past can be forgotten. I can try to forgive yours." He stood up and went to the door. "A young lady, feeble witted as you are, can be easily swayed by the likes of Leary, but you'll soon forget him. Best you do that quickly—he is dead, after all." He shut the door behind him.

Will sat in the tent for two days, listening to the wind whirling outside, peeking through the flaps at the snow falling. Four Bears didn't return during the storm, just the woman with food and water twice a day. It was the third day. He was lying on the caribou-fur mattress, his arm in a leather sling she had fashioned for him. Four Bears pushed into the pole lodge.

"How are you feeling?"

"I can make it back to my claim."

"Can you walk?"

"I walked all the way here from the mountains."

"One supernatural achievement doesn't necessarily lead to another. I will help you."

"Why are you doing this for me?"

"I don't do it for you. I do it for your brother—the man they murdered. He seemed like a good man and didn't deserve a dishonorable death like that. I'm helping you because that is what he would have wished."

"Thank you."

Four Bears helped him up and out of the lodge. Several Indians stood whispering among themselves, watching as he emerged into the dull sunlight. Three Han children were playing with sticks down by the frozen river fifty yards away. They stopped and ran back when they saw him.

"I want to thank you all for taking me in, for giving me food and shelter." He reached into his pocket for some banknotes. "I want to give this to you." Four Bears shook his head, but the woman who'd brought Will food stepped forward to take them.

Four Bears spoke to the others, ten in all, including the three children. He reached forward to kiss the woman who'd taken the money from Will before picking up one of the children. He hugged the young boy before putting him back down.

"Your wife and child?" Will said as they walked away.

"Yes. Couldn't you tell when she took the money against my wishes?"

"I should have put the pieces together."

Four Bears reached down for some food packed into a fur-lined bag and tied it to his belt. Will walked behind him.

The weather was fine, and they followed the river for several hours, talking little. He thought of killing Bradwell. He would kill him first, then Milton. He would save Carrick for last. *But what do I really want—to become like them?* He had little chance against Bradwell and his men. Word of his arrival back at the claim would spread quickly. They would be ready for him. Even if he did manage to kill them all, the Mounties would take him down or hang him.

Six months ago, none of that would have mattered. Will Leary would have avenged Silas's death no matter the cost. If it meant his death in doing so, so be it. But he was a different person now. His life mattered. He wanted to go on. He wanted her. The gold was nothing. He could sell his claim to Schmidt or Fox or one of the other wealthy prospectors. He was sure they'd offer at least $60,000 for it, and he could live the rest of his life in comfort on far less. He could hide out until spring and go back to the outside a rich man, but the money was nothing without her. It mattered only as leverage to get her back. The Mounties could deal with Bradwell and his men. They would hang for what they'd done to Silas. They would pay for what they'd done to his brother. Somehow. They weren't worth hanging for. His future with Anna was worth finding a different way.

"Silas," he whispered. "I know you're still with me. Thank you. I won't let you down."

Four Bears knocked on the door of the first cabin they saw. An old man with a French accent opened the door. The Frenchman brought Will inside, not offering Four Bears the same invitation. Will refused, holding out fifty dollars for a ride back to Bonanza. Ten minutes later, he and Four Bears were sitting on a sled, the Frenchman driving the dogs. It was dark as they arrived back at the cabin. Four Bears stepped off as Will approached the Frenchman.

"I have one more favor to ask."

"I must get back to my cabin before the night traps me here," the man said.

"Just wait a few minutes."

Will pushed open the door to their cabin. He'd expected it to be ransacked, but it was as they'd left it: Silas's bed made and his clothes tucked underneath. He went to his own bed. He reached under the mattress for the wad of banknotes that was somehow still there. The Frenchman gasped as Will walked back out to him.

"I'll give you five hundred dollars to take this man into town and back tonight. Just give me a few minutes to write the letter I need you to deliver. You remember who to search out?"

"Yes," Four Bears answered.

The two men stepped into the cabin as Will lit the stove in the corner. They waited in silence as he put pen to paper. Will reached under Silas's mattress. The letter was there, folded into an envelope addressed to Silas's parents inside his journal. Will took it out, holding it as if it were an injured bird. He cried as he read it. He cried like a little boy, just as he'd done the day Silas had brought him home and insisted that his parents take him in.

The doctor hadn't come back that day, and Anna's face was throbbing as she woke. She rolled off the bed. Thoughts tripped over one another, and she had to stop and take a deep breath to order them in her head. She went to the mirror, stepping back as she beheld her face. Her right eye was swollen and blackened. Her bottom lip was as big as her finger. A long cut extended across the ugly black bruises covering her right cheek. Startled by her grotesque appearance, she stumbled back onto the bed. How long had she been out? The clock on the wall said it was seven o'clock, but what day was it? Will and Silas were dead. She went to the bedpan they'd left for her, retching, but nothing came, and she collapsed back on the bed. A knock on the door jarred her from her misery.

"Who is it?" she shouted. Anyone but Bradwell—she couldn't bear to see him.

"It's Betsy," came the whisper through the door. "I have something for you. Don't tell. I have to go."

An envelope came under the door and settled a few feet from her bed. She waited until Betsy's footsteps had faded before getting up to take the letter. The envelope was blank and unsealed. She pulled out the piece of paper inside, her hands shaking.

> Dearest Anna,
> I am alive. I don't have long to write this letter, so I'll tell my story. Carrick and Milton lured us out of town on the promise of a new gold strike. We followed them to the mountains east of the claims into unexplored territory, but it was a ruse. We were on a mountain pass when Carrick and Milton shot our horses in a most cruel and cowardly fashion. We plunged off the ridge. Silas fell to his death. Even writing those words stirs grief in me. I managed to escape with the help of a friend and made my way back to the cabin, where I am writing this. My anger at Bradwell is tempered only by the love I feel for you. I'm coming for you.

> Don't be afraid. Bradwell and his men will pay for their murderous treachery. We will have the future together we both dream of, and Silas will receive the justice in death he was never afforded in life.
>
> Stay strong. I am coming for you.
>
> All my love,
>
> Will

She ran her hand over the letter that he had touched just hours before. Hope reignited inside her but only as a single lantern in the darkness. What could he do alone against Bradwell and all his men? He should forget about her. He should take the money he'd won from the evil bastard and run all the way back to the "outside." She held the letter to her chest. How could she write back to him? She had been a prisoner in here these last two or three days. Was Betsy coming back? She delivered her meals three times a day. The muffled chatter of the patrons downstairs told her that she was in the Palace, but there had been no sound of carnal activities from the walls on either side of her. Perhaps Bradwell's morals forbade his fiancée from hearing such things. A knock on the door came like the splash of cold water, and she jumped on the bed, scrambling to hide the letter as the key turned in the lock. She shoved it under her pillow as the door opened. Bradwell. Dread crept through her like a virus.

"I decided to bring your dinner myself tonight," he said with a joyless smile. "You're going to have to get used to my taking care of you."

She sat still as granite as he placed the tray of food on the bed beside her.

"Not hungry?" he said. "You can eat it in your own time." He moved the tray aside as he sat on the bed beside her. The letter was two feet away. "I can promise you that I'll try to find it in my heart to move on from these last few weeks and months. We can leave this behind and begin our lives together."

"Will is dead. We both know why. You murdered him. I have nothing and no one. Just let me go. Don't hurt me."

"My conduct is entirely dependent upon yours. I don't even know how we got to this place between us. The people of this town love me. I'm revered wherever I go here. Like all good leaders, I can be merciful as well as powerful. I can try to forgive you if you can behave like a lady."

"I will, I swear," she said. It was almost impossible to look at him.

He reached over and took hold of the pillow she'd hidden the letter under, placing it on top of the one beside it without looking. Her heart froze. "Lie back. You need some rest." She didn't move. "Lie back, I said."

She moved her legs onto the bed as if in slow motion, the letter visible a foot away from her. He placed the tray on her lap. "That's better," he said. "Now . . ." His voice trailed off as he saw the piece of paper. He had it in his hand before she could speak. "What's this, a letter home?"

"No, it's nothing. Please don't." The words tumbled out of her mouth as she reached for the letter. He held it beyond her grasp, pushing her back with his free hand.

"I can't trust you, even if there's nowhere to send this letter now. You're not in your right mind." He got off the bed and opened it up. She took the tray off her lap and went to him.

"Let's not worry about that now," she said. "We should do as married couples do. We're in bed already."

"I'm delighted to hear you say that. I knew you'd come around, but let me see this first," he said, pushing her away once more. He began to read the letter.

She stood back.

"So your little boyfriend is alive." He shook his head. "I should have done it myself. Those fools couldn't be trusted to pick up a loaf of bread. But don't worry—he's coming for you." He struck her across the face with the back of his hand, sending her flailing back onto the bed. "You were conspiring with him against me?"

"I only just received it a few minutes ago."

"Who delivered it?"

"I don't know. I found it under the door." She reached a hand to her lip. It came back red. He'd opened it up again.

"I can never trust you. The wedding is off. If you want to act like a whore, then you'll be one. It's what you were meant to be."

"I'll never be your whore."

"Oh, you will. You feel that itching under your skin and the depression surging through you? That's the morphine withdrawal. That's what Dr. Krupp was giving you—morphine. You're probably addicted already."

"I don't feel any itching, and any depression I feel is from being around you, you disgusting piece of filth!"

"Not addicted yet? Oh, no problem. You soon will be, and then I won't even have to pay you. You can work for your daily fixes. We might even get six months out of you."

"You keep that filth between your legs away from me. You're going to lose anything you touch me with."

"Brave words, but words won't save you now. We're going to have a little meeting with your Irish boyfriend. You're going to watch him die—slowly. He's going to cry out your name so many times you'll be hearing it in your dreams for the rest of your miserable life."

"Don't do this. Please let him go. He doesn't deserve this."

"I'll be back soon," he said and walked out.

She got up off the bed as if in a daze. She picked up a hand mirror off her dresser and looked at herself in it before smashing it down and sending shards of jagged glass to the floor.

Will was awake on his bed. It was night outside. He'd make his way into town the next morning to report Silas's murder to the Mounties.

It would be his word against theirs. Four Bears's testimony as a native would hold little water against white men. The horses' corpses would be some evidence. The bullets in their bodies would serve as his proof, and he was sure Carrick would give up Bradwell in seconds if the Mounties promised him immunity. It would be up to Will to exact punishment on Carrick then. The sound of dogs outside the cabin cut through the night. He reached down for his gun, cocking the trigger as he got off the bed. The knock on the door came.

"Leary, Mr. Bradwell wants to speak to you. He has a final offer for the claim. He says he'll give you the girl. He doesn't want her anymore," came the voice through the door. "Open up. I won't harm you in any way. I give you my word."

Will got up, the barrel of his revolver pointed at the door. "Who is it?"

"My name's Ray. I work for Bradwell at the Palace. He sent me to bring you to him. I don't want trouble any more than you do, but things will get ugly if you don't come voluntarily. Bradwell says he'll kill the girl if you don't see him."

He remembered Ray from the bar. He was a young kid from Michigan. Will opened the door, managing to keep the gun in his good hand. Ray held his arms in the air as he saw the gun.

"I don't want any piece of this, Mr. Leary. I've no fight with you. I was just sent here. Bradwell threatened to banish me from town if I didn't, I swear. There's no one else," he said, gesturing into the darkness. "I just need you to come with me. Bradwell found a letter from you to Miss Denton. He wants to buy you out and send the girl with you. The only condition being that you both have to leave tomorrow. Hear him out."

"He said he'd kill her if I didn't?"

"He's gone insane. She has bruises all over her the size of dinner plates. I only saw her tonight for the first time in days. He has the poor girl locked away."

"We're going to the Mounties first."

"Whatever you want. We just gotta leave now. You don't want to keep Bradwell waiting on this."

He went back into the cabin, leaving Ray in the cold without another word. It was a trap. He was almost certain of that. The time for buying him out had long since passed, but what choice did he have if Bradwell was going to kill her? He put the gun down on the table and reached under Silas's bed.

"What are you doing?" Ray had walked in behind him.

"I'm just getting the papers for our claim. I can't exactly sell it to him without them."

Ray had his gun drawn. "I'm going to need you to come with me now. Leave the pistol where it is. I'm sorry. I can't afford to get slung out of town. We won't be going to see no Mounties neither. Mr. Bradwell was real clear about that."

"What if I were to offer you some money to pretend you never saw me?"

"There's no money you could offer me better than the future he's promised me. I can run this whole operation one day. I won't jeopardize that for you or your money."

"Looks like he has me exactly where he wants me," Will said as he slipped the journal in his pocket. Ray led him out to the sled, and a few minutes later, they were speeding through the freezing Klondike night.

Ray hid the gun under his coat as they approached Dawson. The Mounties were all over and would stop anyone as soon as they caught sight of a firearm. He stopped outside the front of the Palace. It was full, as it always was at eleven o'clock at night. A band was playing in the corner, the music mixing with the sounds of conversation and laughter. Will got off the sled, his feet sinking into the sludge of the street.

"I'm sorry, Leary," Ray said. "He's up in the office. I wish you good luck in there. I had no choice in bringing you here." He looked at Will, likely with the expectation of getting a reprieve that he didn't offer. He stayed to watch Will walk through the door into the Palace. Milton came around the bar.

"This way," Milton said.

"Keep your filthy mitts off me," he said so only Milton could hear. Milton didn't answer and led him through the crowd and toward the stairs. The pain in Will's side came again. He kept his head down as he went, not making eye contact with any of the patrons they pushed past. It took them ten seconds to ascend the stairs. *Forgive me, Silas, for what I'm about to say and do. I have to provoke him. It's my only chance to save her.* He saw Silas nod his approval as Milton jabbed him in the back. Will was ready, and he pushed the door open.

"Anna?" he said as he saw her standing behind Bradwell, who was seated at his desk. Carrick stood to the side, his arms crossed, and Milton shut the door behind them.

"I'm all right," she said.

"Make sure our Irish friend isn't armed."

Milton patted him down. "He's clean."

"What did you do to her, you animal?"

"Nothing more than she deserved."

Will bit down on his lip and surveyed the room. Neither man had guns on their hips, but that didn't mean they didn't have them hidden in their coats.

"What am I doing here? The kid said you had an offer for me."

"Oh yes, the 'offer,'" Bradwell said and began to laugh. "You're going to die tonight. That's my offer."

"Henry," Anna said.

"Shut up, you ridiculous whore," he said before focusing back on Will. "You're going to die horribly, and then I'm going to take back my claim."

"You can't do that," Anna said.

"Oh, we'll make it look like an accident, and if we can't—if we go a little overboard in making you suffer—I'll wait a few months after you're declared missing. Your case will go up before the Miners Association—of which I'm chairman—and they will rule in my favor. Did you really think you could come here and make a fool out of me, the King of the Klondike? This is my world, Leary. You exist here only if I say you can."

"You vile bastard," she shouted and slapped Bradwell across the face. He stood up and took her by the arms. He let her go when Will spoke again.

"How much did he pay you to murder my brother?"

"Five thousand each and a share of the claim we were going to take back from you," Milton said. "It was just business."

"There was no discontent between you and Bradwell, was there? It was all a setup."

"My men are loyal to me. We came up with the plan together and worked it out to the last detail."

"Except I'm still alive."

"Not for long. Carrick, come here and keep hold of her." He let Anna go. "I want her to hear this. I want her to see what's about to happen."

Carrick walked over behind the desk, holding Anna by the arms as she struggled against him.

"Do what you want to me; just let her go."

"I will do what I want to you and to her too," Bradwell said. "I wanted to marry Anna—truly, I did. I would have, even after I heard about your sordid meetings with her, but the news of her conspiracy with you was too much."

"She had no idea I was still alive. I sent that letter four hours ago. She didn't even have the opportunity to reply."

"Is this true, my dear?"

"Go to hell," she replied. "I'd rather be a prostitute for every prospector in the Klondike than have you touch me ever again."

"And so you shall be. Leary, your girlfriend is going to be my prize whore. I won't be sending any money to her family either—just a letter explaining why she decided to partake in her new life working on her back."

"Your quarrel is with me, not her. You've already murdered my brother." He stepped forward. "Carrick, please. You loved Silas once."

"What?" Carrick said. "What the hell are you talking about?"

"Silas—you and he were lovers. I have his journal saying so here." He reached into his pocket, holding the leather-bound diary. "Look into your heart and spare the girl, Carrick. Talk to your boss—"

"What is he talking about?" Bradwell said.

"Believe me, I have no idea." Carrick let go of Anna and reached into his pocket. "You can't lie your way out of this. Keep babbling. I'm going to enjoy prolonging your agony for every second I can."

"It's no lie. I have the proof right here. Can I read?"

"Put that journal away. We won't listen to your lies," Carrick snarled.

"What is this?" Bradwell said.

"'I know by the way Carrick held me that night in his cabin that it was neither an accident nor the first time he'd taken a man to his bed. I saw the shame in his eyes that first time we met afterward. It was all too familiar. I hope he somehow finds peace. I hope I do too.' That is you he's mentioning in the entry, isn't it? There's no other Carrick in the Klondike he could be referring to? Don't you think your friends should know you prefer the company of men? I mean, what if you come after them next?"

Carrick roared as he threw Anna aside, ripping a knife from his coat as he leaped across Bradwell's desk. Will stepped aside as Carrick slashed down at him, falling into the side table. The decanter of expensive whiskey they'd shared a few days before shattered on the floor. Carrick raised the blade again, but Will ran into him before he could bring it down, shoving him back against Bradwell's desk. Milton seemed stunned but began to move in, pulling his own blade. His movements were languid and slow. It was as if he was in shock or too afraid to intervene. Bradwell recovered himself and reached into a drawer for a hidden revolver, leveling it to aim at Will. Anna reached into her dress and drew out a shard of broken glass. Bradwell shouted out in agony as she plunged the jagged glass into his shoulder, and the gun fell to the floor. The old man turned to try to slap her, but she was too fast and ran around the table, grabbing at Carrick's arm. Will took his opportunity and shoved Milton back onto the floor with his good arm before turning to catch Carrick with a fist to the jaw. He fell back, visibly stunned. Anna ran to where Milton had fallen and kicked his knife back toward the door. Will picked up Carrick's knife. He whirled around behind him and put the point of the blade against the skin of his neck.

"This is for my brother," he said and brought the edge across his throat. Carrick just had time to call out before he collapsed to the floor, blood pouring from a neat red line below his beard. Milton raised himself to his feet. Will took the bloody knife between thumb and forefinger and threw, catching him square in the chest. The top half of the blade disappeared into his torso. He stumbled and fell still.

"Anna!" Will shouted, reaching for her hand as they ran for the door together. Bradwell had the gun again, holding it in his left hand. He took aim at them as they ran out. A bullet struck the doorframe above them, showering splinters of wood down on their heads. He fired again as they made for the stairs, his tormented screams filling their ears. He was running now, following them down and shooting. An innocent prospector took one of his bullets to the chest, falling back against the bar. They darted through the scattering crowd. The band dropped their instruments and ran for their lives. The only sounds now were of screaming, panic, and gunfire.

An armed Mountie appeared at the saloon door, holding up his pistol, shouting at Bradwell to drop his weapon. The Mountie tried to level his gun at him, but the prospectors bolting past him impeded his view. Bradwell caught sight of the Mountie through the crowd and brought him down with another bullet. The wounded Mountie fell to the floor, spilling his gun. Will had Anna's hand as they made for the door. A fleeing prospector came between them as they ran, colliding with Will, sending both men to the floor as Anna stumbled to the side of the rapidly emptying saloon. The prospector got up to run again as Bradwell caught up. He stood over Will's prone, helpless figure on the saloon floor.

"Don't do this. It's over," Will said. "You just shot a Mountie. Your men are dead."

Bradwell laughed, raising his gun. "This is my town. No one crosses me here." The crack of gunfire rang out. The pain didn't come. Bradwell coughed scarlet blood, his pistol clattering to the floor by his feet. He raised his eyes to Anna, the Mountie's smoking revolver in her hand. "You?" he said. "How could it be . . . you?" He toppled backward to the floor of the saloon he'd built. His body shuddered a few times and went still. She dropped the gun onto the smooth wooden floor. She took Will's face in her hands as the Mounties poured in, their bloodred uniforms filling the room like water.

Chapter 18

Dawson City, Yukon, July 1898

The sun was already high in the sky as Will woke. The clock on the wall said it wasn't even six in the morning, yet the sun's radiance suggested an hour nearer noon. Living under the midnight sun took some getting used to. He settled onto his back, reaching a hand across to where Anna slept beside him. His hand settled on the gentle curvature of her hip beneath the blankets, and he lay still a moment to listen to the rhythmic humming of her breath. The sound of a cart sloshing through the mud on the street outside brought him back to the moment, and he let the blanket fall as he rose out of the bed.

Dawson City was coming to life outside. He could hear the sound of construction, of hammers driving nails and lumber being delivered. The town was thriving now. New prospectors, both those who'd been stuck on the Chilkoot Trail or at Lake Lindeman, waiting for the ice to thaw, and those just arriving from the "outside," still came every day on the largely false promise of staking their claim in the boom. Few would succeed. Certainly not like he had.

Will went to his wardrobe and picked out a fine suit he'd had tailored the week before. It had cost him hundreds of dollars more than it should, but it was a beautiful cut. He ran his hand along the smooth fabric. The tailor had told him he'd learned his trade on Savile Row in London. Will hadn't been in a position to question him and didn't haggle on the price. He'd put the suit on later in the day, but for now, he knew the mud of Dawson would ruin it. He put on something more fitting and turned to glance at Anna one last time before he shut the bedroom door behind him.

Betsy sat alone in the saloon and looked up with a smile as he came down. "Good morning," she said.

"You're up early."

"I'm up late, Will. You're the one who's up early."

He reached the bottom of the stairs and went to her. "Business good last night?"

"Yeah. It's a bit different from lying on my back, but I'm getting used to it."

"You're a natural—the perfect person to manage the Palace. Who else is going to look after the girls as well as you?"

"I hope that new owner thinks the same."

"He will. I told you, he's keeping you and the girls on, exactly like it is now."

"We're going to miss you around here. When's the steamer?"

"This afternoon."

"You're gonna have me crying now."

"It's time for us to leave. Anna wants to get back to see her sisters, and it's high time I met my in-laws!"

"I don't envy you that." Betsy put down the coffee she was drinking and stood up. "There is something else—I hear congratulations are in order."

Will laughed. "She told you?"

"You think she wasn't going to tell me? The girls and me had a party when we found out. You'll be a fine father, Will."

"Thank you," he said as she embraced him.

The boy was waiting outside with the horse he'd arranged, and Will put a coin in his hand before climbing into the saddle. Father Spring, the new priest in town, waved from across the street as Will trotted past. Father Jones was gone now. Will had paid his way out of town on the first steamer after the ice broke.

He rode past the courthouse, where he'd been cleared of any wrongdoing after Bradwell's death. Ray had testified to him being taken to the Palace under duress, and after Anna's testimony, the judge soon realized that Will had acted in self-defense in Carrick's and Milton's deaths. Anna wasn't even arrested for shooting Bradwell. The verdict was greeted with a round of applause from the large crowd who'd packed into the tiny courtroom to hear it, and Will had been greeted by handshakes and slaps on the back from the people waiting outside.

It was only a minute or so before he left the town behind. He made his way down toward Lousetown before taking a trail to follow the river east. He rode an hour along the river, past Bonanza Creek on the south side, where the claim he'd won, which he and Silas had worked together, still produced enough in a month to make a man comfortable for a lifetime. He said goodbye to it in his mind. The man from Oregon he'd sold it to could take his chances with it now. He rode on, the trees seeming to close in around him as the river grew wilder and all signs of man diminished. He rode another half hour before he saw the lodges covered in animal fur, just where the prospector he'd spoken to the day before had said they'd be. Several children played outside the tents, stripped to the waist in the warm sun.

Will brought the horse to a trot as a woman emerged from one of the tents, the sunshine like a seam of gold in her black hair. A spark of recognition came across her face, and she went back inside the tent without uttering a word. By the time Will was off the horse, Four Bears had emerged from the tent, a smile spreading across his face as he moved to embrace Will.

"You look a lot better than last time I saw you," he said.

"All thanks to you, my friend."

"Come. I have a fine salmon I caught this morning, perfect for sharing with an honored guest such as you."

Will sat and ate with Four Bears and his family. The other members of the tribe sat with them as Four Bears recounted the tale of how Will had survived the attempt on his life and stumbled through the wilderness to find them.

"They all know the story already," Four Bears said to Will, "so I put in some extra details to make it interesting to them."

"Tell them I killed a wolverine with my bare hands—that'll be sure to impress."

The two men sat until the food was eaten, then stayed and talked some more. When it was time to leave, they embraced one last time as men who knew they'd never see each other again did. Will set out, back toward town, with the laughter of Han children in his ears and the light of love in his heart blurring out the visions of the dead Lakota in his mind.

It was two hours before Dawson came into view, but he had one last stop to make. He rode up the hill outside the town, past the cemetery for the Yukon Order of Pioneers, where Bradwell was buried. Will gave the old man a few seconds' thought. Anna never had laid claim to any of Bradwell's riches. The lawyer had found his sister in Missouri. Rumor had it that she'd fainted when told the amount of money she had coming her way. Will brushed Bradwell from his mind once more as he rode past the cemeteries for Catholics, for police and government officials, until it came time to get down off his horse again and lead it by the reins.

The simple grave markings told the story of what had happened in the town below. Almost all the occupants of the graves were men, almost all of them under the age of forty. Bradwell must have been one of the oldest here. And they had come from all over the world—Russia, France, England, Ireland, Mexico, Bolivia, China, the United States, and of course Canada. All with the same dream—now diminished.

Silas's grave was at the end with a view of the town and the river below, which sparkled as if sprinkled with diamonds. Will took his hat in his hands.

"Today is the day we leave. I don't know if I'll ever make it here to see you in person again. In fact, I'll bet Anna is wondering where the hell I am right about now. Just like you used to." He raised a hand to wipe sweat off his brow. "I told you Anna was pregnant. I made sure to make an honest woman out of her just in time, didn't I? And, of course, we don't know if it's going to be a boy or a girl, but I have a feeling, and I think little Silas Leary will be honored to know who he was named after once he's old enough." Will stood in silence for a few minutes before he took out his watch. It was almost three. The steamer was in two hours. "I have to leave you now. I don't want to. I'm so sorry for what happened to you, Silas. I miss you. I suppose I always will, but I know you'll always be with me, and I'll never forget that everything I am today is because of you."

Will knelt to touch the name, running his fingers along the lettering before he stood up.

"Goodbye, brother."

Epilogue

Newton, Massachusetts, September 1900

The gold rush in the Klondike was over now. It had ended just three years after it had begun. The saloons and taverns of Dawson had lulled to a hush. Those lucky few hundred who had managed to fulfill the dreams of millions were back in the "outside" now. Most of those who had gotten rich quickly squandered it in the same way. Only a rare few joined the elite class that all had aspired to. Those who never found fortune in the Klondike soon found another dream to chase. Another stampede began. The fever for the color drove those still left in Dawson to the beaches of Nome, eighteen hundred miles west of Dawson near the mouth of the Yukon River in Alaska. The gold there was said to litter the shore like pebbles. Some had gotten rich, but like the Klondike, most had gone home poorer than they'd started out. But the transformation of the north had begun. Many stampeders found fertile ground for farming and, with little money or recourse to return, had set down roots in the Yukon or Alaska. Some others discovered gold in creeks far short of Dawson and stayed to prospect there. Many stampeders cut their journeys short and, upon realizing that the dreams of an easy fortune were beyond them, had stayed to develop the land. The mystery surrounding Alaska and northwest Canada had disappeared. A new frontier had opened up.

Anna took baby Silas in her arms, holding him close as she stared into his teal-blue eyes. He had held up well considering his age and the sheer length of the trip from their home in Evanston. She thought of their new house in Illinois—just far enough from her parents but just close enough too. Her father had made a sincere contrition, particularly after Anna had told him who exactly Bradwell had turned out to be. She accepted his apology. It was easier than the alternative. His business went under, and he admitted that even Bradwell's money wouldn't have saved him. He was running a restaurant now that Will had bought in the city. It was thriving.

The joy of being home and close to her sisters, getting to know Mary's new husband, and their getting to know little Silas was worth more than all the gold in the Klondike to her. So was Mabel. The doctors had called her recovery a miracle, even with the radiation therapy. But Anna knew better; she knew Mabel's fortitude and sheer refusal to admit defeat had carried her through, and that it always would. It was impossible to say if the cancer would come back and if she would live the long and happy life they all wished for her, but she was healthy and alive, and there was all the money available for treatment she'd ever need.

Will was nervous. He didn't want to admit that, of course, but his mannerisms made it plain enough. Anna handed him the baby, to calm him as much as anything else.

The carriage pulled up. Anna raised her head as Will tried to smile at her. She peered out the window. The house was exactly as he'd described it—white with square windows and a rolling lawn leading to the front door.

"This is it," he said.

"Are you quite ready for this?"

"Yes."

"This is your grandparents' house," Anna said to the baby, taking him back from Will. "This is the house Daddy and Uncle Silas grew up in."

The carriage door opened, and Will climbed out before the driver came around to help Anna and the baby down onto the sidewalk. The gray clouds above their heads had gone to reveal a clear blue sky. Will took the letter he'd promised Silas he'd deliver out of his pocket. He let his eyes drift across the words one last time, though he knew each line by heart now. Anna took his hand, baby Silas in her other arm, and led him up the garden path toward the front door.

ACKNOWLEDGMENTS

Massive thanks to Karl Gurke, the resident historian at the Klondike Gold Rush National Park in Skagway, for the enormous help he offered me. Thanks, as always, to my beta readers for their patience in dealing with the clumsy early drafts of my books. Thanks to Betsy Frimmer, Carol and Ed McDuell, Jackie Kosbob, Chris Menier, Morgan Leafe, Nicola Hogan, Shane Woods, and Jack Layden. Thanks to my marvelous agent, Byrd Leavell, for believing in me when it didn't seem like the prudent move. Thanks to my wonderful editors, Jenna Free and Will Bennett, and of course the fabulous Chris Werner at Lake Union, who looked out for me when it mattered most. Thanks also to all the terrific staff at Lake Union who make publishing a happy and friendly business.

Thanks to my siblings, Conor, Brian, and Orla, for all your support over the years. Thanks to my parents for igniting the love of history and learning within me, and especially to my mum for all those extra reading lessons she gave me before I even started school—look at me now, Mum! Thanks to my beautiful, kind, and hilarious wife, Jill, for making every day one more piece of the heaven we've constructed together. And of course, thanks to my maddening, beautiful, and wonderful sons, Robbie and Sam. You are my motivation, my reason for being, and the personification of the joy I feel in my heart every day living with you.

ABOUT THE AUTHOR

Photo © 2017 Jill McDuell

Eoin Dempsey is the author of the Amazon Charts bestselling novel *White Rose, Black Forest* as well as *Finding Rebecca* and *The Bogside Boys*. Born in Dublin, Ireland, Eoin is living his dream: writing full time and waking up to his wife and two sons every morning. Eoin and his family reside in Philadelphia, Pennsylvania. To learn more, visit www.eoindempseybooks.com.